PRAISE FOR MELODY GROVES

"Readers should make sure their saddles are properly cinched."

— *ALBUQUERQUE JOURNAL*

"Groves' breezing writing style puts the reader in the story...plenty of action."

— ANNE HILLERMAN, *NEW YORK TIMES* BESTSELLING AUTHOR

"The author...is a daughter of the modern West, but her heart is in the Old West."

— *ALBUQUERQUE JOURNAL*

EAGAN'S REVENGE

ALSO BY MELODY GROVES

Lady of the Law

The Colton Brothers Saga
Trail to Tin Town
Showdown at Pinos Altos

Nolan Gang Unleashed Series
The Making of the Texas Kid

EAGAN'S REVENGE

NOLAN GANG UNLEASHED
BOOK TWO

MELODY GROVES

WOLFPACK
PUBLISHING
— EST 2013 —

Eagan's Revenge
Paperback Edition
Copyright © 2024 Melody Groves

Wolfpack Publishing
1707 E. Diana Street
Tampa, Florida 33609

wolfpackpublishing.com

Paperback ISBN 978-1-63977-531-6
eBook ISBN 978-1-63977-530-9
LCCN 2024937607

EAGAN'S REVENGE

CHAPTER ONE

BLANCO HILL, TEXAS—SEPTEMBER 1871

THE CLEAVER MADE A SATISFYING *thunk* AS IT sunk deep into the leg, right at the joint. I twisted the blade, and the lower leg came loose. I was pleased my hand-eye coordination was improving, although I was still an apprentice. But enough cutting for today. Da was about to turn the store's *Open* sign around, pull down the shades, and lock the front door. My second favorite part of the day.

My favorite part was opening the door first thing in the morning and watching customers come in. Or maybe it was meeting my best lads at Sam's Emporium after a long day of work. That was planned for tonight and I couldn't wait.

My fingers fumbled with the apron knot behind me. My apron, which started out bright white but was now smeared with blood and various offal from the meat I handled today. It was one of the unavoidable results inherent with the trade of meat cutter or butcher's helper. Da and I came home smelling of carrion and ofttimes looking like we'd just wrestled in a freshly butchered steer.

I yanked and pulled. Jerked and tugged. Snugged around my slim body, the apron simply wouldn't unleash me. Guess I'd tied it too tight this afternoon after returning from eating my noontime sandwich.

I waited for Da to finish with Mrs. Watkins, a steady customer who bought four times a week, usually choosing the plumpest pork chops and roasts. I was sure her husband and five boys made short work of her meals. Chuckling softly, I nodded to her. No matter who was taking the last of today's steak, I was ready to go. I'd been on my feet all day. Nothing new there, but this was Friday. Pay day.

Of course, I'd be at work first thing tomorrow morning, the busiest day of the week. And that was fine because we closed an hour earlier than the other days. Plenty of time left during the summer months to walk home, eat supper, then wander over to my friends' houses. Usually, we'd pal around a porch or go down to the creek and tell stories, some of which might be true.

I didn't have a girlfriend to take up my lazy hours. I liked girls, and they seemed to like me, despite the limp I got as a baby from falling out of the back of a wagon. My oldest brother, Tate, spurred himself sometimes because he was supposed to have been watching me. But he was only four or five back then, so unless he had pushed me, which he hadn't, I'd told him hundreds of times it wasn't his fault. Besides, I'd always walked this way and it didn't bother me.

"Can I help, Eagan?" Mrs. Watkins' kind voice brought a smile to my face.

"Yes, ma'am. I'd appreciate the help. Fingers are

kinda stiff." I figured with six men in her house she was always tying or untying something. I turned my back to her where she stood at the counter and within seconds, I was free.

Before I could properly thank her, Da handed over two large brown paper-wrapped packages of our best pork chops. They'd have a feast tonight, I was sure. Da held the door, the little bell over it tinkling. "Thanks again, Mrs. Watkins. Haste ye back."

I was pulling the apron over my head as Da closed the door, turned around the *Open* sign, pulled down the window shade and locked the door. I let go a huge sigh. Another long day on my feet, done. Another day working with raw meat and hungry customers done.

My aprons weren't quite at the stage for laundering, dunked in hot sudsy water, scrubbed with lye soap, and hung to dry behind the store. Another day and then that chore would be a great ending to a Saturday. And since I was the junior member and Da's only employee, usually I got that job. I looked forward to someday telling someone else to do it.

"Let me put this ground meat in the icebox, Eagan, then we'll walk home." Da turned to me and raised an eyebrow. "What d'ye think Ma's got on the stove tonight?"

I could smell her fried chicken and potatoes and pulled in imagined aromas. "Our favorite, Da. But think I'll be a little late."

He frowned at me. "Late?" Then his mouth turned up at both ends. "Ah, I see, lad. Got yourself a *chailín* ye do."

Heat warmed my cheeks. As much as I wanted that to be true, there was no sweetheart on the horizon. I'd have to fess up. Da always brought honesty out in me. I hung my head and wagged it. "No. No girlfriend. And wishin' doesn't make it so, Da." I looked eye-to-eye at him. "Me and Jimmy and Zeke are meetin' down at Sam's Emporium. We're all gettin' paid today and we're celebratin' with a pint."

Da stood back, his gaze scanning me head to toe and then back to head. "G'way outta that. Sam pours ye wee ones beer?" My da's Irish accent came out strong.

"We're not youngsters anymore." One of my hands fisted on my hip. "Jimmy's already nineteen, Zeke's thinkin' of gettin' married, and I'm comin' up on eighteen. Old enough."

Da's chuckle launched into a hearty laugh. "Reckon ye are at that. I forget ye're all grown men now." He reached into his pocket and pulled out four one-dollar paper bills and two one-dollar Liberty coins. "Want me to take some of this home for ye? Or ye plannin' to spend it all on ale tonight?" He waggled a finger at me. "We gotta work tomorrow. Bright and early."

As much as I wanted to feel that money jangling in my pocket, I knew he was smart. He should take most of it home. Then again, I'd have riches for a few hours. I'd have all my money in my pocket and maybe, just maybe, I'd get in a poker game and win more.

Plucking my hat from the peg near the back door, I fitted it down tight while Da did the same with his. I inspected the hand he held out with my money in it. "Guess I'll take the coins,"—my chest rose and fell with the excitement—"and the rest of it." I scooped up the cash and stuck it all into my vest pocket. I patted it, enjoying the sound of metal on metal. "Plenty to buy one for me and maybe a round for the lads."

The money burned in my pocket while I said goodbye to Da, assuring him I'd be home in an hour or two. Not to wait supper on me. After making a show of putting his own money in his pocket, from the back door of the butcher shop, Da turned left, heading down the alley for Main Street where he would walk four more streets to supper. I turned right, threw back my shoulders, and swagger-limped toward Sam's Emporium for what I hoped would be a memorable evening. My best lads and me didn't get together often, especially at a saloon, and I'd been looking forward to this all week.

Not even a handful of people were out and about this late in the day. Women were home fixing supper, children busy doing chores, and men coming in from the fields or other work. No one was rushing toward Sam's Emporium. Inside awaited women of questionable virtue, games of chance, and beer. Plenty of beer. I wasn't interested in the fallen angels. I'd played poker only with my two older brothers, but I'd had beer. More than Da and Ma knew about. Probably.

My wide-brimmed hat doing a poor job shielding my eyes from the setting sun, I held out one hand, managing to block the blinding rays. With no other people on the sidewalk, I enjoyed not bumping into anyone. Felt odd, but great at the same time.

And then, from the darkness of an alley, two men stepped in front of me, facing me, while a third came up behind. I froze. Glancing around, I narrowed my eyes, hoping to see if these were friends or at least acquaintances playing a trick on me. I'd been teased and taunted before, but never found the experiences close to amusing.

I didn't recognize any of them.

Finally, sense flooded my brain. Hands relaxed, I eased forward. "Excuse me." Did my words warble?

They took a step toward me. Now I was close enough to see both of these fellas needed a shave, last week.

Probably the one in back, too. Unfortunately, they were taller and more muscled than me. A bit older, but not by much. "Can I help you?" Maybe a polite question would disarm them.

"Ain't you the cripple from the butcher's?" The man on my right, his shoulders wider than a horse's rump, chinned at me. His crow black hair hung in thin strands at those shoulders, and his eyes—bulging, midnight black—bore a hole clear through my chest. I couldn't breathe.

"What d'you want?" Why would they pick on me? I had no horse, no gun, no money worth taking, no nice clothes, and not even my hat was all that new.

The man chuckled and looked at the man at his shoulder. "Hear that, Purdy? He don't know why we're here." He shrugged and pretended to wipe away a tear. "That mightly hurts my feelings."

"It do, fer sure, Clyde, it do." A sneer raised Purdy's thin mustache.

Shorter than Clyde, Purdy made up for lack of height with girth. He hadn't missed many, if any, meals. While he didn't appear fat, I hated to think the bulges under his shirt and vest were muscles.

Clyde stepped even closer. His breath, reeking of whiskey and cigars, turned my stomach. He grabbed my right arm so tight that all feeling immediately stopped. So, if they were going to hurt me, or rob me, I vowed I wouldn't go down easily. Throwing my shoulders back as far as I could, standing taller than I thought possible, I snapped at the man, hopefully growling. "I'll ask again. What d'you want?"

"Oh, looky here, Purdy. We got us here a real honest-to-gawd, ferocious she-bear."

Purdy grabbed my other arm. "We want your money."

"Don't have any." I wrenched my arm out of the man's claw-like grip and fisted my hands. I knew I was strong from cutting meat all day, but could I run, too? No. Then I'd give them a fight they'd remember.

A man stepped from around behind me, the resemblance to Clyde remarkable. Words slurred, still he made his intention clear. "Hell, Clyde. Hurry up an' rob 'im 'n be done. I'm powerful, thirsty and in need of a whore. Bad." He leaned in at me, breath as foul as his brother's. His gaze roamed up and down me, boots to hat. "Hell, you'll do." Filthy hands pulled at my shirt, buttons popping off.

I slapped at his hands just as Purdy grabbed my arm again, and swung it up behind me. Had my shoulder snapped? Pain rippled down my body.

The other Clyde kept ripping at my shirt, the buttons flying into the street. My vest came off with the shirt. "Ain't had me but couple other boys." He glanced at his brother. "'Member that last one? He was prettier'n this one."

"Yeah. Fought damn fine." Clyde snickered and gripped my arm tighter. "Didn't do him no good, though."

Wriggling out of Clyde's grip, I swung with everything I had. My fist connected with his jaw, and he flew back, crashing to the boardwalk. Fists plowed into my stomach and my face. My nose crunched, and blood poured. I kicked, swung, grunted, tried to scream.

Clyde's brother, bigger than him, pounced on me, knocking me to the ground. Purdy let go before I landed on my arm. We rolled into the street, where he managed to get me on my back, him sitting on my hips like a cowboy on a bucking bronc. He ripped off the rest of my shirt, while his brother and Purdy held my arms above my head. I kicked up but connected with nothing. I screamed. Grunted. Wriggled.

Bigger Clyde ran his dirt-encrusted hands down my belly and ripped at the buttons on my trousers. He pulled. Hard. My trousers now down under him, he clawed at my underdrawers while rubbing against me. His body writhing on top threatened to bring up everything I'd eaten this week. Jeers, rude words, hands running over my tender parts that were now hurting.

"Leave me alone!" My words sailed into the evening air. I thrashed side to side. He grabbed me through the cotton underdrawers.

Like in a dream, he flew backward off me and rolled. Zeke plowed his fist into Little Clyde's face. Clyde let go. Purdy found his feet, scrambled away, disappearing into the alley.

I lay there, dust and dirt attacking my nose. Tears clouded my vision and my head rung. Jimmy's face appeared. "You all right?"

Of course not. Instead, I nodded. Jimmy and Zeke each grabbed an arm and hoisted me up to my feet. The Clydes bolted into the dark alley after Purdy.

I wasn't sure what to do first. Wipe my nose, put on what was left of my shirt, grip my head, or start crying. I'd never been so terrified in my life or shook so hard. Not even when my older brother Joe got robbed and hit on the back of the head at the telegraph office.

My friends nodded at my trousers about halfway down to my ankles. Shame enveloped my entire body. Icy cold daggers pounded into me. How could I ever look at them again? They *knew*. *Knew* what had almost happened. The ultimate humiliation discovered and seen by my best lads.

I pulled up the britches and avoided looking at my

saviors. Top button was missing, but the rest seemed to be intact. I shrugged the shirt over my shoulders and discovered nothing to button with. Ma would not be happy to have so much to mend.

Zeke placed a hand on my back and nudged. "Let's get you down to Doc's so he can patch you up." He inspected my face. "Looks like you're gonna have a helluva shiner there, my friend."

"Don't touch me." I wrenched my shoulder out of his reach. "Leave me alone." A brass band marched through my head, trumpets blaring louder than the tubas. "No doc. I'm fine." Swaying, I grabbed Jimmy's sleeve, then immediately shoved him away. I'd be all right in a minute or two, despite fiery ribs and a throbbing face.

"Like hell you are." Jimmy helped me into my vest, then slid dollar bills and coins into my pocket. He pointed behind me. "Found these on the street. Guess they wanted your pay. You tell 'em you don't have much?"

Big Zeke raised both eyebrows and looked past my shoulder. "So, since you didn't have money, they were gonna take it out in flesh?"

Like a giant wave, the assault engulfed me. The sandwich I had for lunch came back up. It splatted all over my boots and the ground. The terror, the feel of his...his body grinding against mine, his grunts, my helplessness all came crashing down. "Leave me alone!" I spun and stumbled fast as I could toward darkness. Somewhere that wasn't here. The other side of Main was dark, only a few houses there. I ran. Lurched. Angry tears clouded my vision. I ran blind.

CHAPTER TWO

LARGE, STRONG HANDS SHOOK MY SHOULDER. Working man's hands. "Late, it is, son. Sure, look it. It's half six. Time to rise up." The voice took a breath and continued. "Lose an hour in the mornin' and ye'll be lookin' for it all day."

I jerked upright, covered my chest with a sheet and scooted back against the wall. Struggling to make sense of where I was, I stared at a face I knew well. Parts finally pulled themselves together. Da.

He reached out to touch my face. "*Ó mo Dhia*! What happened to ye?"

I recoiled, clutching the sheet tighter.

Da leaned closer and poked my quite tender left cheek. "Got into a bully fight, ye did!" He lowered his voice. "Did ye win?" He winked.

Swallowing a wad of something in my throat, I nodded. "I'm gran'." Hell, he didn't have to know, wasn't going to know, what really happened. I'd pretend to be the winner. Not the loser I actually was. Not the terrified kid who almost got violated. Not a man who fought back and won. It all flooded into my mind. Reliving the terror, the embarrassment, the feel of exposure, I shook. I gazed up at Da who was halfway out the door.

He spoke over his shoulder. "Breakfast in two shakes, son. Best get washed up. Leg it." And he was gone into early morning grayness.

I sat there, in bed, covers under my chin, trembling. I hurt. All over. Especially down there. Could I stand in the butcher's all day, aching, throbbing? I ran my tongue around my mouth. All my teeth seemed to be where they should be. And my shoulders weren't quite as sore as I thought they'd be.

All right. Get up, I told myself. Be a man. Face the day. Face what happened last night. Big breath of air pulled in, a second one, and then I stood. I swayed and sat back down. That brass band had returned and were busily warming up. Not one instrument was in tune.

I was such a *gobshite* for being taken. Could I ever face my best lads? What would Ma say when she saw my face? And I'd have to give her my buttonless shirt. Could I be sick today and not go to work? Hell, Da would never allow that.

I stood again, and this time, the room stayed still. New clothes made me feel a mite better, as did cold water on my swollen, bruised face. A cut above my eye and split lip didn't stand out too much. However, the black ring circling my right eye gave me a bit of a pirate look. I wanted to smile at the thought, wishing big brother Tate was here to see me. He'd point at me and say things like, "Arrr! Shiver me timbers, matey. Quite the shiner, ye got there, ye scallywag, ye."

Buttoning my shirt and coming back to the here and now, I realized my hands were still shaking. A knot in my stomach refused any idea of food coming down. In fact, what I hadn't lost yesterday was threatening to come back up. A closer look in the shaving mirror and I was pale. Paler than usual. I really, truly wasn't feeling well. Could I take the day off? I'd ask Da.

I limped into the dining room which was a luxury here in this hill country Texas town. Most people ate in their kitchen. Ma was putting plates in front of Da and my usual chair. She smiled up at me and then her eyes widened. She gasped.

"Ah, Jasus, Mary, and Joseph!" She made the cross. Rushing to me, she held my chin and gently turned my head. She inspected my face, hands, face and then scrutinized me front to back. "Me poor lad. Who did this to ye?" She didn't wait for a response. "Where'd this happen? Don't tell me ye was down at Sam's. Ah Jasus!" She crossed herself again. "I was worried about ye when you didn't come to supper. Ye must be hungry. Are ye hungry? Come sit."

I loved Ma more than anything, but right now, she made my ears ring and my head thump worse. I swatted away her hands like she was a nagging fly. Her eyes narrowed but she said nothing.

"Sorry, Ma."

Easing into my chair, everything on my body resented movement. I groaned, too loudly, I guess. Ma stood behind my chair and wrapped me in a soft hug, which surprisingly, I needed. I squeezed my eyes shut, trying like the devil to erase memories. Their faces. Clyde, Purdy, and the other Clyde. The Three, as I thought of them. I'd never forget them, their images etched on my memory. Stomach roiling, I scooted the chair back taking Ma with it, doubled over, and tried to bring up any leftovers of yesterday's lunch. Nothing but drips of something tasting acidic. I wiped my mouth with a napkin.

"Sorry." I looked from parent to parent. "Da, don't think I can come in today. *Tá mé tinn*. Real sorry."

His fork clattered against his plate rim. "But today's Saturday. Busiest day of the week. I need ye there."

Ma placed a hand on her hip and used the other to point to me. "Now, Ciernan. Our boy is sick. Look at his face. Pale and bruised." She tsked. "If ye must, tell yer customers Eagan's a bit under the weather. They can just show a little patience."

More lunch or whatever it was, surfaced. I tried to grip my head and stomach at the same time. Ma helped me to my feet. "Ye'll lie down right now and when ye feel better, ye can go to the shop." When Ma made a declaration like that, Da stayed quiet. Guess he knew when to fight or to give in. And he probably knew I'd be worthless helping today. The thought of raw meat, hacking and sawing it, brought up new gobs of whatever in my stomach.

I crawled back into bed and pulled up the sheet. Closing my eyes brought back The Three. Only this time, the other Clyde succeeded in having his way with me. I fought him, thrashing against his muscled body. I hollered, "Get off me! Get off!" He was brutal, chuckling and then laughing, loudly. The other two held me so tight I couldn't move.

"Saints, Eagan."

Ma's voice unraveled part of the haze.

"Ye're hollering like a *banshee*, ye are." She eased to an edge of the bed and sat. "Brought ye some buttermilk. 'Tis fresh. Mr. McGruder brought it by jest now."

I elbowed my way up to sitting, waiting for Ma and the milk glass to take shape. Still shaking, but not as badly as earlier, I took the glass and sipped. Milk swirled in my stomach, threatening to rise. I waited, then sipped more. This time, my stomach settled.

"There ye are, boy." Ma patted my leg. "Sure, and it's the Irish flu. Ye'll be gran' in no time." She beamed at me in a hopeful, but worried way. Skin on the side of her eyes crinkled as she smiled. Standing all of five feet, her hair pulled back in a bun, wisps of gray cascaded around her face. For a moment, I thought she was an angel. Well, she was right then.

She leaned over and touched my sore shoulder. "When ye need to talk, I'll be for listenin', *mográ*. Bet it was a glorious fight but looks like ye got the worst end." Ma stood in the doorway. "Told yer brothers more'n once to stay away from Sam's. Looks like ye learned yer lesson, too." She wagged her head, soft mutterings following as she walked away. "The hard way. Always the hard way."

So she thinks it was a barroom brawl at Sam's. Fine. I wouldn't tell her or Da any different. How could I face them if they knew? I downed the last of the milk, put the glass on the floor, pulled up the sheet and lay there thinking.

Jimmy and Zeke were the only ones who knew what had happened. I lay there, miserable, hurting, not knowing what to do. Who, if anybody, to talk to. The new priest? Maybe.

"What d'ye mean he's still abed?" Da's booming voice rushed down the hall and crashed into my bedroom. "All day? He's been abed all day? What kinda *spalpeen* did ye raise?" Clomping footfalls came down the hall and into my room. I threw off the sheet, put my feet on the floor and before I could stand, Da marched in, stopping inches from me. "How ye feelin', son?" The satire fairly dripped.

How to say I was physically better, except my split lip throbbed and my private parts were still tender. Ribs probably weren't broken and the band in my head had decided to knock off and go home. But the rest of me...

"I'm grand." I struggled to my feet. At my height of almost six feet, I looked Da eye-to-eye. "Sorry for missing work today. I'm better, though." Was I? That gigantic knot remained large in my chest, and I jerked at every noise. "I'll be there early, Monday."

"Right ye are there, boyo. Needed ye today, I did. Extra busy, I was." He took a breath and seemed to calm. His gaze roamed over my face. "Eye's black like coal. That's a gran' shiner yer havin'. Who gave it a ye?"

Before I could make up a name, Ma called us to supper. My stomach rumbled at the thought of real food. Guess I truly was on the mend.

* * *

MA HAD MADE her finest supper—fried chicken, diced potatoes, and greens. She even made apple pie for dessert. She must've really been concerned about me, usually making pies only in the late fall and winter when it's cold.

Last bite of pie, followed by a second glass of buttermilk, sat in my stomach, and at least for the moment, didn't threaten to come back up. The three of us were sitting at the table, in no hurry to get up and wash dishes, when a knock at the door startled me.

"Wha' now?" Da stood before I could. Within half a minute, he returned to the dining room, followed by Jimmy and Zeke.

Breath caught in my chest, and I'm sure I paled as my face turned cold then hot. Ma pointed to the pie behind her on the counter. "We've finished, but there's plenty for you boys."

The lads, hats clutched in hands, shook their heads. Jimmy produced a wide smile. "Thank you, ma'am, but we've already ate. Looks tasty, though."

Da shook hands with both and then excused himself to the front room to read and smoke. Ma picked up plates and I grabbed mine, ready to help with cleaning up. Instead, she took the plate from my hand. "Eagan, go outside with yer friends. I'll wash up."

I didn't want to see them. Not now. I'd much rather wash dishes and scrub floors than face those two.

"Just thought we'd see how he's doing." Zeke cocked his head toward me. "Didn't see him around town today."

Ma set down the plates and used both hands to chase us out of the dining room. "Ye boys go on outside and enjoy the night air. Tis finally cooled a bit this evening." She flapped her hands again. "Now shoo."

"Yes, ma'am." Jimmy and Zeke spoke in unison.

We nodded at Da in his chair as we passed through. The air outside was indeed soft and cool. But tension, like a bobcat stalking a doe, caused me to limp worse than I normally did. The screen door slammed behind us as we made our way down to the creek. It wasn't too far from the house, but distant enough, Ma and Da couldn't hear our conversation. My brothers and I had spent many hours down here plotting and planning, but mostly talking about girls.

My boots scuffed through old leaves. I threw rocks into the water. Jimmy perched on a boulder while Zeke found a stump and stretched out his long legs. They made small talk while I threw more rocks.

"You know it wasn't your fault, Eagan. You know

that, don't you?" Jimmy's words echoed against my chest. It didn't matter whose fault it was. It happened. And I let it happen. I'd never forgive myself, not in a million years.

Jimmy pushed off from the boulder and moved a bit closer to me. "You know we'd never tell anybody what we saw. Never."

"Unless—" Zeke scuffed his shoes in the dirt.

"Unless what, Zeke? Unless what?" My words came out harsher than I'd intended, but if he was my friend, he'd *never* tell. Ever.

"Unless the law asks."

"That bit o' *shite*? Wagner don't care." I spun around and faced my friends. "Don't you see? I didn't defend myself like I should. If you hadn't come along when you did, well...you know what would've happened. I had to have others save my butt. I can't live like that."

"But we—"

"Have you been assaulted like that? Either of you? Your shirt ripped...pants down...man on top of you wiggling like..."

I was on a roll and nothing I could tell myself would make me stop. I ranted until tears blurred my vision. I sniffed, rubbed my eyes, and wiped my nose with my shirt sleeve. Both lads stayed quiet, letting me say my peace until I ran out of words and energy. I sagged to the ground and leaned against an oak.

Silence wedged into the evening. Night frogs croaked greetings to others, and cicadas sang their last songs since fall was in the air. Still, I sat, my chest full of anger, fear, self-loathing.

Zeke walked over and knelt on one knee. "That was a helluva thing happened to you, Eagan. Helluva thing. But don't let it rule you. Don't let it keep you from doing what you like."

"He's right." Jimmy stood close. "Sure it's embarrassing and it hurts. Your eye tells me that. But you gotta put it in its place and move on."

"Move on?" I looked up at them and knew they were right. Enough whining and feeling sorry for myself. I wouldn't let those three devils ruin my life. If anything, they'd make it better. Make *me* better. I would *move on* by getting revenge.

How, I wasn't sure, but one thing I knew, I'd get it. I stood and shook hands with my mates. We walked back toward the house when Jimmy's words stopped me cold.

"By the way," he said softly. "Didn't know if we should tell you or not."

Icy cold flooded my body. "Tell me what?"

Zeke kicked at a rock and glanced at Jimmy. "Those three fellas. We spotted 'em in town today going into Sam's."

"Well, hell. Figured they'd be long gone." Now I'd have to look over my shoulder and into every dark alley day and night.

"We'll keep an eye out, too." Jimmy thumbed toward Zeke. "I'd like to tell the sheriff, so he can watch, too. But"—he held up a hand before I could interrupt—"we won't. Your attack stays between us three. Promise."

CHAPTER THREE

EVEN THOUGH I DIDN'T WANT TO, I LIMPED MY
way to church the next morning. Ma and Da insisted I
go. Since supper last night and breakfast this morning
had stayed down, I had no good reason to stay home.
How could I face anybody? I was sure I had *almost-rape-
victim* written across my forehead and *Donkey* across my
chest. Everyone would turn and gasp as I walked inside.
No doubt. Maybe I could sit in the back. No, we always
sat in the second row up front. Always.

We said our Hail Marys and sang a couple of hymns.
We stood, kneeled, sat, and then chorused from the
Good Book and listened to the priest talk about...well, I
wasn't sure because I didn't listen. Instead, I watched
people around me. They all knew. It was obvious. Eyes
sliding sideways at me, no one sitting too close, a furtive
smile and nod as I walked in. No pats on the back or
handshakes as usual. Like the lady in the *Scarlet Letter*
book I'd read in school, I was a marked man.

I couldn't get away fast enough. At long last, we said
our final Amens, and I bolted out the door. Not bolted,

but limped as fast as I could. While still warm and a bit muggy, the Texas air never smelled so sweet. Now, I'd go home and hide out from the world until tomorrow. That familiar knot expanded my chest. Tomorrow I'd have to go to the butcher shop and see customers. Help them with their Hamburg steak or lamb chops or roasts. Maybe I could be sick again tomorrow. My eye was still puffed and quite black, my ribs still throbbed, but according to what I saw in the shaving mirror this morning, my usual face color stared back at me. Not pale anymore.

Ma and Da stood in the churchyard, chatting with their friends. They'd be busy for an hour or so. I caught Da's eye and pointed toward home. He nodded in understanding and off I went. I reached the far side of the yard when I heard my name called. I stopped, turned around and about ran face to face with my lad Jimmy.

"Where you going?" Jimmy's words, a bit out of breath, were full of warmth and compassion. While he was taller than me and had an extra year under his belt, I regarded him almost as a brother. In fact, Jimmy knew a few things about me that neither Tate nor Joe knew.

I pointed over my shoulder. "Home. Still not on my pins, proper. Bit o'the collywobbles."

"Wanna show you something before you go." He nudged my shoulder toward the creek a quarter mile away. "You'll like this."

Curiosity bloomed into full swing. "What is it?"

"Come see."

While we walked, two other boys joined us. Finn and Maine Murphy, the only boys from a family with five girls, trailed alongside. They were friends, but not of the caliber Jimmy was. Banter back and forth relaxed my chest a bit. They didn't seem to be judging me. In fact, they talked like they didn't know. Didn't realize who I now was. Who I had become.

For a second, I felt normal.

Crystal-clear water in the creek gurgled along like it had nowhere to go, like it was about to take a nap. I picked up a rock and chucked it into the water. On the opposite bank, a frog leaped out, seemed to glare at me then hopped off. Finn splashed through the water in search of the frog. We laughed when he caught it and held up the amphibian. Trying to extract himself from Finn's clutches, the bullfrog wriggled up and out, smacking into his face. Finn ended up with frog goo and mud in his eyes. He blinked in shock.

I doubled over, laughing. Holding my still-sore ribs, my laughter, along with the others, turned into good-natured kidding. We called him Frog Face Finn, wondered if he'd Croaked, and if he'd Hopped to church this morning. We were merciless.

Ribbing went on for a good five minutes until we ran out of frog jokes, and Finn had dunked his entire head in the stream, scrubbing like he had the pox. At long last, Jimmy waved us together.

"Wanna see what I got?"

Of course, we did.

He glanced behind me and then left and right. I thought if he didn't show us right then and there, I'd burst. Digging deep into his vest, he pulled out a gun. We gasped. "This's a thirty-six caliber Colt Navy revolver." Jimmy ran his hand down a long barrel, then spun the cylinder, showing us there were no bullets lodged inside.

"Where'd you get it?"

"This's yours?"

"Can I hold it?"

So many questions and comments flew through the air, Jimmy asked us to lower our voices. Guess he wasn't supposed to have the revolver.

"Now," he held it like he would a baby bird. "This pistol'll do lots of damage. Kill a man down dead. Gotta be careful holding it. And Pa says never, ever point it at someone unless you mean to use it."

We all shrugged, we understood. I'd heard those same words from Da at least a million times.

Jimmy turned to me. "Wanna hold it?"

I couldn't nod fast enough. Heavier than I'd remembered, although I'd held one before, its power exuded through my hand, down my arm, and into my body, which brought smiles to my face. I held it shoulder high, aimed down the barrel, locating a limb on a nearby tree. I pretended to pull the trigger and shoot.

"Boom!" My hand recoiled with the imagined shot. Like ghosts arising from the mist, my attackers stood in front of me. I scrambled back two steps, terrified they'd try again. My heart pounded along with my head, and I struggled to breathe.

Jimmy's hand on my shoulder brought me around. He held out his hand. "Maine wants to hold it now."

I looked at my hand. I had a gun. It was lethal. I nodded to no one in particular. I'd kill those three sonsuvbitches by shooting them. So I wasn't as big and strong as they were, but this Colt definitely made me an equal.

My shoulders threw themselves back, and I stood straight. The answer was right there in my hand. Literally. I ran shaking fingers down the barrel, caressing it like I would a wounded kitten. Instantly, I became one with the Colt revolver.

"Jimmy said I could hold it." Maine pulled at the revolver.

I looked at him like he'd come from the moon. This was my gun. Gonna get revenge. Kill three men. Take away everything from them, like...

Jimmy lifted the Colt from my tight grip. "Give it over to Maine, Eagan. He gets it next."

As if in a dream, I gave my prized possession to Maine, watching as he hefted it, aimed at the sky, and pretend fired. "Blam!"

Finn held it last, but instead of once, like the rest of us, this time he shot at least six times.

Jimmy pried the gun from his hand.

Maine ran to a bare spot under the tree. "Looky there, Finn. You got 'im. That crow you were aimin' at is all done in. Good shootin', brother!"

The four of us chuckled and pretended to admire the dead bird. Comments about what you serve with crow for supper, the amazing shot of hitting one while it flew by instead of the bird sitting on a branch, and breathtaking that all five nearby birds were killed, all dead.

Killed. That's what I wanted. The three men, all dead. I froze. What was I saying? Kill somebody? How could I think that? Was my humiliation worth a man's life? I'd have to think on that. Maybe Jimmy was right. Maybe I should go to the sheriff. Let the law punish them. But what if—

"You got that look on your face, Eagan." Jimmy's words in my ear made me jump. "You all right? That shiner's growing darker and you're shaking."

I turned my attention to Jimmy and wagged my head. "Just thinkin'." Pointing to the gun he tucked into his vest pocket, I asked, "Where d'you get it at? You buy it or is that your da's?"

We glanced toward Finn and Maine now totally engrossed in picking up "dead birds." They laughed and chased each other around, trying to rub an imaginary bird on each other's back. They darted in and out and splashed into the stream. No doubt their ma would be thrilled when they got home.

Jimmy lowered his voice. "My uncle John give it to me few years back, but since Pa said I was too young, he put it away, high up. Now that I'm near grown, he reached it down yesterday and give it to me. Even have more bullets at home."

I was too awed to say anything. Sure wish I had an uncle John to give me a gun like that. Da, I knew, owned a gun. I'd seen him clean it once. Since he owned the butcher shop, he didn't go hunting like most men in town. We got meat any time we wanted.

Soon as I could, I'd get home and count the bills and coins I had stored in my sock drawer. Tate hadn't come home for a bit, so my money hadn't been "borrowed" by my older brother. Not that I minded when he did that. But from now on, my money had a purpose.

CHAPTER FOUR

LIKE WE ALWAYS DID, DA AND I WALKED INTO town early Monday morning. We owned one horse, a mare Da officially named Kilkenny Canterer, but I called her Banshee. Usually, I called her simply Horse. But since the shop was close to town, we walked. Plus, where would we stable her? She was much happier back in her own barn.

Da seemed to enjoy the early morning sun and coolness. No doubt it would get hot today, being as it was only September and days didn't cool until close to November. The Texas Hill country was like that. Da softly whistled to himself and greeted the few people out and about with a nod and touch of the hat brim. All were customers or potential customers, being as he was, the only butcher in Blanco Hill.

All I managed was to cringe every time someone moved in close to me. I knew logically, no one would bother me, but the instinct to run or fight was in full force this morning. Since my breath was held and my nerves on high alert all the way to the shop, I let Da do all the talking.

We rounded the last corner to Main, and I stopped to focus on the sign over the shop's door right in front of me: *Nolan's Meats*. Normally, we'd continue around back, through the dark alley and I'd wait for Da to tuck his key into the lock. The back door would creak open, and we'd step inside. But, I knew, just *knew* that Purdy and the two Clydes would be in there waiting. Taking no chances, I remained on the boardwalk by the front door.

"How about I make sure it gets clean out here? I'll tidy up and come in when you unlock the front door. All right?" Part of me wondered where my bravery had high-tailed it to, the other half knew this was the smart thing to do. They wouldn't jump Da. Probably.

But were they hiding in the store? I should go with Da to protect him. I stood frozen. Go? Stay? How much of a coward was I? Where was a gun when I needed it?

Da pulled the keys out of his pocket. "Sweep? *Ye're* offering to sweep the boardwalk?"

Anything was better than facing those men. "Sure, Da. Why not?"

He shook his head and headed for the dark alley. "Ye *never* volunteer to clean. Broom's just inside the front door." More words trailed behind him, but I was too busy peering up and down the street to really listen. Why did it take so long to open a stupid door? Five minutes, ten minutes, what felt like an hour passed until that distinctive click opened the shop for another day of business.

I wrenched open the door. "What took so long?" I jumped inside, slamming the door shut. I made sure the *Closed* sign was still turned outward. We'd officially open in a few minutes.

"Long? Don't know how ye count time, but it could'na be more 'n a minute."

I tugged the apron over my head and wrapped the not-very-white material around my front. Maybe this afternoon I'd wash it. Maybe tomorrow. Da and I set about doing our usual morning routine. My first chore was to retrieve meat from the icebox in the storage room after emptying the water tray under the tin-lined wooden box. I peered inside the room, dark and full of places to hide. Figures towered in the back, boxes stacked next to them. Was that them? I stood and listened. Da opening a cash register, coins clicking into the drawer, his low humming was all I heard. Eyes adjusting to the dimness, I realized the figures I'd seen were nothing more than stacked crates that I had put there. A bit relieved and feeling a wee foolish, I stepped inside, and nothing moved. Another step. Again nothing. Maybe they weren't in there waiting for me. But where were they? A third step inside and still nothing. A long sigh of relief lowered my shoulders. Safe for now. Probably.

I brought out Hamburg steak, pork, and lamb chops, one plump roast from the icebox. Within minutes, Mr. Atherton should be stopping by with a couple of chickens he's dressed out this morning. Ready-made chicken was a true indulgence since most people raised and butchered their own. But customers such as the Widow Sellan didn't like eating animals she raised. She tended to name each one, which kind of forced her to buy from us.

Sliding the meat trays under the glass counter, I arranged each piece to where the best side was up toward the customer. I'd just finished when Mr. Atherton knocked at the door. As fast as I could, I rushed over, unlocking it. The bell tinkled.

He held up two chickens, heads off, all plucked,

innards in separate bags. I'd been told the giblets were good in gravy, but since I didn't cook, I didn't know for certain. Ma had mentioned it a time or two.

While I took the chickens and arranged them inside the showcase, Da and Mr. Atherton chatted for a bit, discussing mainly the weather and local politics. My mind went to the fact we'd be needing more ice today. Not today. *Now*. Most of it I had used in the front counter with today's meat selection, and the icebox was about empty. Maybe Da would go down to Solano's Ice Barn and I would stay and mind the store. I knew how to make change, wrap the meats, and discuss the best ways of fixing pork chops. But it was Da's store. I, merely the helper. As usual, it would fall on me to go. But what if *those* men were out there on the street or down at Solano's waiting for me? I struggled to swallow.

"See ya tomorrow, Eagan." Mr. Atherton's words brought me back to the store. I nodded and followed him to the door where I turned the sign around to read *Open*.

Da plunked the last of the coins into the cash register and regarded the money as he spoke. "Best get over to Solano's before the day gets too hot." He held out a fifty-cent coin. "Get about fifteen pounds. Tell ye, Eagan, we get any more busy, we'll be havin' to buy a bigger icebox, we will."

Peering through the front window, I searched for *them*. No strangers passed nearby. Maybe they were gone. Out of town. Out of Texas. No, Zeke said he'd seen them in town Saturday. At noon, I'd visit the gun shop and buy me a weapon. And bullets. Just in case.

I patted my vest pocket. This morning I'd brought all my money with me. I'd counted nearly thirteen dollars which surely was enough. I wouldn't tell Da because he'd say no, and then we'd have an argument. I didn't want that. What he didn't know, wouldn't hurt him, I told myself.

"Eagan? You hear me?" Da joined me at the window. "What's got yer attention, boyo?"

I stepped back. "Nothin'. Just looking."

He patted my shoulder and nodded toward the storage room. "Best get that wheelbarrow and get a move on. Customers'll be arrivin' soon and I'll be needin' ye here."

"I could stay." I pointed to the coin he held out. "You go to Solano's. Give you a chance to visit with him." I shrugged. "You say you never get out and about. Well, here's your chance."

Before he could say no, I started toward the storage area. "I'll even get the wheelbarrow for you."

As if on cue, that irritating bell over the door rang and in stepped one of our best customers, Mrs. Watkins, ready for more fare for her brood. Da greeted her, then led her to the case, the glass shining from the early morning rays streaming in. He turned to me. "Go on now, Eagan. Tis ice we're in sore need of." He shooed me toward the storage room, and since he had a customer, I was obliged to go.

I knew *they* weren't in the room's darkness, but still, I squinted at the boxes, located the wheelbarrow, and made my way out of the room within a minute. If I could get down to Solano's at the end of the second block without being seen, maybe I'd be left alone and back at the store within ten minutes. Fifteen pounds of ice wasn't much, as I'd carted forty a time or two before, but still, it could be cumbersome.

I chose to go out the front door instead of the back into the alley. Da frowned at me and dipped his eyebrows when I waved a goodbye. Was I acting strange today?

Probably, but I'd do anything not to relive Friday's encounter.

The wheelbarrow, its wooden wheel and heavy body, rolled along with the confidence I didn't have. It was old, tough, and sturdy and I wasn't. Pushing it, I cast my eyes right and left, and even glanced over my shoulder a time or two. A couple ruts in the street, thanks to the one rain we'd had last month, made me lose control. It tilted, nearly tipping completely over, but I managed to keep it upright. More people were out and about than when Da and I had come to work this morning. But it wasn't busy like a Saturday. Or when the County Fair was in town or the big doings for the Fourth of July. I concentrated on remembering the glory of the fireworks until I spotted Solano's Ice Barn.

It was more like a barn inside a barn. The outside structure resembled a barn and may have been one back in the day, but inside was another barn with a rounded roof, this one buried halfway down in the ground. Resembling what I figured a cave looked like when I went in, it was cool, a bit damp and dark. Mr. Solano lit the lanterns only when a customer came in. He had told me that he buys ice from the Louisiana Ice Manufacturing Company and they ship tons during late winter to Texas where he gets a smaller shipment. I smiled at the aroma of wet straw that he said kept the ice frozen. A good insulator, he'd said. It seemed to work well because stacks of ice blocks towered over me and I was just shy of six feet.

He hacked off what I figured was fifteen pounds, dumped it in the wheelbarrow, took my fifty-cents coin, returned a couple of pennies, and off I went. Back into daylight, I squinted. I pushed the barrow out of the big barn, which opened to the main street. A long survey left, then right and behind me, revealed no one of any significance. So far, so good. Looked like I'd make it back in one piece, after all.

I had to take my time on the return trip. Those road ruts seemed to jump in front of me with every step, and navigating with weight was tough. I avoided toppling over twice. Two riders on horses trotted past, tipped their hats, and greeted me. No way could I wave back, so I offered a raised chin.

Now, almost halfway back to the store, I relaxed. There were enough people on the boardwalk that if those three men accosted me, I could scream, and help would come running. I was going to be all right.

Still, in the dirt road, I passed the Shoo Fly Café, my favorite place to eat, besides my house. Just then, the door opened and out stepped Purdy and the two Clydes, all three with toothpicks in their mouths.

I picked up speed, but Purdy's long legs reached me within seconds. "Well, well. Looky who we've got here. If it ain't the cripple from the butcher's."

I gripped the handlebars hard and inched forward. "Excuse me." By now the Clydes moved in, all three surrounding me like ravenous coyotes stalking a chicken coop. "Don't want any trouble. Excuse me." I pushed forward.

Clyde Two used his boot to push the top of the wheelbarrow over. Ice slid out onto the ground. They gave hearty belly laughs, and Purdy slapped my back. "Looks like you got yourself a mess."

"Leave me alone," I spoke quietly, but the words were strong between gritted teeth. "Now." While I struggled to right the barrow, Clyde One grabbed one side and dumped it the other way.

"Oops. Just tryin' to help there, Crip."

Purdy hefted the ice block and tossed it farther into the street, startling a passing horse. "Look what you made me do, boy." Purdy wiped his hands down his trousers. "Got me dirty and here I was tryin' to help, too."

Clyde Two ran his hands down the front of my apron and stopped near my crotch. "Let's go finish this."

"Get away! Leave me alone!" I slapped at his hands which made him move in close enough I could smell coffee and bacon on his breath.

Facing me, he moved in even closer, grabbing my most private parts. I growled, "Leave me the hell alone!" Using every muscle I owned, I reached out and popped him in the face. He snarled and returned the favor. Hard.

Back and forth, we exchanged punches. Stars blurred my vision.

"What's going on here?" A voice I didn't recognize stopped us mid-strike. I turned to look at a face I didn't want to see. Walter Wagner, my brother's nemesis, and Blanco Hill's Sheriff. Tate and he had gone to school together, and when Wagner became deputy, a year or so back, he and Sheriff Fritz Becker made my brother's life a living hell. Tate couldn't take a breath without being beaten and locked up. Which was why, now that Tate worked on a ranch milesaway, he was out of the badges' immediate reach.

My brothers and I had hoped things would be different when Becker was hurt in a major barroom brawl two months ago and couldn't fulfill his duties as sheriff. We were hoping somebody else would take his place. Maybe the other deputy, Tommy O'Sullivan. He was reasonable—and Irish. But of course, the town fathers decided to make Wagner county sheriff and Becker town marshal. They tended to rule the town. However, a glimmer of hope came in the form of Sullivan being appointed deputy. There was always a chance sanity would reign.

Wagner looked from man to man. "I'll ask again. What's going on?"

I wanted to shout out, explain what had happened Friday, and what was going on today. But like a statue, I stood still, eyes blinking. Air refused to enter my lungs and let me put words to my thoughts.

Clyde One helped turn the wheelbarrow right side up. "Well, Sheriff. This poor boy done tipped his barrow over and that ice just slid right out." He pointed to his friends. "We was only trying to get him upright with his load, but he didn't want our help. Got mean, he did."

"We weren't doing nothing, Sheriff. Just finished our vittles and tried to help." Purdy held one hand over his heart, another hand toward the sky. "That's gawd's honest truth."

Clyde One pointed at Clyde Two. "That's right, Sheriff. Just look at my brother's face, all bruised and bleeding." He then pointed at me. "I'd say he's a scrapper, sir. An evil youngster that's plain mean. In fact"—he regarded his two companions—"think we ought to file a complaint. Legal like." He nodded to Wagner. "You should probably oughta lock him up."

"He's tellin' true, Sheriff." Purdy moved his toothpick to the other side of his mouth, his thin lips rising. "Fact is, he promised to pay us if we'd help and then he welched on the deal. Told us to leave him alone and he wouldn't pay."

Purdy shrugged and continued. "At first, we told him we didn't want no money, seein' as helping's a right neighborly thing to do."

Clyde Two pointed at my chest. "But he insisted."

Looking down, Purdy shook his head. "A young boy like that. It's a shame, Sheriff. Pure shame."

Wagner turned to me, eyes narrowing as he examined my face. "Hell, yeah. Looks like you got yourself a black eye from a day or so ago, other old bruises under new ones. Just like your worthless brother Tate, you're a true rabble-rouser. A no good nothing. Don't surprise me none what you did." He took a breath. "Too bad they didn't clean your plow."

Finally, I thawed enough to speak. "But I didn't do anything! They attacked me!" I couldn't bring myself to mention Friday's encounter. "Sheriff. I was pushin' this cart when they came out of the café, knocked it over and scattered the ice. It was them who wrecked it all to hell."

"He's lyin', Sheriff. Pure and simple." Clyde One's eyes cast downward, and he looked up under his bushy eyebrows. "But tell you what, Sheriff." He chinned at me. "If he'll pay us what he promised, we won't press assault charges, although we rightfully can."

"I'd say you can. And should." Sheriff Wagner frowned at Clyde Two's face. "But if you'd rather have the money, I think that'd be fair enough." He turned to me. "How much d'you promise?"

"Nothing! I didn't promise them nothing! They started it."

Wagner gripped my upper right arm tight. "Empty your pockets."

"What?"

"You heard me. Empty them pockets. If you got any money in there, it belongs to them. If not, you'll spend your time behind bars until your pa comes to bail you out." The sheriff dug around in my vest pockets hidden under the apron. He held up all my money.

"That's exactly right, Sheriff." Purdy's smile stretched

his cheeks and pointed to the bills. "That's what he said he'd give us."

Wagner didn't bother to count, instead handed the bills to Purdy. That rotten lawman turned back to me. "Let that be a lesson, boy. Don't go back on your word." He pointed toward the butcher shop. "Now get this contraption and that ice out of the street. Get going."

I looked around for onlookers who could come to my defense but spotted only the backs of two children on their way to school and a man and woman entering the mercantile down the street. I stood my ground, trying to figure out how to get my money back. Wagner grabbed the back of my shoulders and heaved me several feet forward. I stumbled into the road, skidding on my knees. Throbbing, undoubtedly, they were skinned. But they didn't hurt as badly as my face. Or my pride.

Picking myself up, I couldn't turn to look at the four men now chortling. Various names were thrown at my back, but I chose to tune them out. I hefted the ice into the cart and pushed it toward the shop. I worked on what I'd tell Da when I walked in.

CHAPTER FIVE

"*Jasus!* NOT AGAIN!" DA HELD THE DOOR AS I struggled to get the wheelbarrow and me inside without hitting the wooden doorframe. "What the hell happened to ye this time, boyo? Ye look brutal."

I knew he was upset. Da rarely cursed, and never around Ma. I hung my head, trying desperately to avoid eye contact. Focusing on not running into the wall or storeroom door, I headed for the darkness ahead. *They* definitely weren't in there, and I was safe. For now.

Da held my upper arm, making me stop and almost dump the ice again. His thick hand gripped my chin, turning my head side-to-side. "What happened?" He drew a breath and looked in closer. "Ye dinna have time to go down to Sam's. Who hit ye?"

I wanted to tell him. I really did. But no way would I. A shrug and quick explanation were all I'd give. "Hit one of those ruts. Barrow fell over with me. Slid on gravel. Face and knees." When he simply huffed, I added, "I'm grand. Really, Da. Just grand."

He stood back, folded his arms, gaze sweeping me

up and down, down and up. I squirmed. He shook his head. "Ara, I've seen me share of fights—bruises and black eyes—and nobody gets marks like yours from falling in the dirt. Not one." He nodded toward the storeroom. "Go finish up your chores. Then I want ye to go home, wash up, change yer clothes, and come right back."

I looked at my ripped trousers and torn shirt. My left cheek throbbed. "But—"

"I won't have a son o'mine lookin' like ye do. Not here in the store. Not waitin' on me customers." He pointed. "Go. Crack on."

Did I look that bad? I certainly felt battered and bruised. I dumped the ice and chipped parts of it into the icebox, arranging the block in there. I upended the wheelbarrow and inspected my clothes.

Da was right. Both knees of the trousers were ripped, and my right shirt sleeve hung by a thread. Good thing I was wearing the apron, or the shirt buttons would have been popped off like last Friday. A soft pat of my lower lip brought blood and its swelling made my mouth hard to open. I ran my tongue around inside. Still had all my teeth. My lip would heal, but a lost tooth wasn't some-thing Ma could patch.

Head throbbing, I touched my forehead. A welt the size of a goose egg over my left eye pulsated. Maybe ice would help. I grabbed a small chip and held it there. The coolness eased the pain. I moved it to my lip. The hurt numbed and tension oozed out through my boots. I sighed. I'd be fine.

Da stepped in. "Ye aren't gone, already, boyo?" He took another long look at me. "You'll be gran' in a day or two. Should be glad you're not kissin' any Colleens right now. Not with that lip o'yers." His eyes sparkled even in the dim light. He chuckled and turned at the bell tinkling.

I waved to Da as I stepped onto the main street now packed with shoppers. Before stepping off the boardwalk, I made sure those three weren't in sight. Looking over my shoulder every few seconds, I limped home slower than usual. My knees were beginning to stiffen, and they hurt every time my boot hit the road.

I pulled open the screen door, stepped inside the front room, and stopped fast. Five pairs of ladies' eyes stared at me. Conversation turned into a collective gasp. A glance around the room reminded me that today was Ma's turn to host her sewing circle. Every Monday, they got together to mend worn-out clothes, work on a quilt, or sew a new garment. Ma was a "piecemeal seamstress," she'd said many times, so this gathering gave her lively conversations and probably a lot of gossip, to make the mending go faster.

"Gracious Mary." Ma put down her lapful of material and rushed to me. She reached to touch my face, but I moved back just far enough to be out of range. "What happened to ye, Eagan? Don't tell me ye were down at Sam's again. This early in the morning, too!" She tsked while peering at my face.

The women sucked all the air out of the room. Two of them leaned back like I had a raging case of pox. All hands hung mid-air, gripping needles.

I held Ma's hand and hoped I spoke clearly. "No, Ma. I wasn't at Sam's." My explanation picked up speed and probably words were lost over my swollen lips. "Went down to the Ice Barn. Coming back the wheel got stuck. The barrow tilted over in the road and took me with it. Skinned my knees." That was as close to the truth as I'd admit to.

Immediately, the women turned into mother hens, all clucking, shaking their heads, and offering various treatments Ma should use on me. If I hadn't been still shaking, I would have laughed.

One of the women pointed to my apron. "My Heavens, he's bleeding!" She put down her needle and sprung to her feet.

Holding up a hand, I rushed to explain. "I'm fine, really. It's not mine. It's from the meat shop."

A sigh of relief rolled around the room, and the woman settled back into her chair. I pointed toward my room upstairs. "Need to change, wash, then go back to work. Da's expecting me."

"Not until *I* say ye can go." Ma's blue-green eyes narrowed, and one hand fisted on her hip. "Go on and clean up. Bring me yer clothes and I'll mend 'em today."

I could feel the stares on my back as I lurched up the steps. And then the jabber dam broke, the women all opining about what had really happened. I'd be the gossip of the group for weeks.

I eased to the edge of my bed, ready to lie back and enjoy a quick nap. But my knees said otherwise, and my face decided it wanted a thorough scrubbing. Not in a hurry to return to work or especially face those women again, I took my time washing, patting, and soothing my bruises. Friday's shiner ringed most of my right eye, and the bruise on my left cheek had turned deep purple. A hint of green lined the edges. Between the cuts, scrapes, and bruises, my copper-colored eyes stood out against my pale face. Was I ever a mess.

I put on a clean shirt, the other pair of trousers, my vest, dusted off my boots, and combed my blond hair, which I hated because it was wavy. Thank goodness it wasn't what they called "curly," but it hung in waves to my shoulders. Ma said it was beautiful, fortunately never in front of my friends. A compliment like that always made my face hot. And of course, in school, I'd been teased. A lot.

A long look in the shaving mirror, and I was ready to present a better version of myself downstairs. I grabbed my apron, ready to start the day anew. Before opening the bedroom door, a thought struck. Da kept his gun in his bedroom, right next door. I knew where it was. Wrapped in cloth, tucked back in a drawer. With Ma downstairs busy gossiping and trading stories with her friends, she wouldn't hear the drawer scrape.

Feeling like a common criminal, nevertheless, I sneaked into their bedroom, located the Colt, and unwrapped the material. Caressing the power in the palm of my hand, I ran trembling fingers up and down the barrel. I opened the gate to make sure no bullets were in the cylinder, discovered it empty, and pressed it sideways to my chest, closing my eyes. It beat against my heart. A sigh the size of San Antonio erupted from my inner soul.

In my mind, I stood up to Purdy and the two Clydes, smiling at the panic on their surly faces. I aimed the gun. The torment ended. The equalizer. Purdy would run away, Clyde One kneeling and asking forgiveness. Clyde Two would wet himself, then raise his pistol at me. I fired first. He spun, took a step back, and dropped his weapon as he spiraled into the ground.

Heart thudding against my sore ribs, I couldn't move. I'd killed a man. I opened my eyes, relieved to recognize bedroom walls rather than a man lying dead on the dusty street. Panic, anger, concern, confusion, fear, and contentment mingled in a cacophony of emotions that flooded over me. The gun shook in my hand as I wiped beads of sweat off my forehead.

"Ho-ly hell," I mumbled. That weapon…its power, its beauty, its finality called to me. I wanted one. Needed one. Had to have one. And Da wasn't using this one. I could slip it inside my vest, and he'd never know. Probably had bullets around somewhere, too.

"Eagan?"

I jumped. Ma had called from the bottom of the stairs, but any second, she'd be up here, looking for me, wondering what was taking so long. "Be right there!" Take the gun or leave it? Take? Leave?

Everything in my being told me to rewrap, put the gun back in the drawer and go downstairs. Then to work.

Instead, I wrapped my apron around the Colt, folded the cloth Da had wrapped it in, and put that back where I found it. This evening, I'd figure out how to return the weapon.

Or not.

* * *

No DOUBT, there was a lighter spring to my step as I walked down Main, headed for the shop. Ma had insisted I have a glass of milk before she allowed me to go and one of the ladies had brought in scones, made fresh this morning. Two of the pastries went down well with the milk.

Fortified, part of me was hoping The Three would step out of the shadows and accost me. This time I'd be ready. Just as I reached the shop's door, I realized I had no bullets. Hard to shoot someone that way. Maybe I could go by the gunsmith's this afternoon and buy a couple. But with what money? Da undoubtedly had coins in the cash register. I'd borrow some.

Gun and apron tucked under one arm, I stepped inside and froze. Must be ten customers waiting to be served. Da caught my eye and waved me in. Automatically, I went for my apron, but with the weight, realized I had to hide the gun first. I rushed to the storeroom and slid it behind a couple of burlap sacks, arranging the material so it was invisible. I hoped.

Donning my smock, I limped back out and offered assistance to a little old lady.

The afternoon turned hectic, and I kept thinking there was a party or a "do" that I didn't know about. Had we lost the invitation? For a Monday, usually calm with few customers, we were kept hopping. And then, before I realized we'd worked through luncheon, the shop turned quiet. Shafts of sun spread across the floor but at a low angle. Must be almost quitting time. My stomach rumbled. Definitely food time.

Da regarded his pocket watch. "Wouldn'na ye know? High time ta turnin' that *Open* sign around." He turned to me. "Wanna do the honors?"

Oh boy, did I. Missing dinner, although it was only a sandwich, my stomach had decided to complain and rumble. I flipped the sign to *Closed*, pulled the apron over my head, and draped the stinky material over my arm. I'd wash it tonight.

The gun! I'd almost forgotten my most prized treasure. I hadn't had a chance to get bullets. And surely, at this time of day, Mr. Krause, the gunsmith, was at home enjoying a plate of whatever Germans ate for supper. Surely, it wasn't as good as Ma's Irish chicken stew. Nothing beat that. I wiped a bit of drool from the side of my mouth and turned to Da as he folded his own apron.

"What say we straighten up the storeroom then head for home, boyo?" Da headed for the back room.

I jumped in front, blocking the door. "I'll come in early tomorrow, Da. I'll clean up back here. I owe you for missing part of the day."

He narrowed his lids, cocked his head, and let out a loud sigh, eyebrows dipping over his olive-green eyes. "What's got into ye, Eagan? First ye offer to sweep the porch, which ye haven't done yet. Then ye offer to stay while I go to Solano's Ice. Ye work through luncheon, and now ye offer to come in early, ye do." He moved in a bit closer. "Ye grand?"

I shrugged. "If you want to bunk off tomorrow, I'll open and work all day. You come in when you feel like it."

Da's stomach grumbled louder than mine. He patted the offending area, tossing a sideways smile at me. "Me belly thinks me throat's been cut." He turned around, grabbed his apron, and headed across the store. "Let's crack on then. I'll think on it while we walk."

I also thought while we walked. My limp this evening was worse than usual. Must be tired. And I was. My knees throbbed, ribs burned, my bottom lip had crusted over, split, then re-crusted. Every time today I had smiled or spoke, it stung, which made me wonder now how I'd chew supper. As hungry as I was, I'd surely manage.

CHAPTER SIX

I'M NOT SURE HOW, BUT I GOT UP EARLY AND managed to head off to the shop with Da's keys, about the time Old Man Gurky's rooster crowed. Snores had floated down the stairs and into the kitchen where I had grabbed a leftover scone from yesterday. I left a note telling him to sleep late and come in only if he felt like it. I had the shop under control. I slipped out the front door, closing it so gently I wasn't sure it latched.

Every muscle in my body complained, especially my knees, while I walked the rutted road to the store. Through the graying morning, my gaze swung right, left and behind me the entire five long blocks. Would *they* be waiting for me? Would I be lucky enough they'd decided to move on?

Deathly quiet. The town wasn't quite awake yet and for that, I was grateful. It would be bustling soon enough, and I'd have to be extra vigilant. A light from the big window at the Shoo Fly Café turned into a welcoming beacon of safety. At least someone else was up and working.

At the shop, I unlocked the front door, peered up and down the street, then across it. Nobody. Not Purdy, not the Clydes. I donned my freshly washed apron, grabbed the broom near the door, and swept the sidewalk. Dirt and dust mushroomed from the boardwalk. I sneezed, wiped my nose, sneezed again. Sun brighter now, I swept clear down to the end of the block, another three stores worth. Hopefully, they'd appreciate the effort.

Back inside, I locked the door and headed for the storeroom. The gun hadn't moved. I held it, caressing the entire weapon as if it were a newborn babe. Running my fingers up and down the barrel, I smiled too hard. My lip cracked, and blood dripped down my chin. Small price to pay for such pleasure. I aimed across the room, focusing on a small wooden crate in the corner.

Bang! Oh, it felt good. The imagined recoil was like butter. Barely felt it at all. I aimed and fired again. *Bang!* Again. *Bang!* Again. *Bang!* Damn, I was a good shot. Hit everything I aimed at. With a tad more practice, maybe I'd be better than Jesse James. Like big brother Tate wanted to be. Hell, I'd be better than Tate and Jesse combined.

Bullets. I needed bullets. Da had left coins in the cash register yesterday. I returned my weapon to its hiding place, closed the storeroom door, and checked for money. Sure enough. Almost a dollar's worth of change in there. I couldn't take it all, and how much were bullets, anyway? I selected five dimes. That should get me at least one. Maybe two. I shoved the coins under the apron and into my vest pocket, then reluctantly turned my attention to meat.

Surprisingly, ice from yesterday hadn't melted too much. Soon, I'd have to make the trip down to Solano's, but for now, I'd use what I had. I put more ice into the front showcases, then hauled out lamb chops, Hamburg steaks, roasts, pork, and various other cuts of meat for display. Now that I had a gun, I could go hunting with Jimmy and Zeke. They liked ducks and knew a place a couple hours away that had hundreds of them. How perfect would that be? I could bring a few back to the store and one home to Ma. We'd have a fancy Sunday dinner.

Tap, tap, tap. I jumped and spun around like an off-kilter ballerina. Heart pounding, I peered at the front door like it had come alive. A tap on the window shook me back to reality. Mr. Atherton held up one chicken. Head someplace else, I'd completely forgotten he'd be stopping by before the day started.

I unlocked the door and held it wide as he stepped in. "Howdy, Mr. Atherton. You startled me."

He chuckled, a low, innocent sound. "Sure did. You about jumped to the moon." Laying

the plucked chicken on a sheet on the counter, he glanced around the store. "Your pa out sick today?"

"No, sir." I rummaged through the cash register to find two one-dollar bills. "Told him I'd open up and he can come in when he feels like it." I held out the cash.

"Did ya now?" He leaned back, then slowly took the money. Cocking his head to one side, he waved the bills. "Ya givin' me a raise while your pa's not here?"

"Sir?"

Mr. Atherton held out the money. "Your pa pays me fifty cents a bird. This's too much." He peered at the cash register, the drawer still open. "How about five dimes?" I went cold. "Or that Eagle half-dollar I see in there?"

I'm sure *stupid* was written all over my fiery face. Obviously, I wasn't ready to manage the store by myself.

I replaced the bills, dug out the half-dollar coin, and stuttered. "Thank you, Mr. Atherton. Thank you for being so honest. Da would've been furious with me."

He lightly thumped my shoulder. "I'm sure he would've." Atherton's light-brown eyes sparked. "But you giving him the day off might've made up for it."

I tried to nod, but my embarrassment kept my shoulders slumped and my gaze sweeping the floor. "Not likely, sir."

"Well, I tell ya, son. Still and all, it was mighty thoughtful." He rubbed his stubbled chin. "Wish my boys would think like you. Maybe I should send 'em over. Ya can give 'em some advice."

It was my turn to chuckle. Looked like I'd done a good thing. First time I could remember that I was held up as an example of decency. My chest swelled, and my lip cracked with the smile.

I waved goodbye, then realized I hadn't swept inside the store for days. A closer inspection showed it was in desperate need. I hadn't turned the door sign around yet, so I had time. I arranged the new chicken in the case making sure the bird nestled on ice, then grabbed the broom I'd left by the front door. Fortunately, the shop wasn't all that big, and I could get it clean within a few minutes. I'd done it at least a million times.

Starting at the counter on the far side of the shop, I swept my way toward the back door. Soon, a small mound of dirt and bits of dried meat accumulated. Thoughts elsewhere, I unlocked the door, pushed it open and took one swipe at the pile. The door squeaked like it was starting to close. Probably the wind, I figured. I pushed on it and spotted a trouser leg I didn't recognize.

My heart raced in pure panic and I slammed the door, immediately locking it. *Need to block the door,* my only thought. A heavy crate nearby would have to do. I pushed the wooden box in front of the door while someone knocked. Hard.

I held the broom handle close to my chest and tried to make myself tiny like a mouse. Breathing didn't come and my hands tingled. My heart thudded so loudly, all I heard was pounding.

And then it stopped. Deep breath. Another one. Nerves calming, I relaxed.

Bang, bang, bang. Front door. The Three were at the front door! I plastered myself to the wall between the two doors, praying they would give up and leave.

"Eagan? Eagan? I know you're in there."

I listened harder. Someone tapped on the window.

"Eagan? Son?"

Da. What an idiot I was. Had become one. "Just a minute, Da." Trembling legs took me across the shop to the door.

I opened it, remembering to turn the sign around. I couldn't shut the door fast enough before Da took to ranting as he stepped inside.

"What the hell's wrong with ye, Eagan?" He tossed two wax paper-wrapped sandwiches on the counter and spun back to me. "Ye leave early, clean up the place, then slam the back door on my foot!" He leaned in close, dropping his words to a tense whisper. "What've ye done, boyo? Ara, what are you not telling your da?"

The little boy in me wanted to throw myself in his arms and cry. He'd make the world right again, as he always had. But the grown-up in me held him at arms' length. No way in hell I'd tell him about Friday night. About the ultimate humiliation. About his gun. About what I planned to do. No way.

He held both of my shoulders and looked into my

sore and swollen face. "Ye can tell me anythin', boy. I've had a few experiences of me own and maybe I can help ye."

Pressure built behind my eyes, but I was determined not to cry. Shrugging out of his well-meaning hold, I stepped back, desperate to keep tears from flowing. "Don't know what you mean, Da. I'm grand. Everything's grand."

With perfect timing, the bell over the door announced a customer. Whew! My smile split my lip again. When I turned to see who'd saved me, I froze like a statue. A girl in the prettiest sky-blue dress I'd ever seen shut the door behind her.

"'Allo there, Miss." Da tied the apron strings behind him while nodding to this angel.

For the second time this morning, I couldn't move. This time, it wasn't due to abject fear. Well, maybe a bit.

She glided into the middle of the room, her lake blue eyes taking in the store—the various meats, the crates of bottles and stacks of brown wrapping paper. And then... me. If I could unfreeze myself, I'd stretch out a hand to shake with her. As it was, all I managed was a weak smile, my lip splitting again.

The beauty, this Heaven-sent messenger, nodded to me and Da. "I'm Molly. Thomas O'Malley's daughter." She reached out a perfectly gloved hand. "Ma asked me to come buy some Hamburg steak."

Da, obviously not as dumbfounded as I was, returned a hand. "Pleased to make yer acquaintance, Miss O'Malley. I've met yer ma a time or two. Yer family's new to the area, if I remember right."

"Yes, sir, we are. Moved from Kansas. Bought the Crawford ranch about three miles north of town. We're raising cattle of our own, but none are ready for butchering yet. We have only yearlings."

Da gave her a wide smile, winked, and nodded, which I thought was way too casual and forward. "Well, when they're ready, let me know. The slaughterhouse, where we buy our meat, is always in the market for fresh."

"Thank you, I will." Her gaze swept the store, and I detected a hint of approval. Her voice, like cherubs purring, filled the room with music. Beautiful music. I could listen to her all day.

"How much steak did ye need?" Da sounded all business while all I could do was stand there like a deaf-mute, addle-brained plowboy.

They discussed quality while Da filled the order. Inch by inch, I thawed. Breath no longer stuck in my lungs, I took a step in her direction. Da turned to me.

"Ah, here then. This is me son, Eagan. Works here full time. Me right-hand man."

Would my tongue and lips work? Together? I opened my mouth and out came, "Ma'am. Pleased to meet you." Yes! I got through a whole sentence.

She stretched out an arm, offering her hand. "Molly O'Malley." Giggling, she glanced down at her button-up shoes. "Molly O'Malley is such a mouthful. Wish I could have a different front name."

It suited me just fine, but could I tell her? No. Instead, I released her soft hand and kicked at the bottom of the wooden case. Da jumped in and saved my humiliation.

"*Tá sé go hálainn.* I think it's beautiful, Miss O'Malley. Good Irish name. Suits ye, too, what with yer strawberry red hair."

She had hair?

CHAPTER SEVEN

THE BELL JINGLED AGAIN, BUT ONLY TO TOLL her leaving. The tinny clang brought nothing but sadness and a long sigh to my chest. I'd probably never see her again.

Da's hand on my shoulder rocked it. "She's a *cailín áiliann*, now ain't she?"

Oh yes. A million times, yes. And *beautiful* didn't do her justice. The back of her blue

skirt waved past the window as she headed home, the wrapped package under a lovely arm. How

could I manage to go visit her? At least I knew where she lived. Did she go to church? Was she seeing someone? Already spoken for? Questions flew around my head until Da swept the broom across my boots.

"Here ye go. Finish up what ye started." He aimed the broom toward the back door.

Way beyond embarrassed, I swept harder than necessary, finding all sorts of nooks and crannies to clean. Once I pushed the crate blocking the door back into place, I stood up straight, pulled air into my lungs, unlocked the latch, and stepped out into the morning air. A long look left and right revealed nothing but empty alley. Not wanting to push my luck, I swept as quickly as possible, then closed the door, locking it with a satisfying *click*.

I kept both eyes open, one a lookout for The Three, the other for Molly. I didn't spot either for two full days. By Friday, my nerves had relaxed as I figured Purdy and the two Clydes had moved on. I hadn't heard of any big barroom fights or other attacks in the street. Everything was nice and quiet.

Which gave me the chance to figure how to go over to Mr. Krause, the gunsmith, to see about bullets and maybe get a few tips on shooting. I couldn't ask too much since he'd probably talk to Da at some point.

At lunch on Friday, I wolfed down my sandwich in record time, then asked Da for a few minutes off, telling him I wanted to try on a new hat down at the mercantile.

"A new hat?" Da put down his sandwich and spoke over a mouthful of ham and bread. "A new hat?" He leaned back and eyed me. "Ara, what's got into ye, boy?"

I shrugged.

"No, now don't tell me. Let me guess." Da's eyes narrowed just a bit. Playfulness ringed each one. "Ye're sweet on Miss Molly O'Malley and want to look the dapper." He tapped my upper arm. "That's it, is it?"

"Does it show, Da?" All right. I'd take that. Best he thought I was out wanting to *look* better rather than *shoot* better. And so far, the gun, hidden in the storeroom, had stayed put. Da hadn't looked for it at home and hadn't discovered the weapon here.

I pulled the apron over my head, folded it carefully, and set it behind the counter near the cash register. I tossed half a smile his way. "I'll be back soon, don't you worry."

He hollered at my back as I opened the front door. "Don't know what's got into ye. Ye've changed."

I waved over my shoulder and closed the door firmly, the bell still tinkling inside.

In case he was watching, I headed west up Main but soon doubled back through the alley and down to the gunsmith.

His store was empty of customers, and Mr. Krause was sitting on a stool behind the counter, running a rod with a cleaning cloth through a gun's barrel. He held up the gun, peering through the bore. He spotted me, raised an eyebrow, then furrowed both.

"Howdy, young Eagan." He lay the gun on the counter. "Didn't expect to see you in here."

We shook hands, and it took me a good long while to stammer out what I wanted. While I did, my gaze roved over the rifles, shotguns, and revolvers he had on a shelf behind him. The display reminded me of being in a candy store as a child. The possibilities were endless, and I could taste each one. Choosing was always the hard part.

Mr. Krauss cupped a hand behind his ear. "Bullets, you say? Yeah, I got bullets." His bushy gray eyebrows dipped. "Didn't know you went around heeled. What kinda gun ya got?"

Well, hell. I wasn't completely sure, and no way could I bring it to him. I dug hard into my memory and recalled Da telling Tate about it. "Sixty Colt Army revolver."

He eased down from the stool and eyed me. "That'd be forty-four caliber."

Sounded about right. I knew a little about guns, but clearly not enough. I just needed one that would shoot straight...one with bullets.

We spent longer than I'd intended when he handed me a box of caps and one of paper cartridges. He assumed I knew how to load my gun, so simply handed me what I needed.

"Fifty cents, Eagan." He held out a gnarled hand.

"Both?" I dug in my vest pocket for the five dimes I'd hidden there days ago.

"Unless you want to pay extra for 'em." Part of a smile crinkled his grizzled face. "Fifty cents for both."

I thanked him, pocketed my ammunition, and started back for the shop. The sun was lower than it should have been, so I hurried my step. Da would kill me for being so late.

I rounded a corner and there stood Sheriff Wagner, the scourge of Blanco Hill. Maybe he'd ignore me and let me pass without too much hassle. But no. He stepped directly in my path, causing me to screech to a halt. He eyed me. "Where ya off to in such a hurry?"

"Work. Da's expecting me. Excuse me." I side-stepped, and he dogged my steps. I raised my voice higher than necessary. "I said excuse me."

"Ain't no *excuse* for crips like you." Sarcasm dripped off every word. "What are you up to?" He chinned at the bulge in my vest. "I mean, seein' as you're supposed to be at work, like you say."

I stepped the other way. "On an errand. I still need to get back. Move aside, *please*." Would I have to resort to hitting him? If I did, I'd end up behind bars. Probably for a long time. A glance up the street and the shop was still a block and a half away. The only good part was I didn't see Purdy or the two Clydes.

Sheriff Wagner stepped in close and made a point of sniffing at me. "Don't smell like you been drinkin'. Don't smell like you had a woman lately, neither. You one of those fancy pants?" He turned up his nose and breathed in again. "No, not a man. A sheep." He poked my chest so hard I stepped back. "That's it. You've been havin' your way with a ewe. That's just like you and your Irish brothers. Can't get a woman so you get yourself a woolie."

Hands fisted, all I could see was Wagner's nose relocated to his ear. That would be glorious. Using every fiber in my body, I fought to keep my emotions under control.

Poking me harder in the chest, he continued taunting. "That brother of yours, Joe? Well, I hear he ran off to Denver. Him and that whore of his. Bet they both—"

"That's enough, Wagner. Ain't got time to stand around listening to you badmouth my brother." Surprised those words came from my mouth, I stood my ground. My shoulders drew back. More than likely the bullets made me bolder. I liked the feeling.

"Well, Sheriff Wagner." A woman's sultry voice behind me made me turn.

Wagner tipped his hat. "Miss Gertrude Van Zant. A pleasure, as always."

"I'll be going now." I stepped right while he made eyes at this Gertrude. Her timing was perfect, and he was obviously interested in her. Neither seemed to notice I was there one minute and gone the next.

All the way back to the shop, limping as fast as I could, I knew I'd feel a bullet in my back within seconds, or at least cold handcuffs around my wrists. But no. At the shop's door, I gazed behind me down the street. Sheriff Wagner was strutting a bit, chatting with three women on the sidewalk.

Teeth gritted, I stepped into the store. Fortunately, two Irishmen from the Ould Sod were busily passing the time with Da, all telling stories at the same time in Gaelic. These were men who came in almost daily and occasionally bought something. So, hopefully Da didn't realize how long I'd been gone.

While I kept an eye out for the Clydes and Purdy, and now the sheriff, I watched for the lovely Molly O'Malley. Guess she stayed close to home, as I hadn't seen hide nor hair of her pretty blue dress. Maybe she had been a daydream. Was she even real?

CHAPTER EIGHT

AND THEN, THERE SHE WAS. SITTING IN THE second to last pew in church. The days since Tuesday had dragged. No, passed as slow as the days before Christmas. I'd looked for her everywhere, my heart always beating a bit harder when the bell over the shop door tinkled. But it was never her. Not until this moment.

Shoulders pulled back, I nodded to her as I walked with Ma and Da to the first pew. They liked sitting up front. I don't know why, but this area was known as the Nolan Pew and nobody else sat there until we did. Today, I'd give anything to sit in the back. Since we were early, I turned around and spotted her among what looked like a dozen red-headed children. A ma and da sat on either end of the line. If size was any indication, Molly was the oldest.

The priest walked in, and I reluctantly pulled my attention away from the most beautiful

creature on earth to a robed man spouting "thees," "thous," and "thys." I sat, stood, kneeled, sung, half-listened, stood again, sat once more, all the time hoping she was back there doing the same thing.

With the final "amen," I scooted down the aisle, out the door and waited at the bottom of the steps. Nodding and giving a quick "hello" to nearly everyone leaving, I figured her entire family had somehow vanished through a back door. Surely, there couldn't be anybody left inside.

Ma and Da stepped out, hesitating at the glaring sun, shaking hands with the priest. Then, down the steps they came.

"There ye are, Eagan." Ma took my arm. "Walkin' home with us, are ye?"

Behind them, I spotted a sea of red hair. I pecked Ma on the cheek and released her hand from my arm. "Sorry, Ma. There's somebody I need to talk to."

She and Da turned around, smiled at the O'Malley clan, then nodded at me. "I see what ye mean." Ma winked at me, took Da's arm, and headed west. "Well. Don't be too late, son. Remember us." She stifled a giggle.

I couldn't respond, what with my tongue stuck to the roof of my mouth.

Molly flashed the widest, most enchanting smile when she spotted me at the base of the steps. My heart must have been beating because something fluttered inside my chest. Remembering my manners, thank you Ma, I wrenched my hat from my head, ran a hand across my hair, and returned Molly's grin. Thankfully, my lip had healed enough it didn't split again. In fact, I was pretty much healed, except for the ugly green and yellow patch under my eye.

The red-haired herd of Lilliputians congregated at the bottom of the steps near Molly and waited for their ma and da to join them. I was surprised the youngsters didn't go scampering off across the wide field. I would have at their age.

"Good afternoon, Mr. Nolan." Molly held out a hand. "Nice to see you again."

Again, my manners kicked in without my thinking. I'd definitely have to remember to thank Ma. "Miss O'Malley. So, you go to church here?" Oh, Jeez. What a stupid question. Could I not have come up with something better?

She glanced up at her folks shaking hands with the priest. "We just started a few weeks back." One of her siblings, a little boy about six, tugged on her skirt and pointed to the grassy field. Molly raised one shoulder. "Yes, go play. But we're leaving soon."

Leaving? I hated that word. "I could walk you home if you'd like. I know it's a ways, but it's a nice day and it's Sunday, so not much to do, except milk the cow. You have a cow, don't you? Of course, horses're already fed, I guess, and chickens—"

"Yes, all done." She giggled—actually giggled at me. And she flashed another dazzling smile, which lit up her blue eyes sparkling like sun glinting on a stream. Could anyone be more perfect?

Her ma and da stepped to the ground, giving a final wave to the priest, then joined us.

"Ma, Pa, this is Mr. Eagan Nolan. The boy I've been telling you about." Molly pointed at me. "Down at the meat shop?"

She's been talking about me? Was it good? What did she say? I reached up for my hat but found only air. It was still clutched in my other hand. What a moron. "Ma'am, sir." Her da and I shook hands, and I nodded to her ma.

Her ma, who I sort of recognized from coming into

the shop, did a mental headcount of children, her gaze pinpointing each one. She also took time to study my face. I hoped I'd remembered to wipe off the egg parts from breakfast.

"Nice to meet you, Eagan." Ma tilted her head. "You're taller than I remember. Younger, too."

"Over six foot, almost eighteen, ma'am." I hoped there wasn't more to the inquisition. I wasn't ready.

"Well, I think it's wonderful, you working with your pa like that." Mrs. O'Malley stepped back and glanced at her husband. "Your family's building something. Good for you both."

I had no idea what she was talking about, but her words were soft, sweet, approving. That's all I needed.

"Time to head on home." Ma waved at two children playing chase in the yard, then shooed the rest toward a wagon across the street.

First looking at her da, then Ma, I took a deep breath. "Uh, I asked Molly if I could walk her home. Hope you don't mind."

Ma flapped a hand. "I don't mind, but it's three miles." She produced a smile similar to

Molly's. "I have a better idea. Why don't you come have Sunday dinner with us? One more mouth to feed won't make a difference. Molly's father can drive you home later."

Oh, Lord. An afternoon with Molly, but then a long drive alone with her da. Choices? I nodded. I'd take the chance her da wouldn't ask hard questions. "Thank you, ma'am, for the invitation. I'd be honored to come to Sunday dinner." A glance at Molly and she raised both eyebrows at me while her mouth turned into a bow. One dimple accentuated her left pink cheek.

Mrs. O'Malley turned toward the wagon and spoke

over her shoulder at me. "Well, come on then, Eagan. Hop in." What must have been twenty children raced for the wagon, the older ones scrambling into the hay scattered in the bed.

Molly and I lifted the youngest ones in, made them sit, then hopped on.

Ma turned on her seat. "We'll stop by your folks and tell them you're dining with us."

Had not seen that coming. All right. I pointed up the street. "We're about four blocks that way. Might even catch up with them before that."

We sat near the end, our feet dangling over the edge. Bumps along the way only served to jostle me closer to Molly. Could this day get any better?

Ma and Da, in their church finery, had just reached the top of the front porch when our wagonload of redheads drove up. Ma waved for everyone to get down, but Molly's ma shook her head.

"Just wanted you to know we're borrowing your son for the afternoon, Mrs. Nolan. Invited him to dinner and he accepted." Molly's ma flapped her hand. "In fact, why don't you two come, also? We could get better acquainted."

Oh, please no, I muttered. No. Not now. This courting thing was hard enough with just me. It'd be impossible and humiliating with Ma and Da.

Ma walked up to the wagon and nodded at Molly's ma. "Thanks for the offer, Mrs. O'Malley. But I've already got stew on the stove. Some other time?"

A huge sigh escaped my chest. Saved.

More brief discussions sawed back and forth but I tuned them out. I had Molly at my shoulder, and she had my undivided attention. Suddenly, the wagon jerked, and I crashed against Molly. We both laughed, she more than me. How could I laugh with my heart in my throat?

At the house, the children asked me hundreds of questions while we waited for the noon meal. Molly helped with the fixings, and the older girls set the table. The rest of us were in the front room playing. Waiting. Asking and answering questions. Waiting. I sat on a brown padded chair, then stood and looked at pictures of stern old people on the wall. Must've been relatives.

Aromas of baked chicken, cornbread, and fresh green beans floated out the kitchen and into the front room. I couldn't help licking my lips a time or two around explaining to one child why my mustache was so light he could barely see it.

Before I formed an acceptable answer for a five-year-old—he said he was five—he continued with questions about cowboys and pirates and outlaws. Another brother asked if I knew Jesse James. This brother was about eight.

A girl blindsided me with, "When are you going to marry Molly?"

Pure panic gripped my throat. I stuttered, desperately needing to be rescued. No adult came to my aid. An idea sprung to mind. I stood and pointed to the door. "How about you all show me your chickens?" That was harmless, right?

An army of little people jumped up and down, clucking, flapping wings and two even crowed. Sounded plenty authentic, too. Problem was they ran around the room, pecking at the rug and occasionally each other. One little girl sat in the corner, desperate to poop out an egg.

"No! Outside, chickens. You live outside!" I opened the door, hoping to shoo them out and in stepped Mr.

O'Malley, Thomas, as he'd been introduced to me. Over the squawking, I hollered to explain. "I'm sorry. I only asked to see the chickens."

A thin smile crinkled his cheeks, then turned to his brood. "All right chickens, wash up for dinner."

Instantly, they quieted, with only few squawks and one more cock-a-doodle-do and headed outside for the water trough. Like a short army, they lined up. I guessed when you have that many siblings, you have to do that. I couldn't imagine having so many brothers and sisters. Two was all I knew, and since I was the youngest, always got the hand-me-downs and had to do the chores my brothers didn't want. When we were younger, they blamed everything on me, but I had a feeling Ma and Da knew better. I wondered how it worked with nine siblings. I had counted nine but might have missed one or two.

Mr. O'Malley stood in the front room staring at my face, and then down at my hands. Up at me, then down.

Once the entire flock was outside, I held up both my hands like I'd just noticed they were new. "Guess I should go wash up, too." I pointed at the door. "Be right back." I limped away as fast as I could and then took my place in line at the water pump. Finally, my turn, knowing a million eyes were watching, I picked up a bar of soap lying on a table next to the pump, lathered up well and washed my face, too. Rinsed off, I held out a hand and a towel appeared. It was wet and used but did the trick well enough.

All clean and now quiet, the entourage took seats at the table. Since I was a guest, I was placed next to Molly and her da near the end. Butterflies stomping in my stomach did nothing for my usually ravenous appetite. Nothing on the table looked edible, although I figured it was tasty. Mrs. O'Malley and Thomas ladled green beans and fresh corn to plates held out by the sea of redheads. Molly and I waited patiently for ours.

Once the younger ones' plates were adorned, we got our share while the parents took what was left. Which wasn't much. But there had been enough fried chicken to go around easily. I picked the smallest of everything, not wanting to literally take food out of mouths.

I answered a few questions that were mainly about how long I'd worked with Da, my future plans, my brothers, and how I liked living in Blanco Hills. I assumed they asked that last question since they were new to the area.

Giving them a quick rundown of the good points of town, I emphasized how lucky they were to be here. Maybe Molly would stay here, too. No need for her to go off to a bigger town. Not like my brother Joe. Of course, he'd gotten married and followed his in-laws to Denver. Probably never see him again. I already missed him terribly and he'd been gone just a couple of months.

Before I realized the meal was over, Ma O'Malley pushed her chair back from the table and pointed to a couple of the children, the older ones. "Eliza, Teddy. Stack the dishes over on the counter." She turned to a third child. "Tommy, start heating the water."

And like magic, they pushed their chairs back and did as told. I was impressed, but also amazed they didn't whine. I would have. Da nodded at me. "Molly, why don't you show Eagan our newest line of yearlings? He might want to see what he'll be selling next year."

Perfect! A chance to get out of the house *alone* with Molly.

I stood and wiped my mouth with the cloth napkin. "Thank you for a wonderful meal, Mrs. O'Malley. It was delicious." All right, I was lying. I hadn't tasted a thing.

Had I even eaten? My plate was clean and decorated with biscuit flakes. So, apparently, I had.

The front door closed behind us, and she pointed north. "Biggest herd's a ways off. Ma doesn't like the smell, so we keep only a few nearby."

Did I truly care about cattle? Live cattle? Not a whit. But if Molly cared, guessed I could too. We strolled east about a quarter mile to a fenced-in area filled with steers. I counted at

least thirty, all sporting black hides, shining in the afternoon sun, gleaming like ebony diamonds.

Molly leaned against a wooden post and hung an arm over the wire fencing. Like family dogs, the wide-eyed black beauties spotted her and wandered over. I guessed looking for treats. Or maybe checking out the strangers. Either way, they came up to the fence, a couple sticking their heads between the wires, extending their necks until they resembled turtles.

I ran my hand down the neck of the closest. He turned his head and licked me. Laughing, I rubbed as much of him as I could reach, and I swear, if he could, he'd have climbed onto my lap for a good overall rubdown. Molly was doing the same with another one, and we shared laughs. She was good to be with. Fun. Not afraid to get all slobbered up. My kind of girl.

We spent the next hour petting, rubbing the animals, then wiping steer drool off our clothes. We laughed, made up jokes, talked about eating these critters, not naming our food, about everything and nothing. It was the most glorious moment in the world.

Molly and I found a Texas oak upwind from the cattle. We sat, backs against the trunk, and raised our faces to the flecks of sun managing to sparkle between the leaves.

Life couldn't be better. I sighed. Loudly. She took my hand.

"I haven't had this much fun in weeks." She giggled again. A true, honest giggle.

"Me, neither. Thank you." I didn't giggle, but sure wanted to.

We sat quiet until she took a breath and asked, "You got a gun, Eagan? You go out shooting with your pa? Your brothers?"

I leaned back, hand still in hers, and studied her pinking face. "I do. Why d'you ask?" Well, technically, I had a gun. And bullets. And I *wanted* to go shooting with my family. So, I lied. But only a half lie.

Resting her head on my shoulder, her silky, golden-flecked red hair draping down my chest, she sighed. "I think a man who shoots well, ain't afraid to stand up for himself, is ace-high." She squeezed our intertwined fingers. "I'd like to get to know him well."

Air refused to enter my lungs. Hell yeah, I'd become that man. Tomorrow. I'd turn cartwheels in a dung heap just to be that man. The man she wanted.

And what did she mean by *get to know him*? Did that mean what I hoped it did? That she'd let me kiss her and rub her all over like we'd done the cattle? Or maybe do more than that. While I didn't have personal experience in that matter, both my brothers did, and they'd talked about it some. Among ourselves, of course, not with our folks. That would be an embarrassment beyond belief. Hopefully, I'd picked up enough to know what to do when the time came.

Sitting up straight, Molly dipped one perfect eyebrow. "Why're you so quiet? Did I offend you?"

Before I could shake my head or offer an explanation, she continued. "I think men who go toe-to-toe with outlaws, bank robbers and curly wolfs are simply grand. All that bravery, that...that toughness makes me tingle all over."

I was tingling all over.

"My pa was a lawman for a while, back in Kansas, where we came from. But he got shot and decided to quit." She moved away from me and smoothed her skirt. "Then we came here. Cattle ranchers." Her mouth turned down, shoulders slumped, and she pulled at grass. "Merely a plain, ordinary cattleman, now. Plain... ordinary—"

"But it's a good job. We need cattle to eat. Your pa feeds people."

A long sigh followed a shrug. "Guess so. But it's so... ordinary."

"At least you still have a pa. I hear lawmen don't live all that long." Now, I was making that up, but it could be true. I considered the two lawmen I knew in town. How much longer would they live?

We sat in more silence until I took another approach. "Turns out your pa and me are alike." I waited for her to look at me. "He raises the food and I sell it. He's at one end, I'm at the other." If that logic didn't change her mood, nothing would.

She gave a slow nod until the light returned to her eyes. "At least you go shooting. With a gun. Maybe I can go with you sometime. I'd like that."

Me, too. But not soon. First, I'd have to figure out how to load my gun. Wait. It wasn't *my* gun. It was Da's. Should I admit my lie to beautiful Molly O'Malley? Absolutely not. I'd figure out something.

Shadows grew, and it was time to go. I hated to end such a perfect day, but I had things to do. Buy a gun. Practice. Show Molly how grand I was at shooting.

Energized, I climbed to my feet, helped Molly to hers and wrapped my arms around her. Soft, oh so soft her body was. Fortunately, I had a good seven inches on her which was perfect. She fit against me like we'd been cut out of quilt pieces and sewed together. We stayed like that for half a minute until I couldn't stand the feelings anymore. I moved back ever so slightly, leaned down and kissed her. On the mouth.

Best yet, she kissed me back. My hands roved over her back as I pulled her closer. I didn't want to stop at her shoulders, but I was a gentleman. For now. We traded kisses until my lips were raw and even then, I didn't want to stop.

"Ummmmber...I'm gonna tell." A child's voice made us both jump.

Molly gathered her wits first. "Jake! Were you spying on me?"

Jake giggled and pointed. "Molly has a boyfriend. Molly's in love. Nanny nanny boo boo." Making kissing sounds, he hopped on one foot in a circle. "Oh...Eagan. You're soooo handsome."

Molly grabbed his upper arm. "Stop it. Stop it!" She shook him. "What d'you want?"

Apparently, some of the fun had run out of the taunting. Jake caught his breath. "Pa says it's time for your *boyfriend* to go home."

Boyfriend? Was it official? That meant I had a girlfriend. What a day this had turned out to be.

She released Jake. "Tell him we'll be there in two minutes. *And*...do not tattle. I'm warning you, Jacob Tyler O'Malley, no telling."

Definitely the wind was out of his sails. He turned

toward the house and kicked at a rock. "Two minutes. I'll tell Pa."

And then it hit me. Now I had to endure the Pa Inquisition. No doubt he knew I'd kissed his daughter. But nothing more. Just a kiss. How bad could that be?

Waiting until Jake was a dot in the field, Molly snuggled into my chest. "Thank you for a wonderful afternoon. I can't wait to see you shoot. Bet you're really good."

"Uh huh." Our lips touched and we locked our feelings into a tangle of tongues and mouths. Her hands ran up and down my back while my hands headed for her chest. Her white blouse buttoned up the front with round pearls. My fingers fidgeted with ones in the middle of her chest. One button was almost undone when she pressed into me. Two round parts of her pushed into my chest and now my hands had a mind of their own.

Under my hand, these round, soft bumps brought sensations to my body I'd never felt before. Ever. I grasped harder. I'd never let go. If this was Heaven, I'd died.

"Molly! Home! Now!" Pa's baritone voice shot across the field.

Like we'd been shot, we jerked apart.

"Holy hell." Molly tucked in her blouse making sure all buttons were done, putting girl parts back into place. "I'm in so much trouble." She took off running with me right behind.

Her da stood on the front porch, facing us, his arms crossed across his muscled chest. The daggers spurting from his narrowed eyes pierced my entire body. I was a dead boyfriend. Really, truly dead.

We stopped in front of him, me fully expecting to get backhanded, stomped by his horse, thrown into the pond, and then used as target practice. A glance at Molly. Her face showing nothing but innocence.

"When I call you to come home, young lady, I expect you to obey me. Immediately." He unfolded his arms, looked at her and then me. "Time to call it a day. Your folks'll be expecting you."

Swallowing panic, I nodded. "Yes sir, they will." I turned to Molly. "Thank you for showing me the cattle." I looked at him. "They'll make good steaks next year."

I don't think he was too impressed with that last statement, but he didn't hit me. Which he had all the right to do. If he hadn't called when he did, no telling what would've happened.

He pointed to the door. "Mrs. O'Malley's in the front room, if you want to say goodbye." He stepped sideways.

I'm sure I flinched when he moved. But I didn't give him much time to spin me across the field because I bounded up the steps, opened the door and spotted Molly's ma in a rocking chair, mending a shirt. My own ma did that all day. "Thank you, again, ma'am, for dinner. Again, it was delicious."

"You're welcome, Eagan."

Before I stepped out, I added, "And thank you for inviting me. I had a good time." I

didn't wait for her to ask questions. She had a look on her face that said she knew what we'd been doing. I took the coward's way out and closed the door.

I climbed onto the wagon seat after Pa picked up the reins. I nodded to Molly. "See you soon, I hope."

She didn't say a word, just waved. I waved back and headed for home.

CHAPTER NINE

"HAD A GRAN' TIME AT MOLLY'S YESTERDAY, I see." Da arranged three pork chops under the glass counter, ice chips pushed up around them.

I leaned on the broom, halting my sweeping long enough to answer. "Why d'you say that?" Was it obvious? I'd kissed a girl. Lots of times. Up until yesterday, I hadn't even held hands with one. And now? Now, I was a different person. She let me touch her, too, in sacred places. Does life get better than that?

"Yer smiling and now sweeping without being reminded! Ya brought back a whole barrowful of ice without dumping it!" Da straightened up and threw me a knowing look. I about melted. "I'd say ye had a *breá* day all right."

I had. That's all I could think about. Last night when I'd arrived home, safe and sound and without too many personal questions from Molly's da, I sat on the porch and smiled. A cup of leftover coffee tickled my throat as it ran down. Remembered heat from our kisses, her fingers intertwined in mine, her hands on my back, my hands on her...well, hell. Nothing could spoil these sensations. I was beginning to understand what Tate and Joe talked about late into the night. Now I could join them.

Both Ma and Da stepped out onto the porch and into the cool Texas night air. I positioned the cup to hide the *sensations*. We all sat on the porch, staring out into darkness. They asked general questions—how was the meal? How many children do they have? Did I see any cattle?

I related the time when the children turned into chickens. My folks laughed, actually laughed, out loud. I chuckled because now, at a distance, it was funny.

They didn't ask and I certainly didn't tell, about the best part. That was between me and my lady. Only us. That got me to thinking about Ma and Da. Surely, they had secrets, special times, just between them. I imagined them, young newlyweds, sailing from Ireland across the Atlantic with a six-month-old baby, Tate. Scary, absolutely, but what a romantic adventure. They'd dropped anchor in New Orleans, a bustling seaport town. Da worked in a meat market, and Ma picked up sewing where she could. And she tended Tate, which I'd heard stories he was quite the little devil.

And it was there in New Orleans, two years later, where Ma delivered Joe to join the family. Must've been hard with two small children and getting used to American society. But my folks did well with Da buying out the meat market within three years, I remember him saying.

But something went awry, I guess. After four in Louisiana, they got the urge to head west, to Texas. Somewhere on that trail, I was born. And then fell off the wagon. But that's a different part of their story.

Would Molly and I be like our folks? Moving elsewhere to start another life? I thought about Joe and Freida. They were still both twenty, much like Ma and Da had been. But Joe moved up to Denver, not millions of miles away across the ocean, with no hope of going home. Joe could come back any time. My folks had left everyone and everything behind. But look where they were now.

I wanted to be like them. And then another thought slapped me upside the head. Molly had said she wanted a *man*, someone who wasn't afraid to stand toe-to-toe with outlaws. One who could shoot well, keep his head when in danger, and I guess, be something of a curly wolf himself. Was I that man? Hell, I was barely a man as it was. Not quite eighteen. No gun. But I had bullets. No horse. No job I'd gotten on my own. I didn't like trouble. Even in school, after being teased, I kept my head down.

But now I was asked to be something I wasn't. Could *I* become the curly wolf Molly dreamed of? And if I didn't, would she settle for me the way I was? Probably not. She'd undoubtedly move on to somebody like Jesse James. I'd have to redefine myself.

Where to start? First, I'd need a gun. Second, I'd have to get some muscles. I had some, somewhere, but they sure weren't all that impressive. And then it hit me. I'd chop wood. More than Da. Or better yet, I'd chop all the wood. I'd also lift the hay bales when Mr. Samuels brought them in a couple of weeks. Usually, he brought a colored man with him to do the work. But this time, I'd sling those bales up into the loft. Heck, maybe I'd even take them down and lift them up a time or two. Surely, I'd get muscles that way.

Or maybe go over to Solano's Ice Barn and lift a few ice blocks. Even fifteen pounds can be heavy, so I'd start with at least thirty. Would Mr. Solano let me do that? If not, when he wasn't looking, I'd lift some on the sly.

I sipped my cold coffee and thought about what I'd become. I'd taken Da's gun without permission, taken fifty cents without permission and plotted how to lift ice without permission. Was I already becoming a curly wolf and not known it? This wasn't like me to steal and lie. Ma always said I was the good son. Kind, caring, respectful.

Not anymore. Not since those three men tried to... well, my life changed right then and there. And now, with Molly on my every thought, I was changing more. Was it for the better? I shook my head. No. I was heading in the wrong direction, but I'd be damned to figure out how to stop it.

Fact was, I enjoyed the feelings, the prospects. I was in love with being bad.

CHAPTER TEN

THE NEXT THREE DAYS AT WORK PROCEEDED AS usual. I swept, arranged the meat in the glass counter, and bought more ice. Mr. Atherton sold us more chickens, women bought fare for dinners, men came in to visit with Da, and I kept an eagle eye out for Miss Molly O'Malley to come in. Or even walk past. I'd give almost anything to see her again. Guessing she kept close to the house what with helping care for all those siblings, I plotted and planned ways to go out to see her. Maybe Sunday after church we could meet again. That thought twisted my stomach, sending butterflies stomping around in my chest. Only four more days and we'd be back, looking at her cattle.

In the meantime, I had to start chopping more wood. And carting heavier ice. And buying a gun. Or at least shooting Da's. So much to do. Four days was not enough time.

I wrapped up the roast and two pork chops Mrs. Rosemond had selected. She rattled on about the best way to cook a roast and that this one was too small for

Sunday company but should be perfect for tonight's supper. I didn't truly listen. She was a nice lady, but did I care? No. She wasn't Molly and that's all I wanted to think about. She was interrupting my reverie.

Mrs. Rosemond handed over a dollar bill, and I thanked her for coming in. When I opened the cash register, I frowned at the amount of money in there. Where had it all come from? Several dollar bills lay in the tray, as did a small mound of dimes and half dollars. Remembering, I pulled out the change from buying ice this morning and plunked it in with the other coins.

A glance around the shop and Da wasn't in sight. Had he gone to the privy or was he in the back? I looked inside the storeroom, and it was empty. All right, I was alone. Now was the time. I picked up a wad of bills and counted twenty. How much did I need for a gun? Twenty would definitely be enough, but Da would quickly see some was missing. I put five back just as the back door opened and Da stepped in.

"What ye doin', Eagan?" He walked closer. "Ara, don't tell me ye're cleanin' the cash now, too." Da's head wagged. "Whatever's gotten into ye, it's rand so. I'm happy out."

I replaced the bills, straightening them up. I hated myself for thinking of stealing. "Just putting them in the same direction." I produced my most innocent smile. "Guess there's not much else to do."

Da gripped the storeroom door handle. "What say we clean up back here?" He opened the door and I rushed over, meeting him in the doorway. Da turned sideways. "What's wrong with ye, Eagan? Ye're actin' the maggot."

"Sorry, Da." I had to think quick. "It's just that I don't want you to work so hard. I'm much younger than you and *I* should be doing the hard work, not you."

He leaned back against the door and scanned me head to toe. Folded arms over his chest gave him a look, saying he didn't believe me. I had to make it look realistic. "Besides, you're much better talking to the customers. I'm better at cleaning." I paused for effect and to see how he reacted. "Right?"

Da shook his head, ran fingers through his salt-and-pepper hair, and breathed out a long sigh. His gaze nearly brought me to my knees. In those eyes, I found confusion, belief, and something I couldn't quite identify.

He held my shoulder and rocked it. "Well, boyo. I'm not quite as old as ye're makin' me out to be, but some of what ye say is true. I'm good with people. Enjoy most of 'em, I do."

Perfect. On one hand, I hated myself for deceiving him, and on the other I was proud of myself for pulling it off. On second thought, I more hated myself than proud, but I'd continue anyway. There was Molly now to think about.

I put a hand on Da's back. "Go take a breather, Da. Let me do the cleaning back here." I stepped away and then stopped. "Of course, when you get busy, just call and I'll come out and help."

One side of Da's mouth raised. "Aye, that's what I pay ye for." He gave me one last long look. "Well, what're ye still standing about? Get to cleanin'."

"Yessir." More relieved than anything, I headed for a crate filled with boxes of brown butcher paper. I sorted and arranged and counted so much that maybe in a year or two, we'd need more. What else was back here?

I spent half an hour organizing and sweeping and another half hour caressing Da's gun, usually hidden under a burlap bag. Sitting behind a larger crate, I aimed the weapon at a high window and shot. Smooth. No recoil. Of course, I hadn't loaded it, but still, the imagined kickback didn't hurt my wrist.

As soon as I could, I'd figure out a way to go shooting. If Molly wanted a curly wolf, then that's what she'd get. I'd practice until I could shoot out a flying bird's eye. I'd be that good. After that, I'd find Tate and he and I would form what he'd wanted—the feared Nolan Outlaw Gang. We'd be better than Frank and Jesse James and Molly would swoon all over me. She wouldn't be able to keep her hands off. I'd buy a wide-brimmed hat, a Stetson I'd heard them called, wear jangling spurs, but most importantly, wrap a double holster rig for both of my Colts around my hips. I'd be the talk of the town, a magnet for women, and somebody men would step aside for.

Tate would be proud of his little brother. Despite my limp, I'd become someone to be reckoned with. In fact, I'd—

"Eagan? Need yer help, here."

I flinched at Da's voice at the door. Returning to the here and now, I pushed up off the floor and held the gun behind me. "Be right there, Da." He stepped away, and I relaxed. No way could he have seen me holding his gun. But I'd have to be more careful.

Hiding the Colt under the burlap bags, I limped out to the showroom. Without my noticing the commotion, at least ten customers had come in. Right now, they were all waiting for someone to help them. That someone, of course, would be me.

I wrapped chops, Hamburg steak, roasts, and a chicken while Da did pretty much the same. The last customer pulled on the door, wishing us a good day, when in stepped Purdy and the two Clydes. Ice water filled my veins while I sucked in air. Dizzy, my legs trembled as I stood frozen in place.

Da greeted them as amiably as he did all the other customers. "Gentlemen." He nodded. "How can I help ye?"

I stood behind the glass counter searching the room for a weapon. My gun was in the back and even if I had it now, my bullets were at home. I'd forgotten to bring them today. What an idiot. Never again. Molly's fault. I was so smitten with her I'd lost any fear of these three. Again...idiot.

Clyde One stuck out a hand to Da. "We're new in town and lookin' to see what all you've got here." Without acknowledging me, he leaned down at the counter where I was standing. "That chicken looks good. Fresh?" He looked up at me where our eyes met. I couldn't move. Couldn't breathe.

"Fresh this morning, sir." Da walked up and then pointed to another counter. "Hamburg steak was ground this morning, too."

Keeping my eyes on the other two, I relaxed my shoulders. I'd probably have to defend Da and suddenly I was glad I'd been chopping so much wood. I was stronger than last week and could surely take down either Clyde. Purdy was a different matter, though. Muscles made his shirtsleeves tight and buttons strain across his shirt.

I still hadn't moved from my spot behind the counter when Purdy and Clyde Two sauntered over. Da and the other Clyde were busy discussing the variety of meats in a glass case across the room.

Purdy stood two, three feet away. "Saw you ride off with a pretty young redhead the other day." Both of his thin eyebrows raised. "She as spicy as she looks?"

I swallowed loudly. "Leave her alone." Was my voice low enough Da hadn't heard?

"Or what?" Clyde Two's mouth raised into a snarl. "You gonna cry? Tell your daddy?"

"Touch Molly and I'll kill you." I hoped every word came out as menacingly as I'd meant. No way would they get their hands on her.

Purdy leaned back and chuckled. "Molly, is it?" He nudged Clyde Two. "We'll have to pay this Molly a visit. Huh, Clyde?"

Like a lightning flash, I leaned across the counter and grabbed Purdy by his vest lapels, tugging him halfway across the counter. "You heard me. Leave her alone." I glared as hard as I knew how. We stood, Purdy and me, bent across the glass showcase, almost nose to nose.

Clyde Two reached over, pulling us apart. His thick fingers wedged between my hand and Purdy's vest. "Don't want no trouble in here, do we, Purdy?"

I let go the moment Da walked up, Clyde One next to him. Da frowned at me, then Purdy.

"There a problem here, Eagan?"

Purdy regained his feet and brushed off his vest. "No problem, Mr. Nolan. Simple misunderstandin' is all."

Like hell it was. As much as I wanted to tell Da who these men were, I decided to keep quiet. We were outnumbered in our little shop and no telling what they'd do. Plus, my gun was stowed carefully under burlap in the back. Empty. They definitely had the upper hand. For now.

Another long look at me and then Purdy. Da flashed a small smile. "Sorry about that. Eagan's usually mild-mannered and polite. A good boy."

It took all my energy not to holler at Da. A *good boy*? *Mild mannered*? Ho-ly hell. How embarrassing. Sounded like he was talking about a dog to an old aunt or somebody.

Purdy held up a hand and backed away. "No harm done. Again, a misunderstandin'."

"We'll be back, Mr. Nolan." Clyde One pointed to the meat, then eyeballed me. "You can count on that." The Three nodded at Da as they stepped outside. That damn bell tinkled cheerfully as they carefully closed the door.

Da turned to me. Tension filled the air as thick as a creosote campfire. "Mind tellin' me what the hell that was?" He pointed back over his shoulder.

Definitely Da was mad. He rarely cussed. But what to tell him? Maybe partial truth. "Said he'd seen Molly and wanted to...court her."

His frown not only narrowed his eyes but brought his eyebrows down low. Da wiped a hand across his mouth. "Ye had supper with her family. Only that. Ye got no right to be possessive." He gripped both of my shoulders and shook them gently. "What's goin' on with ye, boyo? What is it with those fellas? Gotta be more'n that."

My gaze swept my shoes. I couldn't look at him. And I certainly couldn't tell him.

He shook me a bit harder. "Eagan? What?"

I shrugged. "Guess I like her more'n I thought. He made me mad, is all." That reasoning would have to do for now. Maybe Da would give me a lecture about love and courting and all that. It would be better than me telling him about the gun and him locking me away for ten years.

With perfect timing, the bell announced an interruption. A customer. Da released my shoulders and stared at me, eye-to-eye. "Don't know what's goin' on, son, but I'm thinkin' ye need some help." He turned around, heading for the shopper.

I turned and headed for the gun. Still where I'd left it. Still empty of ammunition. Still hadn't shot it. All of that I'd change today. The Clydes and Purdy were becoming dangerous, more so than last week, and I'd have to do something about that. Tonight, I'd bring the gun back to the house, and after supper, go outside down by the creek. There, I'd put the bullets in and pretend to fire. At least I'd get that much experience.

My best mates Jimmy and Zeke probably knew how to shoot. Jimmy had a gun now and Zeke was almost two years older than me, so surely he could shoot. Unfortunately, the three of us didn't live close to each other. I'd have to make a plan to stop by Jimmy's. He was closer than Zeke by at least a mile.

Around closing time, I'd hatched a plan to visit Jimmy. He was an apprentice to the farrier, so he often worked past dark. Horses tended to throw their shoes at any time and if they weren't stabled right there, Jimmy would work past supper. Yep. On the way home, I'd definitely stop in at the livery stable and have a chat with Jimmy. Da couldn't object too much.

He turned the *Open* sign around, locked the front door, arched his back, and rubbed it. "Long day, eh, boyo?"

Nodding, I still had to get to the storeroom without Da seeing me. I untied the dingy cloth around my front, folded it, then pointed behind me. "I'll put this and the meat away, straighten a few things and then be along shortly." I limped toward the door, then spun around. "Oh. Almost forgot. Jimmy asked me to stop by the stable after work today. Wants to show me something."

I guessed Da was focused on going home. He didn't ask the million questions I thought he would. "Grand.

Don't be too long. Ye know yer ma serves supper at half six."

Relaxing, I nodded. "Be along shortly." And then another plan hit me. "You go on home. I'll lock up here. I'm behind you, maybe ten minutes."

That frown of his made my heart race. What was he thinking? He shook his head and handed me the key and his wadded-up apron. "Don't know what's got into yer head." A stop at the back door, one long last look at his shop, at me, then opened the door and stepped into a warm Texas evening.

Was it that easy? And why did I feel so guilty? Because I'd lied to him, stolen from him. What sort of son was I becoming? One who was in love, or maybe lust. And one who was terrified of three men.

I cleaned, hung up aprons, and brought out the Colt. It was shinier than I'd remembered from earlier. With no rig to buckle around my hips and no holster to secure my gun, I tucked it under my waistband, hoping my vest was long enough to cover the bulge the cold steel made.

Jimmy was washing his callused hands when I poked my head in the area where the forge and anvil stood. Coals still glowed but lacked luster from earlier in the day. Apparently, even they were tired and ready for supper and sleep.

I kept my voice low. "Hey there, Jimbo."

He about knocked over the water basin when he jerked around at my voice. "Hell and damnation, Eagan! Why'd you come sneakin' up behind me like that? I about wet my britches."

"Sorry, I scared you. Didn't mean to."

That look on his face—eyes wide, mouth turned down, both hands fisted—made me laugh. Out loud. Smudges of black on his face turned him more into a clown than a startled lad. When he failed to see the humor as I did, I toned down my chuckling. He'd probably had as long a day as me.

Wiping his hands on a dirty cloth, he leaned against a wooden rail. He cocked his head toward a mare in a nearby stall. "She didn't want new shoes. Imagine a gal like that not wanting new shoes." Jimmy tossed the rag on a table filled with pliers, hoof nippers, nail pullers and picks, along with other tools I had no name for. His thick cowhide gloves lay on top.

Jimmy was the kind of lad who'd give the shirt off his back if you needed one. He worked hard and played even harder and had turned eighteen several months ago, back in late winter. I wasn't sure if he'd ever kissed a girl and I'd never asked. Now, it was important to know. Besides helping me with the gun, maybe he could give me advice on women.

"Now that my heart's not racing and I can breathe"— Jimmy tossed a smile my way—"what's going on?"

I surveyed the shop. No one else close enough to hear our conversation. The sun's rays were at a low slant and where we stood was shadowed. Perfect. "Remember those three men who...well, who—"

"Can't forget."

I mumbled, hating those men and their making me so fearful that I was embarrassed. "Well—"

"They try it again?" Jimmy stood straight and looked toward the street.

"No." I held up a hand. "Worse."

"Worse?" He rubbed his stubbled chin. "What could be worse?"

I dropped my voice even though our conversation couldn't be heard nearby. "They came into the shop today. Threatened me. Talked about Molly."

He whistled softly. "Takes a lot of—" Jimmy stared at me. "Who's Molly?"

Of course, he didn't know about her. I hoped. Our courting had been a rather sudden event, and I hadn't seen my lad for a couple of weeks. My chest swelled with...I wasn't completely sure what had enveloped me. Love? Lust? Ownership? Feelings I'd never experienced before had taken up residency in my body. Had that happened to him, too? I breathed in and gave a quick rundown of the past week. Especially Sunday's supper... in detail. I didn't think I was the "kiss and tell" type, but while I was talking, that came to mind. I needed to protect my lovely Molly O'Malley's reputation.

Jimmy stood stunned. I waited for him to at least nod. Instead, he slapped at his chaps, raising clouds of dirt. Uncinching them, he draped them on a hook, then turned to me. "A girl? Hell, Eagan, you're purrin' like a clump of cats in a creamery."

"She *is* real pretty. And did I mention her red hair?"

His head bobbed. "Three times." He looked at the sun making its way to the horizon. "I'm happy for you, but I best be gettin' home. Ma's making ham and biscuits tonight."

My stomach gurgled at the thought. I briefly wondered what Ma was cooking. "Those bastards. Came into the store. Found out about Molly."

"Damn them." Jimmy threaded his arms through his vest. "Did you get a gun like you said you would? Looks like we're gonna have to convince them to leave town."

I nodded. "Law won't do anything, so we'll have to. I got a gun and bullets"—I leaned in close—"but I don't know how to shoot."

A smile the width of the Rio Grande stretched Jimmy's face. "Then we gotta go target practicing."

"Hoping you'd say that." I pulled out Da's Colt. "Look what I got."

He whistled and smiled at the same time. "Fine lookin' shootin' piece you got there. When d'you buy it?" Jimmy held out a hand. "Mind if I hold it?"

I handed it over, proud as if I'd made it myself. "Not loaded. Bullets're at home."

Jimmy turned it side to side, aimed and dry fired at nothing. He hefted the piece, nodded, and returned the weapon to me. "Didn't know you bought one."

Looking everywhere except at my best lad, I mumbled. "It's Da's." And added. "Gonna buy me one real soon. Soon as I get paid."

Returning my gun, Jimmy patted my shoulder. "Sure need to go practicing, and soon. How about this Saturday after work? We'll have an hour or so of daylight to plink at cans."

Two more days. Two more days of being afraid. Two more days of jumping at every shadow. After that...I wouldn't be afraid of anyone, anymore. They'd be afraid of *me*.

CHAPTER ELEVEN

SHOOTING AT CANS WAS ALMOST AS MUCH FUN as kissing Molly. Almost. Parts of me tingled when that empty green bean tin jumped into the air, after I'd aimed carefully and squeezed the trigger. Of course, that hadn't happened often. Maybe twice out of twenty or so bullets. Thankfully, Jimmy had extras and used the same caliber as me.

We stood under an oak down along the stream about a mile west of town. This time of year, the sun didn't set for at least another hour, so we took our time aiming, shooting, talking, shooting, talking about guns and girls. Turned out, he'd had a sweetheart last year, but her folks didn't like him, so the whole family had moved away. Although his folks liked her just fine, apparently, their courting came to a screeching halt when her ma caught them kissing a bit too...enthusiastically. Jimmy blushed at the fact unbuttoned blouses and pants were involved. That was the end of a budding relationship.

His story gave me pause for two reasons. First, why hadn't I known about her? We'd been best lads for years.

But knowing Jimmy, he'd probably kept it quiet just in case. Like me, those feelings were new.

And second, I'd have to be more careful with Molly. Like Jimmy and his girl, our kissing could also become too enthusiastic. In fact, as fine as she kissed and cuddled, that was a distinct possibility. No telling where that kind of "enthusiasm" would lead.

At our usual time, Da and I had closed up the store. He headed for home, me for Jimmy and the farrier shop. Now, here with Jimmy and the sun setting on the horizon, we decided to call it a day. It had been a glorious time and I hated for it to end. Who knew shooting was such a thrill? Now I understood what Molly was talking about. If I could practice more—with my own gun—I could indeed become a shooter, the curly wolf, maybe the outlaw that Molly wanted. Yeah, it was all possible.

I stood at the creek bank, staring into the future as the last rays of daylight slid along a meadow. Crickets chirruped, something small dived into a patch of old leaves on the bank, and a dove made its final flight until morning. Tomorrow was Sunday and I'd be sure to be at church extra early. Maybe Molly and I could sit by ourselves. Maybe. Afterall, we were grown adults now and should be allowed to sit wherever we wanted. We could even hold hands on occasion.

Tingles fluttered up one side and down the other. Was this love? Had to be.

But to be the man she wanted, first and foremost, I needed my own Colt. Should I ask Da for an advance on my wages and buy the weapon Monday? Or wait another long week until payday and then buy it? I tried telling myself another week didn't matter, but it did. Maybe she'd find somebody else during that time and we'd never get to kiss again.

All right. Decision made. I'd ask for my wages in advance.

"What're you staring at?"

A gentle whack on my shoulder sent me a step forward. I turned and glared at my best lad. "Just looking." My words were harder than intended.

He stepped back and held up both hands. "Sorrreee. Didn't mean to rile you." Jimmy pointed over his shoulder toward town. "Gotta be gettin' back. See you around."

I spun to face him and grabbed his sleeve. "No, wait. I'm sorry. Just lost deep in thought and you startled me."

His gaze ran over my face like he was deciding if I was a prized yearling. He certainly took his time. Finally, a long breath out and a shrug. "You've changed since you met this Molly. You sure you like what's going on?"

How could he see right through me? I'd been thinking that exact same thing. I nodded and raised one shoulder. "Maybe it's the real me coming out." I pointed toward town, same as him and walked with him. "I'm tired of always being picked on. Called names. Tired of being timid and a *good boy* as Da says."

"Dunno. I kinda like the original Eagan." Next to me, Jimmy walked as slow as I did. Most people walked fast and then had to wait for me to catch up. He continued. "Besides, I don't think you're timid. You're just quiet... sometimes. Except when talking about Molly." He slid his gun into its leather holster. "You're the one," he emphasized *you're*, "who sees what's going on. *You're* the one who's true and honest. Of the three of you brothers, *you're* the best. I'd go riding the trail with you any time. Maybe Joe. Not so sure about Tate."

That gave me lots to think over. I wedged my gun, Da's gun, into my waistband in the small of my back and hoped it didn't fall out. With my awkward gait, anything was possible.

Me and Jimmy turned east to town and sauntered toward home and supper.

The first Blanco Hills buildings came into sight, their windows aglow with warm lamp light. Most windows were open, several screened doors taking the place of wood doors. A warm night, it was close to perfect, except for voracious mosquitoes the size of hummingbirds. They clouded around us like we were fresh meat. We swatted, smacked, cursed, and even threatened to shoot a couple. Nothing worked.

"Well, looky here, Clyde." A gritty voice came out of the shrubs. "If it ain't two of Blanco Hills' little baby boys off playin' shooter."

"And they're out here all by themselves. Surprised their folks let them out at night."

That sounded like Clyde Two. I recognized his slurred drawl. Clyde One had to be close by. I froze, hands clenched, expecting the worst.

Jimmy nudged me forward. "Let's go, Eagan. These boys are just funnin'."

I knew they weren't and that my best lad and I were in a world of hurt. We were too far from town to get the law, like he would help. Hell, Sheriff Wagner would no doubt side with these curs. The gun grew warm under my belt like a reminder I wasn't alone.

Holding my hands out to my sides, I chose to take a chance they'd walk away. "As you know, I'm heeled. Hate to shoot you, but I will."

Jimmy picked up where I left off. "I'm heeled, too. How about we all go home in one piece?"

Purdy leaned over cackling. The two Clydes guffawed,

pointed, and mimicked Jimmy. "In one piece!" He laughed louder. "Which piece?"

Both Clydes hooted. "I'll take an arm. You want a leg?"

I glanced at a paling Jimmy. "Let's get outta here." We stepped forward.

Purdy moved directly in front of us. His breath hitting my face. "Where ya goin'? We ain't done yet." He glanced behind him. "Are we?"

Like joining a barn dance, the two Clydes slid in on either side of Purdy. Now it was three against two, and even though we carried guns, odds were not in our favor. Plus, they probably had guns, too, just not showing them yet. But why hadn't they?

A wave of anger flooded my entire body, boots to hat. I'd just told Jimmy I was tired of being afraid and here I was. And I was right. I wasn't afraid. I was angry. Mad. Furious. Years of being teased and made fun of balled together, manifesting in my fists.

"Move." Had I actually said it like that? Damn, I felt good. A short step forward, but the three didn't back up. I glanced at Jimmy, whose eyes were wide. He'd follow my lead, I was sure. "Move, I said." I took a breath. "Won't tell you again."

Ho-ly hell. Who was this man?

Like they had practiced, together the three moved forward a full step. Purdy's hazel eyes narrowed, and his thin lips curled into a snarl, his face a combination of defiance and stupidity. Whiskey on his breath was strong and recent.

Jimmy's shoulder against mine bolstered my increasing strength and courage. I narrowed my eyes, too. "Move." With my heart thundering in my chest, I couldn't hear if he'd said anything, the pulsating in my ears blocking out all noise. Without too much thinking, and like going into a hornet's nest, I pushed Purdy aside, and eased forward, knowing he was a rattlesnake about to bite.

Before I could take another breath, fists pounded my side, my head, my back. I swung, plowing my pent-up rage into someone's jaw. One of the Clydes yelped, which I smiled at. Unwilling to give in, I gripped Purdy's vest, kicked his shin, pulled him down, somehow managing to push his face into the dirt. Victory! Sweet victory! I'd show that bully I wasn't taking anymore.

He flopped over, scissored his legs around my waist and tossed me over his head. All the wind knocked out and lying flat on my back, boots danced around me. Sucking in bits of air, my world turned from black to brown to white. Bright white. Colors slowly returned in time for me to see Jimmy and Clyde Two tangled in a dance of arms, legs, and cursing.

Couldn't let Jimmy get hurt! I rolled, forcing my body to its knees. I'd stand in a minute. A boot to my stomach knocked me the other way, landing me in the dirt on my side. I spit lunch. Twice. I wiped away goo and blood cascading from my nose.

Jimmy grunted and crashed to the ground near my feet. Anger exploded. I sprung up, lowered my head, and like a bull, roared into Clyde One. I took him down with the strength of a hundred men. I pummeled, punched, pulled his long hair until some of it came out in between my fingers. His cheeks turned bright red, and bands of blood spread across his face. His lip bled worse than mine had.

I was on top, and I'd stay there until he didn't move anymore. Until he couldn't hurt me anymore. Until he was dead. Even in my red-hued bloodlust, I didn't want him dead. I simply wanted him to leave me and my friends alone. I leaned back, sank my fist into his cheek, then stood. I looked down at this bully who wasn't a bully any longer.

A fist upside my head spun me around. Clyde Two, crimson welts dotting his face, kicked my shin, plowed a fist into my belly, then used that fist to come up under my chin. My teeth clacked together as I spun again.

"I don't wanna have to shoot you, but I will." Jimmy's voice.

My vision straightened enough for me to see him standing nearby, holding his gun on Purdy. He then changed his aim to Clyde Two. "Walk away now! Leave us alone!"

My gun! I felt it was still there in the small of my back and briefly wondered how it had stayed in place. Wobbling but standing, I reached behind and pulled it out. Now there were two of us with guns. "Leave! Now!" I aimed squarely at Purdy.

Purdy lurched forward, grabbing my gun. Caught in a deadly tango, he and I twisted, turned, pushed, pulled. "Let go!" I ordered. He kicked me. My ironclad grip loosened enough for him to aim the Colt downward.

Bang!

I jumped back, surprised the gun was still in my hand.

"You little…son of a…"

I didn't hear anything he said except for a roaring in my ears. Purdy hopped on one foot. I looked down. His left boot hung in leather shreds and blood was quickly coating a bare sock and foot. My stomach turned.

Shock wearing off, I turned to Jimmy locked in his own lethal dance with Clyde Two. They gripped Jimmy's gun and each used their free hand to punch and hit.

Clyde One lay on the ground moaning, rocking side to side, thanks to my uncontrolled fury, and Purdy was now on the ground holding his bloody foot.

Gun aimed, I hollered. "Stop it! I'll shoot you, Clyde!"

Without warning, he released Jimmy's arm and dove for me, hitting me square in the chest. The impact made me squeeze the trigger. *Click.* I squeezed again. Another *click.* Wheeling back and air knocked out, I hit the dirt, knowing he was about to kill me. Gun still in hand, I covered my face, brought my knees up like a little kid, and prayed.

Bang! Leaves rained from the Texas oak we were under.

"You're done, Clyde. Hands up!" Jimmy waved his gun away from me.

Clyde did as told, growling the entire time. Anger distorted his face while the arteries in his neck throbbed. He glared at me as I struggled to get upright. "You'll pay for this. And pay with everything you got." A glance at Jimmy and then back to me. "I'll start with that Molly. She sounds delicious. Can't wait to lather her—"

"Leave her the hell alone, Clyde." I pushed my gun into his chest, knowing the bullets were used up. "She's got nothing to do with this. Leave...her...alone."

"She ain't your property." Clyde licked his bottom lip, spreading blood corner to corner. "Besides, I hear she works at Sam's. One of the upstairs gals. She won't mind my coin or company."

Enough was enough. I head-butted Clyde, and he landed on his back. I jumped on him and we tangled into a knot rolling toward the stream. We each got in a couple of good licks, a punch to the jaw, and I managed to pull out more hair.

Tangled like we were, we rolled into the water and came up gasping like drowning fish. My hair hung down over my eyes, and when I pushed it aside, I realized my gun was gone. I flopped against the stream, patting the rocks and dirt for hard metal. Clyde sat, pushed what was left of his hair out of his eyes, then climbed to his feet.

"You boys at it again?" A stranger's voice came from the shadows. "What in the hell tarnation are you doin' out here, Nolan? Funny time to be gettin' a bath." Sheriff Walter Wagner emerged and pointed his gun at us. "Both of you. Out." He turned sideways toward Jimmy. "You. Over here where I can see you."

The three of us stood in front of the sheriff, two of us dripping, one of us frantic to find his gun.

Wagner waved the gun to his right toward Purdy and Clyde One. "Over there."

The five of us gathered like scolded schoolboys. Clyde One was now sitting, rubbing his head, while Purdy sat next to him, holding his bloody foot.

Wagner held out a hand. "Your guns. Hand 'em over." He looked at me first, and I shrugged. I held my arms out at my sides. "Don't have a gun, Sheriff. Check me, if you want."

He patted me quickly, I guessed not wanting to get wet. He spun his pointed finger to have me turn around. Of course, he found nothing and took out his frustration by cuffing me across my mouth. It stung and bled. "I don't believe you. I know you have one. Where is it?"

Touching my lower lip which had split where it had just healed, I mumbled, "Don't have one. Told you."

Another *whap* across my face brought moisture to my eyes. But I stood my ground. He wouldn't see me cry, whimper, or beg. No, I was a new man.

"Now you." He nodded at Jimmy, who reluctantly placed his in the sheriff's hand. Wagner stuck the weapon in his belt. "Now you three."

Each fished a small caliber gun from their vests. I still couldn't figure out why they hadn't used them, except they looked puny compared to mine and Jimmy's. Wagner regarded each pistol with disdain and then put them in his vest pockets.

Purdy pointed at me. "He's got a gun, Sheriff. Looky what he done. He shot off my gal damn foot!" He held it, rocking back and forth. "You gotta arrest him for attempted murder."

"Who? Which one of these fellas shot you?"

Purdy pointed at me. "Him. That one. The mean one."

Inside, I smiled at being called *mean*. I liked it. But I had to object. "Wasn't me, Sheriff. It was that fella over there." I pointed to Clyde One.

"Me?" Clyde One eased to his feet. "Me? Hell, it was you, Nolan. We all saw you do it."

"No, you didn't. You were out cold."

"It was Nolan, for a fact, Sheriff." Purdy nodded at me. "Hell, just ask him. He'll brag about it."

Wagner held up a hand, the other still holding a gun. We stood quietly, not wanting to get shot. The sheriff drew in a breath and let it out. "This's gettin' to be a habit. You all foolin' around. You *five* is making my supper cold. I hear gunfire, come runnin' only to find you scrabblin' with each other like old wet tom cats. And what exactly do I find?" He pointed to Clyde One. "This one here's on the ground, groaning." He pointed to Purdy. "This one's hopping up and down spewing out every curse word I ain't never heard."

I was hoping he'd leave so I could find Da's gun. It was one thing to borrow it, but something else to lose it.

"This one"—Wagner pointed to Jimmy—"standing on the bank watching these two yahoos tussle in the water." He wagged his gun at Clyde Two and me. "These two decide to go larkin' through the water, although the bruises and blood on their faces—in fact all your faces—tell otherwise."

Would he ever get to the point? I pictured Da's gun rusting in the water and itched to retrieve it.

"Fact is," the sheriff continued, "I need to know what all y'all were doin' down here, why the hell you're shootin' your guns, disturbing the peace, and who shot this fella."

Nobody spoke. Figuring silence was best, as all sorts of explanations stayed firmly locked up in my head. Without a gun, I'd be instantly cleared. Which left Jimmy. No way in hell could I let him take the blame, but I wasn't supposed to have the gun in the first place.

Purdy stood. "Sheriff, told you, it was Nolan. He shot me. Now I gotta get to a doc. My foot's all busted and hurts like a—"

"Go ahead. I'll know where to find you." Wagner turned to the four of us as Purdy hobbled off. "All right. If you won't talk, I gotta lock all you up. Nolan, your daddy's gonna be real happy when I go knockin' on his door." His shoulders shook with laughter.

"I can explain." There. The words loosened.

"Not here. Not now. You're guilty. All you Nolans are guilty. Don't care what you say." He pointed. "Let's go."

The Clydes and a crestfallen me dragged our feet.

"But, Sheriff." Jimmy trailed behind. "Eagan and me didn't shoot these fellas. We'd been target practicing and were on our way home. We used up all our bullets."

"Save it for the judge." Wagner chuckled long and loud. "Always wanted to say that." He cocked his head toward town. "You first."

We trudged the half mile to the center of town where the Sheriff's office took up a northeast corner of Main. Thankfully, this time of day, most people were inside fixing or eating supper, preparing for a good night's sleep. On my way over, I was sure, just *sure*, that Molly would be on the boardwalk, waiting for me. I would never been able to look at her again, her father and mother would make sure of that, but my pride wouldn't let me, either. Fortunately, with the stores closed, downtown was deserted. Tinny piano music rolled out of Sam's Emporium at the other end of town. I'd much rather be there than here.

I remembered the inside of the jail, when a couple of months ago, I'd stopped in to visit my older brother, Tate. His charge was much more serious than mine. He'd been accused of murdering a priest. Tate was a bit wild and maybe didn't have all the morals he needed, but he'd never in a hundred million years kill a priest. The judge declared him innocent but with conditions. Tate would have a three-month probation of working on a ranch, which had turned out to be best for him. Last I'd heard, he was thriving as a cowboy.

Sheriff Wagner tossed Jimmy and me in one cell and the other two in the other. I guess he knew we'd kill each other closed up together.

Click. The cell door locked. Wagner's smile stretched his cheeks. "Hell, Eagan. If your brother hadn't skipped town, I'd have the privilege of locking up all the Nolan brothers. Guess two out of three ain't bad." He shook his head as he jingled the keys and headed for the wooden door between the office and cells.

Still dripping wet, I sat on the bunk under the window, put my head in my hands, and fought the pressure welling behind my eyes. Jimmy took the other cot and did the same. I'm sure his thoughts were similar to mine. Except mine involved a borrowed and lost gun and a da and ma who would be more than a little upset. I'd destroyed their faith in me and could never be trusted again. Half of me was more than sorry, trying to figure out how to make it up. The other half was glad. I now knew how to shoot a gun and stand up to bullies. Molly would be proud of me, and I figured that was what was important. I was a new man. Still had a long way to go.

I was on my way.

CHAPTER TWELVE

DA STOOD IN THE DARKENED ROOM WHERE stars and the beginnings of a moon threw vague light through the open cell window. He simply stood, arms folded across his chest, feet shoulder-width apart. His breathing was heavy, forced, through his nose. He stared straight at me, as if I was Satan himself.

When he first opened the door, Jimmy greeted him, but Da—manners ignored—didn't utter a word. Not one. He didn't acknowledge Jimmy or the other two in the room. Like one of those pointer-hunting dogs, Da focused on me.

I stood on the other side of the bars, holding them like the ceiling would collapse if I let go. The only part of this I liked was that Ma wasn't standing next to Da. If she had, I'd probably have broken down and cried, big ol' tears running down my bruised face, mixing in with the blood from my nose and lips. I was a mess, and she didn't need to see me like this, still damp and muddy. I liked staying clean, even though I worked cutting meat. Sundays, I was always neat and washed.

Da's image grew fuzzy around the edges. The anger and disappointment—his lips pressing tight, stony expression on his face—was painfully plain to see. I patted my right eye, surprised to find mostly puffy and tender skin. Guess it was almost swollen shut. My head thumped like it'd been hit by the butt end of a rifle, and my shins ached where I'd been kicked. But my face had received most of the damage, the cheeks stinging and throbbing in rhythm with my beating heart. I wanted to lie down and sleep. Maybe tomorrow I'd wake to find this had been a dream. No, a nightmare.

And still, he stood. Jimmy was smart enough to sit on the far end of his bunk, trying to be invisible. The two Clydes sauntered over as close as they could, gripped the bars and started in.

"Your boy done shot our friend." Clyde One waited for a response. Receiving only stony silence, he tried again. "He's down at Doc's right now. Ol' Purdy was simply standing there, talking to these two jaspers, just like we were"—he cocked his head toward me—"then *your* kid draws iron and shoots him in the foot. For no reason."

Clyde's brother reached through the bars and pointed at me. "Eagan's one mean nut, Mr. Nolan. He beat Clyde here near half to death." He looked over at Clyde One. "Ain't that right?"

"Sure is."

"I mean"—Clyde Two wiped blood from his mouth, smearing it into his beard—"you oughta consider locking him up permanent like. He's a sunuvabitch curly wolf gone real bad."

Da never looked at them nor responded.

They both grew quiet when Da didn't answer. What had to have been five more minutes dragged by with Da simply standing, staring, glaring. At long last, he shifted his weight and let out a long stream of air.

I looked at his blue eyes so full of, well, I wasn't sure, but it wasn't good. "I'm sorry, Da. Don't know what got into me. I'm real sorry." Would he at least speak to me now?

He blinked, pulled in air, straightened his shoulders, turned around and marched out. The door slammed behind him.

* * *

IF I HADN'T BEEN CAGED up there with these men, I'd have laid down and cried. How could I let my folks down when they'd been nothing but kind to me? What was I thinking? I didn't have to go the curly wolf route like Clyde had accused me of being, although part of me liked the moniker. I had nothing to prove. Being mean didn't feel right to me. I liked being helpful and

polite and friendly and kind and someone people enjoyed having around.

On the other hand, Molly liked those rowdy kinds of men. And I liked Molly. Maybe even loved her. So, what was the harm doing some shooting and having a good brawl now and then? I'd laid there most of the night thinking about Molly and my family while listening to snoring. Loud, put-holes-in-the-wall, snoring.

Sun rays hit the ceiling and ran down the wall. I turned on my bunk. Tried to turn was a better description. I was sore. All of me was sore. Down to my toes and my hair, I hurt. Using all my strength, I pushed up onto one elbow. Jimmy was still asleep, probably having the same regrets as me. His da had come in last night after mine. Difference was, his da talked to him. It wasn't a pleasant conversation, either. It was loud. But Jimmy had explained the events and his da listened, even asked questions. He said he'd bail him out today since this was his first arrest—and it better damn well be his last. At least Jimmy knew where he stood.

The Clyde boys yawned and stretched and scratched and spit. They grumbled, making mean remarks and questioned my manhood. As I was figuring out how to reach through the bars and pop them good ones, Jimmy sat up and smoothed his hair. I did the same and realized my hat was gone. Lost somewhere on our fighting ground. Or maybe lost in the water. Well, it was gone. No way Da would buy me a new one. I'd have to go around bare-headed until my wages came in. If they did. I'd thought about that last night, too. Was I still employed? Da had every right to fire me. But if I had wages, first I'd have to pay off his lost gun. How many weeks would that take? Then buy me a hat. And then my own gun. That's assuming I still lived at home. Room and board would take all of my wages, nothing left for a gun.

Could I be any more sad? Here it was Sunday, the bell had pealed a few minutes ago, and I wanted to be in church, sitting next to Molly, holding her hand, looking forward to inspecting her steers again. But here I was, locked up like a common criminal, regretting yesterday.

The door to the office opened and in walked Deputy Sheriff Tommy O'Sullivan,

balancing two trays, each brimming with plates. Smells of scrambled eggs, ham slices and beans sailed in behind him. "Sorry breakfast's late. Being Sunday, the café opens up late." He chinned at the Clydes. "Back against the far wall and I'll get your tray in there. Don't try anything." He waited for them to stand, backs to the wall, then set one tray on the floor, unlocked the door, pushed it inside the cell, then relocked. He did the same with mine.

"I'll get all y'all coffee. Be right back." He disappeared into the office and returned with four mugs, two in each hand.

Mine was the perfect temperature. A long slurp lifted my spirits. Maybe things would work out.

O'Sullivan waited by my cell as I wolfed down the food. Guess I was hungrier than I'd thought. He looked me up and down, then Jimmy. Back to me. "You're Tate's youngest brother, ain't ya? There's Tate, Joe, and then you."

I nodded, not knowing where this was heading, but sure it would be unpleasant. "I'm Eagan. Met you out at the Carmichael ranch for one of their Sunday suppers, few months back."

Snapping his fingers, he nodded. "Of course. That's where me and Imogene made it official. We're a couple." He beamed bright enough to light up the town. "Fact is, we're getting married soon. Maybe around Christmas."

At least someone in here was happy. I forced a "Congratulations" and returned to eating. Who did I care he was marrying?

O'Sullivan nodded at me. "Fact is, your brother Tate used to court Imogene when they was in school." One corner of his mouth turned up. "Glad they broke up. I got the girl and I'm one lucky fella."

From what I'd heard around town and in the shop, this deputy sheriff was liked by pretty much everybody. He was fair, they'd said, polite almost to a fault, willing to help when needed, didn't drink to excess like the sheriff before Wagner, and an all-around good man. Until

Molly, that's what I thought I wanted to be like. Now, I wasn't so sure.

Conversation over, he pointed toward the office. "Gotta run my rounds, Eagan. Sorry you're in here."

Well, that made two of us. He closed the door behind him, and I looked at Jimmy. "Suppose he's as nice as they say?"

He shrugged. "Suppose so. He didn't yell at us. Or hit us, which is great."

I finished the eggs and ham, and about licked the coffee mug edge. I wanted more. Over the years, I'd found coffee much more satisfying than the tea of my youth. The tea Ma still made. I lay back on my bunk and closed my eyes. No telling how long I'd be here.

Sleep was right around the corner, when the door opened and in stepped Sheriff Wagner with Jimmy's da right behind. Wagner scowled at my best lad. "Get your things, Jimmy. Your pa's bailed you out."

If he was like me, and he was, he had nothing to get. He'd lost his hat, too. We eased to our feet, both of us groaning. Shaking hands, we had nothing to say. No words would come to mind.

Wagner shooed me to the back of the cell while he unlocked it. Jimmy stepped through, turned and gave me a sad look. His da draped an arm around his shoulder. "Let's go home, son."

"My gun, Pa?" Jimmy's words trailed behind him.

"Already got it."

And with that, I was all by myself in my cell, two of the three bullies caged next to me. Now, alone, I was fair game. I was sure they'd taunt and tease me for hours.

And so they did. I'd been called every name they could think of, threatened with hours of torture, in exquisite detail. I had nothing to say back except that I wished I was heeled and wouldn't mind shooting them. They laughed at that. Clyde Two, bruises under both eyes and a cut down his chin, laughed so loud the sheriff came in to see what was so funny. We all shut up until he closed the door.

I lay on my bunk deciding if being a curly wolf was a good idea or was it better to be a kind lawman, like O'Sullivan. Each held possibilities. Lost in thought and with my eyes closed, I missed the door opening.

"Got someone to see you, Eagan." Deputy O'Sullivan stood in the doorway in front of my da. Stomach knotting, I had no idea what he'd say. Da wasn't the kind to hit me, so that wasn't a concern. But would he speak?

Da and the deputy stood in front of my cell. I eased up from my bunk and held the bars by the cell door. "Da. I'm so sorry. Don't know what got into me." That's all I had. I'd spent hours trying on different apologies and nothing stuck.

Da pulled in a deep breath and ran a hand across his mouth and chin, his beard neatly trimmed this morning. No doubt he and Ma had gone to church as he was wearing his nice clothes.

He started to speak and then stopped. Started again and took yet another breath. "Eagan. I don't know why you're actin' the maggot, but it has to stop."

The deputy nodded. "Eagan, bail was set at fifty dollars. Your pa just paid it. All of it."

Fifty dollars? Was my freedom worth that much? And where did he get the money? My gaze swept the brick floor. "Thanks, Da. I'll pay you back, soon's I can."

Silence stretched. "*Mar dhea*. You're right. You will. It'll come out of your wages."

Wages? I was still employed! Hallelujah! Now I could buy a hat and a gun.

O'Sullivan fitted the key into the lock and swung open the door while the Clydes complained. I stepped into freedom the same time Sheriff Wagner walked in.

"See your daddy bailed you out. Ain't that touching?" He glanced at Da then turned back to me. He reached behind his back and pulled out Da's gun. He held it out, far enough away I couldn't touch it. "Look what I found this morning. Right where you were fightin' with these scoundrels."

Relieved it had been located, I blurted out, "Was it in the water? Is it dry?"

Da scowled at me. "*Dia diabhal!* You took my gun?" He moved within inches of me. Maybe he *would* hit me. "Stole it from home?" Grabbing my upper arm, he shook it. "You took my gun and went target practicing? Without my permission? Then you get in a fight? Ara, who do you think you are?"

Clyde One hopped on one foot. "He even shot my friend's foot. Almost clean off. Purdy's probably still at Doc's, it was that bad."

I looked at Da, both lawmen. "I didn't shoot him. He pulled the trigger when he tried to take it from me. He did it his own self!"

"Na ah." Clyde Two pushed an arm through the bars and pointed at me. "He did. I saw. Wanted to kill us, he said. Ain't that right, Clyde?"

"For a fact, Sheriff. I been telling you that."

Wagner glared at the Clydes. "Save your breath. Trial's a week, Tuesday."

"Tuesday? A week?" Clyde One counted on his fingers. "But that's six...eight days from now. We're supposed to sit in here all that time?"

"What about Purdy? You gonna lock him up too?"

Deputy O'Sullivan nodded. "It's ten days, and yes,

unless you come up with bail, you'll be guests of the county that whole time."

Not to be outdone, Sheriff Wagner added, "After Nolan's gone, I'm haulin' in Purdy. He's barely hobblin' but he'll make it here just fine."

Da gripped my arm even tighter and held out his hand to Wagner. "May I have my gun? Eagan needs to clean and oil it."

"I suppose. Bring it to the trial next week. Judge'll want to see it." Wagner held it out, butt first. "I can trust you, Mr. Nolan?"

Da flashed fire at the sheriff and took the gun. "Let's go." Thrust through the office by Da, out I went into fresh air and freedom. At least for a few days. Walking to the church where Ma waited, I realized I hated being in jail. It was lonely and scary. No, terrifying. Felt like a sitting duck waiting for somebody to come in and shoot me. I couldn't get away.

The several blocks walk down to the church took at least a day and a half. I did most of the talking, explaining, apologizing. Da grunted a time or two but didn't say much else.

We met up with Ma standing on the walk, in front of the church. Ma and two women with her recoiled at my black, swollen eye, bruised face. Clothes, I'm sure reeked of whatever I'd rolled in.

"Holy Mother of…" Ma extracted a handkerchief from her sleeve and daubed at my split lip and then held it to her nose. "What happened to ye?"

I glanced at a woman standing next to Ma. Molly's ma, of course! Could I simply die? Maybe Da wouldn't tell them where I'd been. Or maybe he should. Molly would like that.

To answer Ma, I pointed toward the stream, my jaw

and mouth not working well. I rubbed the right side of my face gently. It was sore and I felt a couple bumps, which told me I looked a sight.

"Hi Eagan!" Molly beamed at me. I hoped my return smile was good, but I didn't really feel like smiling. I nodded, words unable to form.

Ma gave me a look that was impossible to figure out. She was mad, that much I knew, but were those tears behind her narrowed eyes? And the tight mouth said more than any words could. I had let them down. How could I make it up to them?

Molly wouldn't take the hint to be quiet. Instead, she leaned in a bit. "Where've you been? Figured I'd see you here at church."

No way would I tell. No way.

Da nudged my shoulder. "Go on and tell her, *buachaill*. She asked you nice."

I didn't like being called a child in Irish or English. But I was in no position to argue. Da nudged my shoulder again. "Go on."

My gaze swept over the sidewalk bricks, over everyone's shoes and boots. Silence strained my chest until I mumbled, "In jail."

"Jail?" Ma gasped, stepped back like I was on fire, shoved the handkerchief back into her sleeve. "Good Mother of Heaven."

Molly looked at her folks, mine, then me. "In jail? *You* were in jail?" Eyes wide, her smile lit up this side of the church. "What for?"

Another nudge from Da.

"Shooting at a fella's foot and fighting."

"Is that fella all right?" Molly's da asked, concern edging his words.

I nodded. Far as I knew. Actually, I wished I'd blown his whole leg off.

Da gripped my upper arm again. "Sorry to cut this short. Eagan's gotta go home and clean...his...gun. And there's chores for him to do."

Molly moved in close for a peck on the cheek but Da pulled me away before any contact. I turned to watch my love wave to me while her ma gathered the children. That'd be the last time I'd see her now that her folks knew I was a jailbird. Who wanted a daughter of theirs courted by a criminal?

Thoughts like that consumed me as we walked home. At least thinking about being behind bars was better than thinking about what Ma and Da would say when we got there. The five blocks couldn't be over quick enough before I could go inside and hide. I'd have to venture out tomorrow to go to work, but I'd be safe from the men who were still in jail. Probably. At least I'd be safe with Da.

Safe. It hit me that, for the next ten days, I'd be safe from The Three. But after that? If the judge dismissed them, they'd be out about in town harassing me whenever they felt like it. Which was about all the time. I prayed they didn't have fifty dollars apiece for bail. On second thought, I was sure they didn't.

My shoulders relaxed. Ten days. What could I do in that amount of time?

CHAPTER THIRTEEN

I DIDN'T HAVE TO WORRY ABOUT STAYING BUSY for the next ten days. Da and Ma saw that I did not only my fair share of chores but then some. At home, I swept upstairs and down, cleaned windows, hauled in buckets of wood I'd chopped for hours, brushed and curried our horse, mucked out the barn, restacked hay bales, cleaned out the chicken coop, pulled weeds, brought in gallons of fresh water, cleaned my room until it sparkled, washed clothes, and fell into bed utterly exhausted each night.

At the meat shop, the work wasn't any easier. I started every morning sweeping the entire boardwalk on our side of the street, then getting fresh ice from Solano's. Da had me clean the store's windows, scrub out each glassed case, and restock it. I even rearranged and inventoried the storeroom. Every evening, I swept and mopped the floor after Da had left for the day. Every other day, I brought home our aprons to scrub them clean.

My half hour for lunch was reduced by half. I now had fifteen minutes to wolf down one of the sandwiches

I'd make of a morning for Da and me, and to gulp the buttermilk I'd bring along for us. He took a leisurely pace of his lunch break, while I helped customers. In fact, he took to sitting outside on a bench he'd provided for townsfolk years ago. From his position on the boardwalk, he had plenty of time to sit and chat with passersby while he nibbled at his sandwich. Once, I muttered under my breath that his long lunch breaks weren't fair, but then remembered what I'd done.

I deserved everything I got.

Wrapping a nice piece of rump roast for Mrs. Ramsey, I got to thinking about Molly. Of course, I thought about her most of the time, but this moment was different. I hadn't seen her since Sunday and that was what, five days ago? She hadn't been by once to see me or even send a note. Figuring she would at least get me a message saying she hoped I was all right, missed me, or some such dispatch, disappointment filled my heart. Like a spark from the Fourth of July fireworks, I realized she was using me to get some sort of thrill, some sort of pleasure having me get in trouble, like a low-down curly wolf.

She was probably in ecstasy right about now with all the trouble I was in.

Well, she'd said she liked men who were a bit rough around the edges, whether they were lawmen or outlaws. What an idiot I'd been, playing right into her hands. Who was I anyway? Certainly not an outlaw, a curly wolf, or a man of low integrity. I was better than that. I was someone with values and morals, a man who knew right from wrong. Standing straight, I threw my shoulders back, thanked Mrs. Ramsey for coming in, put the money in the cash register, and right then and there, decided I was done with Molly. No way would she get me to do something or be somebody I wasn't. I was a *good boy*, after all, as Da had said.

Once I got this trial over with and done, assuming I wasn't locked up, I'd find Deputy Tommy O'Sullivan and ask what being a lawman was like. How could I go about being a deputy, too? Maybe I could be a part-time deputy and learn from him. From my point of view, being a deputy was better than cutting up meat all day, cleaning out icy meat boxes, and washing bloody aprons. No, being a deputy, I'd be out riding the range, looking for no-account bank robbers and scalawags, or I'd be out and about in town, visiting Sam's Emporium just to make sure everyone was playing nice. I'd pass the time making my rounds and talking to the townsfolk. Plus, I was sure it paid more than I earned now.

Yep, that's what I'd do.

The bell tinkled as Da walked in, wiping crumbs from his beard. A fella I recognized, Mr. Dunfield, followed Da in and continued their discussion. "Duck season's gonna be slim this year, Ciernan."

Da tossed the empty canvas lunch sack to me and I folded it and put it in the back room. I could hear Da loud and clear. "Ducks haven't come down yet, Fred. Still too warm up north, is what I hear. Which is too bad. I'd love a good duck roast."

"Well, hell, me too." Mr. Dunfield pointed south and east. "Ain't there a breeding ground or meadow half a day's ride from here? I heard hunters go there and get nice fat ones."

I mentally snapped my fingers. Maybe, just maybe, Da, Jimmy, and me could go Sunday. I was sure that's where Jimmy suggested, or was that Zeke? I'd check with Jimmy first and then Zeke, if Da said yes. Most of me resented having to ask permission to go, but the smaller half remembered I didn't own a gun and the trouble I was in was because of that fact. Maybe I really was *actin' the maggot*, as Da would say.

Once Mr. Dunfield left, I asked Da about duck hunting after church. I thought it would be a great outing, and the more I thought about it, the more I wanted to go.

"Sorry to disappoint, but two reasons no." Da shook his head and held up a finger. "First, you're still under arrest, out on bail, but still under arrest, and you can't be holding or shooting a gun. Mine, yours, any gun."

Well, hell. I hadn't thought about that.

"And two," he held up a second finger. "Not duck hunting season yet. Gonna be couple more months." With my mouth turned down and shoulders slouched, my disappointment must've shown. Da added, "We'll go when we can. I'll teach you how to shoot."

My world turned rosy and right. Da offered to teach me to shoot and to go hunting with him. Everything would be ace-high, I was sure. And with that, my attention turned to the upcoming trial in five days. Four and a half, if I was counting right. I fought down panic, but something trickled down the side of my head, anyway. Up until now, I hadn't given the hearing a great deal of thought, but I *could* be going to jail. It all depended on what the judge decided and what I said and what Jimmy said. Surely, no way would he listen to the Clydes and Purdy. No way. But then again, maybe he would. Especially if they said what he wanted to hear and said it just right.

I stood frozen by the Hamburg meat counter. What was the chance I'd be found guilty of shooting Purdy? If so, what kind of sentence would I get? Hanging didn't sound right, but ten years behind bars? Five? Hell, even five days would be unbearable.

I tried swallowing, but nothing happened. Rooted in place, my world turned shockingly white, then red. I could run. Not exactly *run*, with my bum leg, but maybe tonight, after closing up, I could head upstream, away from town and strike out on my own. No one would find me. Maybe I'd head into Mexico. I knew a few words of Spanish.

Before I uprooted my life and went on the owl hoot trail, maybe I should find out how much trouble I was actually in. Maybe Da would know. But how to ask.

I waited until near closing time and the shop was empty, with Da busy counting the day's money in the register. A smile on his face told me we'd done well today. Now that the sign was turned around to read *Closed*, I grabbed the broom and brushed toward Da, working up the courage to ask the big question.

Taking a deep breath, I slowed my sweeping. "What d'you think the judge will say on Tuesday?" I looked up at Da. "Am I gonna hang?"

Da snapped a look at me. "For shootin' a fella's foot? Hardly likely. If ye'd killed him, yes. Just a foot. No." He finished counting, then closed the drawer. "Ye could get a year or so in prison, though. Ye thought about that? Was it worth it? What'd that fella ever do to ye to make ye want to shoot him?"

Again, I wasn't about to give the whole story, but part I'd share. "Told you. I was holding the gun since I didn't have a holster. He wanted to hold it, I told him no. He grabbed it, I forced the gun downward, and he pulled the trigger. Shot his own damn foot." Oops, I'd said *damn*. We didn't curse, especially around Ma.

"Watch yer language, son." Da rubbed his chin.

"Depending on the judge, he may give ye time, a probation, or a warnin'." He untied his apron and tossed it to me. "I'm goin' home. See ye there."

Da fitted his hat, opened the door, then turned back at me. "Ye worked hard today."

And with that, he stepped outside, closed the door, and walked east toward home. A compliment. He gave me a compliment when he didn't have to. I'd worked hard all week, and he recognized the efforts. Whistling, I finished sweeping and went to the storeroom for the mop and bucket.

Someone knocked at the door. I wanted to ignore the noise, since it was obvious we were closed. A second knock, this one harder, I peeked out from the back room and recognized the deputy, O'Sullivan. I waved and he waved back. Da had given me a spare key fortunately, so I dug it out of my pocket and let in the man I'd wanted to talk to.

We started with chit chat and then he got down to business. "I've been listening to those three mongrels yap—all day, all night. Didn't know there were so many useless words in the world." He shook his head. "But they don't like you, that's clear." Lowering his voice, he asked the all-important question, "What d'you do to make them so mad at you?"

How to respond? What should I tell him? After a pause, I chose the truth. I leaned against a cleaned-out counter, took a deep breath, and scanned the floor. "Nobody knows this but my best lads Jimmy and Zeke. They came to my rescue."

"All right. I won't say anything—unless it's necessary."

That had to be good enough. I knew I couldn't trust Sheriff Wagner, but this deputy seemed different. Trustworthy. I told him everything that had happened, what almost happened. Then later, how they dumped over the wheelbarrow of ice and Sheriff Wagner took their side and my money. Words poured forth, and I couldn't stop them. I talked about the gun, target practicing, and then Purdy's stupid foot. I had to give O'Sullivan credit. He never once interrupted or gasped or seemed to judge. He simply stood, also leaning against the counter, and listened.

"Well, Eagan, that's quite a story. I can see why you didn't tell your folks."

"But I've been working to get stronger and meaner. Don't want that to happen again."

O'Sullivan stood up straight and patted the gun on his right hip. "You know, I kinda felt like you before I got this. Now, I feel almost like I have a shield around me and sometimes I do stupid things. Nearly been shot a time or two because I wasn't thinking. Having a gun doesn't really solve problems. It only causes them."

We chatted a bit more then he left, walking toward Sam's Emporium, no doubt checking to be sure everyone was minding their manners. I finished mopping, all the while thinking about what he said: *Guns cause problems.* He was right on that account. But still, I'd feel safer with one on me. How much longer until I could buy one?

The sky a dark gray now, I hobbled home as fast as I could. No doubt Ma and Da would be angry with me for being late, but I had a good excuse. As I walked, I realized I'd forgotten to ask him about being a deputy. Maybe I'd see him tomorrow.

Indeed, they were angry at my tardiness, but when I told them who'd stopped by, I was partially forgiven. My supper was cold and Da hated cold food in general. Seemed I couldn't do anything right, as everything I did went sideways. Maybe after I'd washed dishes, dried, and put them away, and swept the kitchen, I'd go saddle Horse and ride down to Mexico. I'd get lost in cantinas and never come back.

It was full dark when I finished with the kitchen chores, and my body demanded I sit at the table for a quick rest before I rode off. I sat, head in one hand, until a firm hand on my shoulder shook me awake. I lifted my head from the table, wiped embarrassing drool from my chin, and took in a blurry Ma.

"'Tis time for bed, it is, son." She ruffled my hair like when I was a child. "Ye've had a long day and will have another tomorrow. Best turn in."

Could I make it up the stairs? I could sleep on the couch. It wasn't comfortable, but it was in the next room, and I wouldn't have to walk so far or up the stairs. I nodded to Ma and waved a good night. I staggered to the sofa, lay down, then jerked open my eyes when Da shook me.

"Get up. Time for work."

No! I wanted to shout. How could it be? I'd just closed my eyes. I pushed my rumpled body up to what I thought was a seated position, swiped the hair out of my eyes and tried to blink myself awake. A pan banged in the kitchen, followed shortly by the aroma of flapjacks. My favorite.

I pushed up to my feet, shook the cobwebs from my brain, and noticed the sunrays bouncing off the wall behind me. Late. Later than I usually slept. I climbed the stairs, changed clothes, washed my face, and shaved the few chin hairs spiking out. Closer inspection showed my mustache was coming along fine. Feeling like a new person, I bounded downstairs just as the first flapjack hit my plate. Da was already seated, hot tea in front of him, flapjack parts floating on his plate, the syrup thick.

We finished within ten minutes, washed again, then headed out the door. He gave Ma a quick kiss and I gave her a smile and thanks. The walk to work was pleasant with the day already turning warm. Our route took us past the jail, but we always walked on the opposite side of the street just in case. Being a bit late this morning, I guessed Clyde One was awake and enjoying the fresh air. His face appeared in the window, bars keeping him from squeezing through. He spotted me.

"Hey, there's the crip! Lookey what's limpin' up the street!" he hollered at me. "Where y'going? Your pappy still babysittin' you?"

"Turn around, pay them no mind, Eagan. They're just bullies." Pa stared straight ahead, his hand firmly on my back, nudging me forward.

Why was I shaking? They couldn't hurt me. But still...

* * *

THE FOUR DAYS waiting for the trial to happen flew by, much faster than I wanted. Before I knew it, Tuesday morning dawned bright and cheerful, unlike what I felt. Could I still hie myself down to Mexico and live out my life as an outlaw? Would I send for Molly? No. I'd already decided she was trouble. But she sure was pretty. And such a good kisser.

At exactly eight o'clock, I stepped into the courtroom, which up until this morning had been the Frontier Tavern, a quiet sort of saloon. No doubt when this was over, by this afternoon, it would be the tavern once again. The court-appointed lawyer, a Mr. Dan Tubman he introduced himself as, pointed to a chair in front of the judge's desk. I sat, him next to me. Da and Ma took seats directly behind us. In some ways it was comforting for them to be there, but in other ways I was thoroughly embarrassed and didn't want them to see what would happen.

And then I thought of the last time I was in here for a trial. It was for my brother Tate's, last spring. I had sat where my folks were now, and we silently prayed Tate wouldn't hang or spend years in prison. He'd already spent nine months there, hating it, of course. Ending up on probation worked well for him and I hoped that's what I would get. I didn't have any criminal record, never even been yelled at by the sheriff—until a few days ago when he made me give The Three all my money. I truly hated him for that.

More and more people filled the small saloon. I spotted Jimmy's parents come in and sit in another row opposite from us. I waved and they returned it. Where was Jimmy? I knew he wasn't still behind bars, when about then, in he walked with Deputy Tommy O'Sullivan. Jimmy's eyes were wide, and beads of sweat stood out on his face. O'Sullivan seemed at ease and was quietly saying something to him. The deputy pointed to a chair next to Jimmy's Ma, where he sat.

Looked like I was going to be first. Murmurs and hushed voices made me turn toward the door. O'Sullivan and Sheriff Wagner marched in a limping Purdy and both Clydes, their wrists in cuffs. Each of them located me, glared their best villainous stares, then were herded to seats up front, same as me, only an aisle separating us. I couldn't breathe, couldn't swallow. My hands shook. Over the last several days, thinking about these men, I realized they were truly criminals, outlaws, and toe-rags. Knackers. I was darn lucky all they'd wanted to do in the first place was…well, I couldn't bring myself to think about it. They could have killed me easily, as they were all heeled. Or probably they were.

Why they didn't kill me, I still didn't know.

A man dressed in a nice suit with a leather rig buckled around his middle, pearl-handled grips sticking out of both holsters, walked to the front of the room, less than five feet from me. "All rise for the Honorable Judge Rickets." We stood, and from the back, in walked a man much taller than I'd ever seen, full black robe on. His stride was about as long as he was tall, and he covered the room in four steps. He reminded me of a black-robed scarecrow about to take down a flock of buzzards. Standing behind his table, the circuit judge surveyed the room, and I guessed, found it to his satisfaction. He sat with a flourish that almost made me laugh. It was too grandiose. I supposed when you're that tall, everything you do is noticed.

"You may be seated." The bailiff stood behind the judge on his left.

Judge Rickets looked at me then my lawyer. He addressed the room. "This is a bench trial, with no jury, as was requested by the attorneys. Therefore, we will proceed, forthwith."

If I hadn't been so afraid, I would have laughed. Forthwith? Really?

The judge addressed my lawyer. "Mr. Tubman, what say you?"

Tubman stood and straightened his jacket. "Not guilty, Your Honor."

The rabble hollered and grunted, like pigs rutting in

the trash. The judge smacked the gavel on his table. "Another outburst and I'll have you disciplined." He waited for them to quiet. "Are we clear?"

They nodded but sniggered, so I didn't believe them.

"Mr. Nolan"—the judge pointed at me—"please come up here and tell your story."

My lawyer stood with me and pointed to a chair next to the judge. Tubman nodded as the bailiff made me raise my hand and put the other on a Bible. I took the oath but prayed I didn't have to tell the *whole* truth.

With encouraging questions from my lawyer, I gave my side of the story, bit by bit. I didn't rush, mainly because my brain was too frightened to hurry. I spoke clearly but never looked at *them*. Instead, I located Jimmy and spoke mainly his way.

I described when Purdy grabbed my gun, but I muscled it toward the ground. "It was, in fact, Judge, that fella over there, Purdy, who pulled the trigger. He shot his own foot."

That brought The Three to their feet, fists in the air, fingers pointing at me, and loud disagreement. I thought I even heard a threat to my life, but maybe it was my ears ringing. The gavel banged while the bailiff and both lawmen controlled the men. Chaos reigned for a good half minute before the men were shoved back into their chairs, each with a hand firmly on their shoulder.

"Sheriff Wagner?" Rickets frowned.

Wagner, still holding Purdy's shoulder, gave him a shake and then nodded at the judge.

"Please go on, Mr. Nolan." The judge scowled at the outlaws, then chinned at me.

I went on, a bit more quickly, explaining the fight. I still had part of a black eye and bruise on my jaw, which I pointed at, to make my point. Clyde One looked a lot worse than me, which, in thinking on it, didn't help my case much. But it was obvious there had been a fight.

When I reached the part when Sheriff Wagner stepped in, I quit. Surely, he would be asked to fill in the rest. Instead, my lawyer asked the question I'd been dreading. Mr. Tubman stood beside me and addressed me as well as the audience, who could hear every word.

"Mr. Nolan, you're known as an even-tempered, friendly individual. You work at your father's store and are well liked." He looked me square in the eye. "What precipitated...er...caused this friction between you and Mr. Purdy and his friends? When did this start?"

I lowered my voice to a whisper and begged. "Do I hafta say?"

My attorney turned his back to the crowd and spoke only to me. "Afraid so. If it's powerful, you'll probably get off completely. As it stands right now, I'm seeing a couple months in jail and probation." He raised a shoulder. "Up to you, son."

Well, I sure as hell didn't want to go to jail, again. I'd learned that lesson. But even more so, didn't want to explain why those men kept at me. I looked at Ma and Da, the question in their eyes. All right, I'd man up and explain. But could I keep from crying? Already pressure had built behind my eyes, and any second, tears would spill.

I took a ragged breath, raised my chin, glanced at the judge, who was looking right at me, and began. I related everything that had happened. How Jimmy and Zeke came to my rescue, and I had been too ashamed to say anything to anybody.

There. Now my big secret was out in the open for

everyone to laugh at. No doubt, as soon as I walked out today, fingers and giggles would be pointed my way. My folks would be the laughingstock of Blanco Hill and we'd have to move. Sell the store. Get out of town. I'd ruined everyone's lives because of being bullied and too weak to defend myself. I couldn't look at my folks, just Jimmy who nodded.

The judge took a half minute to quiet the room, then spoke to the defendant's lawyer. "Mr. Flaherty, you may cross-examine Mr. Nolan."

What? I had to explain, again? Relive it, again? My hands shook too hard to drink from the water glass my lawyer gave me. Mr. Flaherty stood, looked at his clients, looked at me. "No further questions, Your Honor."

Purdy and the Clydes exploded. "What the hell, Judge? What the hell? What kinda trial is this?"

Clyde Two shrugged out of the bailiff's grip, shot up to his feet and rushed the judge. On his heels was the bailiff who tackled him to the floor.

Rickets' gavel pounded the table. Women shrieked. Men jumped up and yelled.

Purdy, O'Sullivan's gun now pointed at his head, slunk back into his seat. He muttered curses and accusations.

Sheriff Wagner aimed his gun at Clyde One's chest, daring him to move.

Whack, whack, whack! The gavel added to the pandemonium. Part of me wanted to laugh, but the other half realized how serious this was. Had become. People could get hurt.

The bailiff wrestled Clyde Two to his feet and shoved him into his chair.

Judge Rickets pointed his gavel at the spectators.

"Another outburst like that and I'll have all of you removed from this courtroom."

I'd never seen anything like that before and wasn't sure I'd want to again. Looking at my attackers was hard, but I did anyway. I wanted them to know, while I was shaking like an earthquake, I wasn't afraid of them. Although I was, in reality, terrified of what they would do, I prayed that on the outside, I looked confident. Mean and confident.

The judge leaned toward me. "You may step down, Mr. Nolan." Did he really say that? And why didn't the other attorney ask me more questions? What was going on?

Somehow, I stood and marched back to my seat. Mr. Tubman pulled out my chair next to him, and I sat, hard. While I could stare at the men, I couldn't turn around and look at my family. I'd have to, eventually, but not now.

"Both counselors approach the bench." Judge Rickets motioned at the lawyers.

As much as I wanted to know what they were talking about, the three heads huddled together, whispering, I really didn't want to know. Was I going back to jail? Or prison, like my oldest brother Tate did, last year? Or maybe, just maybe, I'd get probation. That was probably the best I could hope for.

After what had to have been a year, at least it felt that way, the two attorneys nodded, turned around, and returned to their respective chairs. I leaned near Mr. Tubman. "What—"

"Shh."

Judge Ricketts pointed at me. "Please stand, Mr. Nolan."

Me and the attorney stood. Surprised my legs held my weight, I trembled and struggled to breathe.

The judge waited until we were upright. "Mr. Nolan, I have no doubt your testimony was difficult to divulge. Your actions of wanting to use the gun are understandable. However, you cannot go around armed just in case someone torments you. There are legal avenues you can pursue instead of shooting, maybe killing someone."

I opened my mouth to argue but my attorney bumped me with his shoulder. I slammed shut.

"I've consulted the attorneys and have considered both your age and humiliating assault." He looked me straight in the eye. "Therefore, it is the decision of this court to give you one month probation, remanded to your mother and father's custody. If, in one month, you've shown good sense and stayed out of trouble, you'll be free to go about your business."

The courtroom exploded. The judge banged the gavel until the room calmed. "Mr. Nolan, I'll see you back here in thirty days." He waved the gavel first toward me and then toward the door.

Mr. Tubman nudged me toward the door.

Outside now, bent over with my hands on my knees, my senses spinning, I waited on the boardwalk for Ma and Da. I knew I had explaining to do and more apologizing, but most importantly, I wanted to stick around to see what would happen to Jimmy.

Several people filed past, most patting my shoulder and giving congratulations. I peeked inside the saloon and discovered Jimmy was up next, and my folks were struggling to make their way through the well-wishing crowd.

When they finally made it outside, Ma wrapped me in

a hug while Da shook my hand. Good. For the first time in a while, I felt good. Relaxed.

"Before we go to the shop," Da spoke quietly, "how about we get a second breakfast? I didn't eat much, and I know Eagan didn't."

My stomach rumbled agreement, over which I heard coming from the courtroom, "Do you solemnly swear to tell the whole truth..."

CHAPTER FOURTEEN

JIMMY STOPPED BY THE STORE SHORTLY AFTER noontime, that silly grin lighting up his face. He always reminded me of a big ol' bullfrog galumphing around when he smiled like that.

"Declared innocent, Eagan! Judge said I was free to go. No jail, no probation, no nothing." Jimmy slapped me on the shoulder. "What d'you think about that?"

We shook hands, my grip tight and sincere. "Congratulations! You didn't do anything wrong. You shouldn't have been locked up at all."

Da leaned on one of the glass-topped counters. "Any word on those *boggin' neds* what caused all this in the first place?"

Jimmy stood still, swallowed, and looked at me, then Da. "Judge said there wasn't enough evidence to hold them." His gaze swept the floor. "He let 'em go."

"Let 'em go?" I hollered despite being close to Jimmy. "Let 'em go? Why? How? Didn't it matter what I said? He let 'em go?"

"Yeah, he did. But..." Jimmy held up a hand. "Told

'em to take a bath, which they needed, then get out of town. Don't never come back."

Great. I'd have to watch over my shoulder for the next hundred years. They wouldn't leave town permanently. Not with Purdy's foot halfway shot off. No, they'd come back, and next time, it would be worse. No matter what the judge said, now I'd have to learn to shoot real well. Carry a gun at all times. Defend myself because the law wouldn't. Seemed like I'd have to become a curly wolf simply to protect myself.

"Sure, look it." Da frowned. "The verdict of those blackguards went arseways, but still and all, let's be happy out. Ye boys avoided the gaol."

He was right. Again. Avoiding jail was paramount. I was glad not to be behind bars.

And of course, that dang bell over the door tinkled right then, announcing Mrs. Ramsey, coming in for yet another roast. Jimmy and I shook hands again as he left, holding the door for her.

I spent the rest of the day mulling over the verdicts. Jimmy getting off was right. My getting probation was a bit much I figured, but I could understand why the judge did it. But them? Hell, they should still be in jail, heading toward a year in prison. Life wasn't fair.

Could I talk Da into loaning me his gun until I could buy one? That seemed logical to me since I was hell-bent on owning one. Maybe Sunday after church, we could go target shooting and he could help me learn. I'd ask tonight on our way home.

"Son, I know you're wantin' to shoot. Eager as any lad I've known. But ye're on probation, which means no firearms. For a month."

"That's not fair, Da." Now I was whining like a *balachan*, a child. I needed to sound more grown up, so I changed tactics. "I can't think of a better teacher than you. Besides, we can go way out of town, and they won't know."

"Four weeks, son. Four weeks. Then, I promise we'll go. Take the whole day." He lifted one shoulder as we walked, now a block and a half from home. "Besides, don't need to go to church *every* Sunday. The Lord will forgive."

I chuckled thinking about the look on Ma's face when Da tells her we're skipping attending that day. She wouldn't be happy, but maybe she'd understand. Maybe in a month it would be duck season and we could bring her supper instead of the roasts and chops which we always brought. I'd take her some Hamburg tonight.

I perked up at the thought of duck. Envisioning a passel of foul slung over my shoulder as we walked into the house brought a smile to my face. The muscles stretched. I hadn't smiled like that in a while.

"What are ye two grinnin' about?" Ma met us at the door, apron tied around her narrow waist, fork in one hand. She sniffed Da like he'd been drinking.

Da leaned down and kissed her, like he did every evening. "We haven't a dram. Just talkin' about the future, darlin' girl."

He always called her *darlin' girl*, especially when he was up to something. I kept his secrets, when he confided in me, like the time he surprised her by their going out to dinner for her birthday last year. Just the two of them. I stayed home and cleaned. She was extra surprised when they got back to a sparkling house.

Aromas of baking ham and potatoes wafted from the kitchen into the front room. Ma was certainly a good cook and she made lots of whatever she came up with. I listened to many different recipes throughout the days at the store and I was sure no one cooked as well as Ma.

"Wash up, men. Supper's about ready." Ma turned toward the kitchen, then spun back around back. "In honor of the trial results today, I made yer favorite meal, son. Ham and fried sweet tatties…and a pie. Apple."

I danced her around the parlor. "Thanks, Ma," and set her back down. "I'll wash up extra special." I took the stairs to the bedroom two at a time. Suddenly, my stomach knew it had never been fed before and was ravenous. I washed my face and hands with soap, combed my hair, re-tucked my shirt, brushed dirt off my pants, rubbed the boot tips on each pant leg, then stood back and inspected what I could in my shaving mirror. I gleamed.

We sat around the table long after supper was done, me chasing the last crumb of crust around my plate, the apple part long gone. Ma and Da sat drinking tea. I stretched, then pushed back to wash dishes.

Ma put her hand on my arm. "Not tonight, Eagan. Ye've earned a night off, fú the noo." She finished her tea and stood. "Go enjoy the cool night air. I'm thinkin' this heat is about to break."

Hoping she wouldn't change her mind, I thanked her, assured her I'd clean up tomorrow, and headed outside to the porch. I'm not sure what I'd have done without that porch. Me and my brothers made so many plans there, discussed hundreds of "important" things, spent our lives on that island. It was the site of our growing up.

I leaned against the rail and stared into the woods on the other side of our field. There lay the creek and those tall, imposing Texas oaks. Pecan trees were interspersed, and in the fall, long about Thanksgiving time, we'd pick up nuts. Buckets and buckets full. Shelling them took time, especially when the outer hull stuck tight, but we always had pecan pie and pecan cookies for Christmas.

Before I could decide what exact problem to think about, there were so many issues, Da joined me at the railing. We stayed silent, simply soaking in the cool and slight breeze, which kept those pesky mosquitoes and midges away. I guessed my biggest problem was how to buy a gun, since all my wages went to Da. Quick reckoning in my head, and it would be three months before my bail was paid. After that, a month of working until I could buy a hat. Truthfully, I needed that worse than a gun. But not by much. If those fellas came back into town, a hat wouldn't do me much good.

The more I thought about that, the more I realized I needed a gun. Now. Not in four or five months. Now. Today. They would return, no doubt, and when they did, they'd take out Purdy's foot injury on me. More than likely, they'd outright kill me. Would Da understand if I pleaded my case again?

I leaned sideways against the rail. "Those fellas, Da. They're coming back." I waited for him to turn and look at me. "Don't care what the judge says, they'll be back. And then I'm in a heap of trouble. They'll find me and—"

"I won't let them hurt ye." Da's face, in the golden shadow from the lantern inside the house, hardened. "Wish ye'd told me sooner, son, but I understand why ye didn't. Yer black affronted. Embarrassed and humiliated and—"

"It is and makes it hard for me to sleep. But I need a gun before they return." I pulled in air and touched his arm. "Please, Da. Let me get a gun. Teach me how to use it. Before they come back. I'll be careful. I will." All I knew was it would be a long four weeks and I'd probably be dead by then.

"Let me do some thinkin' on this Eagan. Sure, look it, it's not an easy decision." Da gazed into the darkening field. "I'll see if I can talk to the circuit judge tomorrow. Maybe he's still in town."

Looked like that would be the best I could get for now. "Thanks Da." In my mind I added, *he'll say no, of course.*

I stayed outside until full dark, and my folks had gone to bed. Alone out here, I was tempted to get on Horse and gallop down to Mexico. I could be there by first light. Hell, I could find a job, easy. I had skill as a butcher. I could learn Spanish. I already knew *carne*—meat—so that was a start right there. But I didn't have any money. I was stuck.

* * *

THE NEXT FOUR days dragged by with me looking over my shoulder every time I ventured outside and cringing each time that bell rung over the door at the shop. I felt relatively safe at home, so after walking with Da, I tended to stay close by. I went back to cleaning up after supper, which gave me something to do besides worry.

I did have time to think, however. I'd given up on the idea of becoming a curly wolf. That simply wasn't me, no matter what Molly wanted. I still wanted, needed a gun, but that was for protection. When I had the chance, I'd go talk to O'Sullivan about becoming a deputy deputy in my spare time.

Sunday finally rolled around, and while putting the finishing touches to my Sunday clothes, I thought about Molly and what I'd tell her. Would it be straight out, honest? I practiced. "Molly. I'm not the man you think I am. You want me to be. I'm a good man. You'll have to find somebody else who's a shooter and curly wolf. I'm sorry. Hope I didn't break your heart too much." There. That sounded good. I practiced more, then joined my folks waiting for me outside. We took our usual seats up front of the church, and occasionally, I glanced over my shoulder at the empty pew in the back, no Molly. Right before the priest waltzed in, Molly and her family slid in and quickly folded their hands.

She was lovely as ever and all I wanted right then and there was to dash back to her, sweep her in my arms and kiss her all over. But I didn't. I couldn't. What was I thinking? I was breaking up with her, wasn't I? But something about her drew me in. She was beautiful, undeniably beautiful. Something about her smell, her turned-up button nose, her flowing red hair buckled my knees. I had to be strong. There would be other girls who didn't want me to be somebody else. Somebody always in trouble. Like Ma says, *there's someone for everyone*. Maybe I'd find someone as beautiful as Molly but liked me for me.

Suddenly, dragged out of my thoughts, I found myself standing, the priest giving last words of...I wasn't really sure of what...and we were done. Briefly, I wondered what he'd talked about, what we'd sung, what we'd prayed, but I didn't think on that much. I had a girl to break up with. Before we moved outside, I spoke softly to my parents. "I gotta talk to Molly, but it won't take long. Wait for me by the steps if you don't mind."

I didn't wait for them to answer. I bolted down the crowded aisle, outside, down the steps and greeted Molly, since they were some of the first to leave.

I nodded to her folks and touched her upper arm. "If you don't mind, I'd like to talk to Molly for just a moment. Won't be long. I promise."

Her da gave me that father look—one of concern. "Ten minutes? Will that give you time? We got chores today."

"Yes, sir. Ten is fine." I turned to Molly, those eyes sizzling right into my core, lighting my heart on fire. "Let's walk down to the creek. You mind?"

"Fine. It's so pretty, down there."

A bit east of church property, which used the creek as a border, was a stand of pecan trees and Texas oak, surrounded by thick bushes. We could speak easily there, without anyone bothering us. Kids played on a field on the other side of the church and parents tended to gather at the front. We were alone.

Arms folded across my chest, I leaned against a tree. Molly stood temptingly close in front. Our eyes met until I had to look away. She ran a dainty hand down my arm.

"You were in jail. And then a trial." Her eyes flared with a grin. "How exciting."

"Wasn't exciting. It was awful. Don't ever want to do either one again."

She reached up and kissed me. It was as sweet and beautiful as the last one. I started to kiss her back and then remembered why we were here.

"I'm not the man you think I am, Molly."

She kissed me again. "You are! You're brave. You shot that man. You've been in jail."

I shook my head, partly to get the marbles back in the right places. "I didn't shoot him. He did. He pulled the trigger." I grabbed both of her shoulders. "Listen, Molly. I—"

The kiss, this time, involved more than lips and

tongues. She melted against me. I couldn't breathe but didn't want to. My arms slid around her, and I pulled her closer. Miraculously, the hem of her plaid skirt was in her hand. Something tugged at the buttons on my pants, which were admittedly getting rather tight.

A deeper kiss. I lowered my hands and found them under her skirt. I gripped flesh. Fireworks ignited in my head and body. And then...then I was hers. We were intertwined, groping and kissing with my most precious parts in her hands. She moaned, tightened in my grasp and I did the same. My head thundered, my heart raced.

We stood like that until we both finally breathed normally. She stepped back and smoothed her skirt. I struggled to button my trousers. I was now thoroughly embarrassed and excited by what we had done. Would I tell her she was my first? Was it obvious?

The blush on her cheeks made the freckles stand out. She was beautiful. How could I have decided to break up with her?

She stood on tiptoes and whispered in my ear. "When you get a gun, we can do that naked." She kissed my ear. "Would you like to?"

I couldn't nod fast enough. I kissed her hard, made sure we were put together, took her hand, and stepped into a field. I spotted her da in the distance, walking toward us. Whew! Good thing he didn't see what we'd done. I never would have seen my eighteenth birthday.

CHAPTER FIFTEEN

NAKED. *Naked.* HER WORD SWIRLED INSIDE MY head until all I could think of was her, naked. Lying on a soft rug. All alone, we would roll and cuddle and kiss and feel each other. Naked. I had no idea what that felt like exactly, but no doubt I'd love it. Just thinking about that made me tingle all over and grow in places that were embarrassing.

This Monday morning at the store seemed busier than usual. The day had started off peaceful, but for whatever reason, more and more customers came in to buy small cuts of meat. I ran back and forth from the storeroom to the front at least thirty times. But I didn't care. I'd had a woman, and soon, she'd be naked. And I'd be naked. We'd be naked together.

"Eagan? Ye comin' back? Mrs. Ramsey would like her roast. Today, if ye don't mind."

Da's holler brought me back to my senses. Oh yes, the roast. I located a nice one from the icebox, took it to the front and presented it for her approval. She smiled, nodded, and thanked me for the service. I couldn't help but smile back. I liked being helpful.

Da wrapped the rump roast in brown paper and string, while I took the money. It felt heavy in my hand. Maybe if I slipped it into my pocket, Da wouldn't notice. If I did that several times this week, I'd have enough to buy a gun.

"Haste ye back," Da called out as Mrs. Ramsey waved under the tinkling bell and closed the door. Da and I were at last alone and I could straighten the remaining meats in the various glass display counters. We had four in our tiny shop, and right now, each one had ice melting into the metal trays underneath and two or three pieces of meat. First thing tomorrow, Da would need to go to Joe's Smokehouse and purchase more smoked meat. I'd haul back at least twenty pounds of ice. We had enough meat hanging in a cold closet in the storeroom to last a few days, but if business kept up at this rate, we'd need to buy more real soon.

Not that I was complaining. This store was our family's livelihood and Da depended on the income to keep a roof over our heads and food in our bellies. And I was glad to help out.

I was helping Da count today's take at the register when I happened to glance through the front window. For a second, I swear it was Clyde One walking past. All I spotted were legs, but they sure reminded me of him.

Frozen, I held two half dollars while ice water poured over me. They were back. Sooner than I'd anticipated. Or maybe it wasn't Clyde One. I couldn't be one hundred percent sure, but I wasn't taking chances.

Thawed, I gave Da the coins. "Thought I saw one of the Clydes walk by. They're back. I just know they are."

He gave me raised eyebrows and a slight shake of the

head. "Kinda soon, ain't it, boyo? If they do return, I'd think it'd be this fall."

"Why this fall?" No matter how I turned the comment on its head, I couldn't figure it out.

"Duck season. People go shootin' and nobody thinks anything of it. Everybody carries a gun around like he's braw...special." He gave me a quick shake of the shoulder. "Duck season. That's what I'd do."

So maybe it wasn't Clyde One I saw go by. Duck season made sense. But they didn't make sense. In the first place, why pick on me? I was merely walking up the street when they attacked. It was my money they wanted at first, but that's not what they got. Twice. Maybe they thought I was good for more coin, more embarrassment. They were sadly mistaken if so. I had nothing but moths in my pockets and would be like that for months to come. Probably not until the new year. Now I was depressed. Here I'd been thinking about Molly naked and now I was angry because I was such a loser.

An hour more until closing time, so I decided to sweep. Gave me something to do besides arranging meat, a chore Da was finishing, anyway. I was in the back storeroom when the bell jingled. I stuck my head out the arch like a turtle coming out of his shell. That was probably The Three coming to find me.

But no. It was Mrs. Ellie Carmichael, whose husband, Anthony, owned the ranch my oldest brother, Tate, worked at. Maybe something had happened to him. Maybe he got fired. Maybe...no, she had a smile on her face and was shaking hands with Da.

I put down the broom and joined them, shaking her hand, too. Kind of unusual for a woman to do that, but she was an unusual woman from what Tate had said. We made chitchat until we ran out of *nice weather*, and all.

"I'll tell you why I'm here, Mr. Nolan. Eagan." She nodded at each of us in turn. I'd only met her a time or two, but I really liked her. "Next Sunday, we're hoisting a social. You know, like the one you came to a few months ago."

"That was a grand time, Mrs. Carmichael. The wife and I had the craic. Really."

Her smile ran ear to ear. "Good to hear. We'd like to invite you, your wife, and Eagan to join us. Tate will be there, too. He's been up on Big Blue riding fence, popping brush most of the summer, and I'm sure he's ready to talk to someone who's not a ranch hand...or a steer."

Now, my smile stretched my cheeks. "Thank you, ma'am. Haven't seen my brother in ages. Like to see how he's doing."

"Tate's been busy. Reports come back he hasn't had any more trouble and he's made friends. He's a good, hard worker, Mr. Nolan. You should be proud."

Da's shoulders pulled back and he stood straighter. "Thank you, Mrs. Carmichael. I *am bródúil*...erm, proud of him. Good to hear he's *nó dosser* and he's stayed out of trouble. Or it hasn't found him."

She extended a hand again. "Then we'll see you this coming Sunday around ten?"

"Ye can count on us." Da escorted her to the door. "We'll be there in our Sunday finest."

She chuckled and turned at the open door. "Be sure to bring a big appetite. You know how Miranda cooks."

As much as I wanted to see my brother and have more of Miranda's fried chicken, missing church Sunday meant missing Molly. Would we be able to have time to ourselves? We wouldn't be naked, but...

But then, Tate had a gun. Probably. And money.

Surely, he'd loan me his earnings. But if not, I would steal them. I shook my head and frowned. No. I don't steal, especially from my brother. So, I continued plotting. If I gave up Molly this Sunday, next week I'd have a gun. Life would be naked. Uh, good.

And even if Purdy and the two Clydes showed up around town, I'd be heeled. They wouldn't have a chance around me. They'd come struttin' down the boardwalk, like they owned the town, then I'd show them who was in charge. I'd shoot their boots, their hats—

"Eagan?" Da's voice interrupted my thoughts. "Ye're 'bout to sweep a hole in the floor, lad."

* * *

I STRETCHED two or three times before throwing off the covers and finding my feet. A glance out the window showed Sunday dawning with a couple of fluffy clouds to the east. The robin's egg-blue sky covered the town. As much as I wanted to see Molly, I wanted more to see my brother. Before he'd moved out last spring, I'd looked forward to having a room of my own. With brother Joe leaving shortly after Tate, I'd spread my belongings everywhere. But now, I missed their company, their late-night whispers, their hiding my things. I missed the teasing and good-natured kidding among the three of us. Yep, it would be good seeing Tate.

Didn't take me long to wash up, shave the wisps of whiskers I'd sprouted since Thursday, put on fresh clothes, pull on boots and slip on my best vest. This was the one Ma had sewn with an extra pocket inside the silk lining. It fit perfectly.

The three of us ate breakfast in a bit of a rush, piled the dishes in the big wash tub, poured water over them, then headed out the door. Rarely did we leave dishes to soak, but today was special. Da had hitched the horse to our buggy, which we seldom used. Horse wasn't too thrilled to have something attached to her rear, but she settled down once Da flicked the reins over her back and said, "Get a crack on."

My spirit was about as high as could be, which made me whistle while my folks sitting on the front bench chatted and chuckled. The road ran up and down hills that leveled out onto a plain, now dotted with sunflowers and other plants with bright colors. Pockets of trees were in full glory, birds flew overhead like they knew where they were going, and three pronghorns pranced across the field. We crossed two creeks, which usually ran more full, than today. It hadn't rained in a while, so I wasn't too surprised at the lack of higher water. Rainy season was still a month or so away.

I spotted the ranch house out in the distance when we crested a short hill and turned into their road. The aroma of Miranda's fried chicken wafted this far. I was sure she'd been doing a lot of cooking, and judging by the smells, there was plenty to go around. We reined up in front of the house where I helped down Ma. Da drove the buggy to the far side of the house and parked between two other buggies.

Mrs. Carmichael met us under the huge canvas tarp that had to stretch twenty by twenty feet. I remembered it from the last time we were here. But the smells coming from the back of the area were more seductive than Molly being naked. All right. Almost as seductive. I followed my nose, while Ma waited for Da to join up. Sure enough, Miranda stirred a huge pot of beans hung over a campfire.

She stood when she spotted me, a grin spreading

across her face. "Ah, Señor Eagan. *Bienvenidos!* So very good to see you again!"

Not sure whether to shake her hand, which had a spoon in it, or give her a brief hug, I settled for the hug. The top of her head coming up not quite to my shoulders, I did a quick lean down and hugged. Could a face beam any brighter?

"Ah, Señor Eagan. *Tus abrazo...Me gusta mucho!* Your hug—*perfecto!*" She stepped back and took me in, her round brown eyes running up and down my head to my boots. "*Guapo*, Eagan. *Muy guapo.*"

Now, I was thoroughly embarrassed. I knew *guapo* meant handsome in Spanish. First, I was a good hugger, then good-looking? Obviously, she'd mistaken me for someone else. I ducked my head and mumbled some sort of thanks.

"Miranda, is this scalawag bothering you?"

The words came from behind, and before I could turn and give Tate a hug, handshake, or punch to the arm, two strong arms wrapped around me. We rocked back and forth, my arms pinned under his. "We don't invite just anybody for Sunday, little brother. How'd you get in?"

I struggled to get out of his capture. Damn, he was strong. I wriggled like a fish, which only brought us both to the ground. Tangled up just like when we were kids, we rolled into a chair, which clattered into another. I knew we were in trouble when we crashed into a pair of legs that belonged to Da. More legs near Tate belonged to Mr. Carmichael, I assumed.

That stopped us. We clambered to our feet, brushed off dirt, ran a hand over my hair, smoothing all the spikes, and sheepishly grinned at the growing crowd.

Tate found his voice first. "Sorry about that, Mrs.

Carmichael. But this scoundrel was bothering Miranda, and I couldn't let that happen."

Playing along, and I suddenly loved her for that, Mrs. Carmichael pushed past the crowd, marched up and slid a protective arm around my shoulders. "For your information, Tate, I *invited* Mr. Nolan here. He's my guest, and I expect you to treat him like one. Put on your best manners and greet him like the royalty he is."

Tate took off his hat and bowed to me like I really was a king. "Your highness," he said. "Please forgive me. I mistook you for my little brother. Now I see, you're much better looking than him. Such atrocities won't happen again."

I waved him off, my nose in the air. "See that it doesn't."

Me and Tate broke out laughing, jabbing each other's arms. The assembled invited guests chortled with a couple bowing to each other. I'd missed him, more than I'd admitted.

About fifteen people gathered under the tarp once the preacher rode up and at last, stood in front of his congregation now crowded undercover. We took our seats, smiles now hidden under our piousness. Sitting there, I tapped my foot, squirmed in my seat, crossed one arm over the other, then reversed them. Tate glanced sideways at me a time or two and then Ma, on my other side, put a hand on my arm. I got the meaning. Except for the standing to sing, I managed to sit "still."

At last, we were done. The preacher raised his hand, said "Amen," and released us. I leaned over to Tate. "We need to talk."

"Alone? Just us?" He stood gazing behind us at Miranda and a cook's helper I didn't recognize. "How 'bout we eat first, then talk?"

We cut around two older men taking their time walking to the food. The spread was as awesome as last time. Miranda had indeed done herself proud. Fried chicken, boiled potatoes, cooked carrots, and a pot of pintos was more than enough. Topping off the buffet were two pies at the end, one some sort of berry and the other peach. Had to be fresh peaches, not canned, since it was the end of peach season. My favorite fruit.

Tate and I filled our plates and found chairs. We turned them to where they faced each other and added two to be used as tables. One by one, people, plates heaped high, sat near us. We passed an hour in small talk and a bit of town gossip to be shared later with the ranch hands.

Two helpings of pie later, my stomach pooched out and there was no way another bite of anything would go down. I wanted to unbutton the top of my pants, and if I'd been home, I would have. But here, surrounded by strangers, I simply groaned and stood. I took Tate's empty plate and mine to an area behind the house to be put into a big tub. Admittedly, I felt guilty for not offering to wash dishes. But I was a guest, and royalty at that, so I wouldn't be allowed to wash or dry. Which suited me just fine.

Tate and I chatted with a couple of people, then walked aways down to the creek. Seemed like every time we had something important to discuss, we always ended up at a creek or stream. Guess that was easier than looking each other in the face.

Events this past month were about to burst out of my chest if I didn't tell him now. A glance over my shoulder confirmed we were far enough away from anyone to hear our conversation. We walked a few more steps and then I stopped. Where to begin?

"Don't know how much you know 'bout what's been going on."

Tate frowned. "Nothing. I've been up on Big Blue." He pointed. "We don't—"

"I got arrested. Had a trial. On probation."

"What?" Tate's eyes went wide, then narrowed. "Why? What'd you do?"

I held up a hand. "There's more."

"More?"

"I met a girl. We did it, Tate. We did it." I danced around, the words pouring out. "I need a gun. *Now*. Can I borrow your money?"

Tate stood still, frozen wide-eyed. He blinked hard then part of a smile crawled up his face. "One thing at a time." He cocked his head. "You had a girl? You still have this girl?"

I nodded, saying I'd explain everything in detail. But first, I swore him to secrecy, because I didn't want word of this personal nature stuff getting around town.

Tate gazed into the distance. "Molly? Molly O'Malley? Don't think I know the family."

"Been in town about three, four months."

We sauntered shoulder to shoulder, only stopping at the creek. Tate picked up small rocks and plunked them into the water. I did the same, waiting for him to say something.

He spoke to the water. "Be careful who you love, Eagan." Tossing another rock, he continued. "You never know the consequences." He paused, then exhaled. "That's where babies come from. You know that don't you? Be careful. That's all I'm sayin'."

I had a faint idea what he was talking about, but Molly and my pleasure far outweighed the idea of having a child. I mean, we were still young. Couldn't happen to us. His mouth had turned into a tight line, his eyes downcast. He was serious.

He let his words sink in for a bit before he tossed another rock, then stared at me. "What about being arrested? A trial? What happened?"

For some reason, that story was harder to relay than Molly's. I told him about the assault and how close I'd come to total humiliation. His hands balled, fisted, relaxed, fisted again. I kept the words flowing without letting him interrupt because I knew if I stopped, I wouldn't get going again. This was the second time I'd told the story, and this time telling it now, brought tears to the back of my eyes and a knot to my stomach. My heart pounded while I felt Clyde on my back, Purdy tugging on my pants.

Tate's sturdy hand on my shoulder brought me back. I was safe. "And they got away scot-free?"

Nodding, I gulped down angst. "Spent a week in jail. Judge threw them out of town, but they'll be back. Might already be."

He balled his hand again. "If I ever get to town again, I'll beat 'em to a pulp. They won't pick on you ever again." He brought up his other hand. "Ever."

I couldn't remember a time Tate had been so angry. This time he was shaking. His cheeks flared red.

"So, you think having a gun will level things? Killing one of them will make it right?" Tate lowered his body to a boulder. He relaxed his hands, then tossed another rock.

"Don't wanna kill anybody. Don't plan to, anyway. Just need to protect myself." Before Tate could ask another question, I explained. "I don't have money. Nothing. First, The Three took all I had—Sheriff Wagner gave it to 'em—then all my wages for the next couple of months I gotta pay Da back for my attorney."

I stopped. "Da's been telling me it's for bail, but since I showed up for the trial, he got it back. Da just lets me think it's bail."

Tate nodded. "But you gotta pay for the attorney. Was he local?"

"San Antonio." I raised one shoulder. "One of the best, someone told me."

"Then it's money well spent." Tate smacked my back.

"Da doesn't know I know. But I also need a new hat, lost mine in the fight by the creek, and then a gun." I looked away to the creek. "Hell, Tate. By then, it'll be Christmas, and I'll be dead."

Tate bounded to his feet and wrapped me in a bear hug. As much as I appreciated the sentiment, I pushed back, out of his grip. His words in my ear rang loud. "Got yourself in a helluva predicament. Maybe you can come work out here for a while. Stay outta trouble." He pointed to his chest. "Worked for me."

"I sorta thought about that, Tate. But I don't run." I held up a hand. "Besides, Da needs me. We've got more business than we can keep up with."

"That's good news!" Tate looked toward the ranch house. "Glad to hear it." He grew serious, eyebrows dipping. "Look. I'm happy to give you the money. Gift from me. But...you gotta promise you'll use that gun only in self-defense. Don't you go lookin' for trouble. It'll find you quick enough."

First piece of good news in weeks! "I promise, I promise."

Tate turned me toward the ranch house. "Gotta be gettin' back. Promised I'd help with dishes."

"I'll help. I'm real good at washing."

"Got a certain gun in mind?" Tate and I talked guns, calibers, grips, cross-draw versus quick-draw, and all things gun-related, while we returned.

Instead of going straight to the dishes tub, we located Mr. Carmichael sitting with the preacher and another couple. I nodded to each and then waited for Tate.

"Mr. Carmichael. I need to speak to you, when you're not busy," Tate said.

"Be happy to right now, Tate." The ranch owner groaned to his feet. "Not as young as I used to be. Maybe it's Miranda's fine cooking." He patted his stomach. "Or both."

We followed Mr. Carmichael to where he stopped out of earshot of the crowd. "What's up?"

"Well, Mr. C, I'm needing my wages you've been holding for me." Tate turned to me. "He keeps them here at the house. I got no use for money, where I'm ridin' fence. We'll start fall roundup in a few weeks and I sure as hell don't need it 'til after that."

Mr. Carmichael eyeballed me. "Let me guess. He's loaning you some so you can court a real pretty gal. Am I right?"

"Something like that, sir." I wasn't about to give him the real reason. Let him think what he wanted. Money for her would be gran', as Ma would say. Maybe I'd have some left over, and I could take her to supper. Or buy her a present. I didn't know how much Tate had, but hopefully enough for a gun and Molly's supper.

We followed Mr. Carmichael into the house, its wooden beams running across a twenty-by-twenty front room, the size of the tent outside. "Make yourselves comfortable." He pointed to a leather sofa. "You want all of it, Tate?"

"Yes, sir. If you don't mind." Tate sunk into the sofa,

his hat in hand. I sat next to him, enjoying the comfort. The leather creaked a bit, reminding me of my saddle. He lowered his voice. "Should have about sixty dollars, Eagan. Two months' wages."

"I can't take all your money." I shook my head. "Only need about half that." On second thought, I could buy me a hat, too. Wouldn't have to wait. "Tell you what, Tate. I'll use what I need, only what I gotta have, and save the rest for next time I see you. How's that?"

"Can't argue with that. It's a deal." We shook hands as Mr. Carmichael walked in, cash in hand.

He handed the bills to Tate, who then counted out sixty dollars, all of it. He plopped them into my outstretched hand. "Here ya go. Spend it in good health."

If I was any less of a man, I'd have cried. My face muscles ached from the smile. "Thank you. I'll pay you back. Won't waste a penny of it."

CHAPTER SIXTEEN

MONDAY MORNING AND WE HAD THE USUAL start-of-the-week customers. I swept outside and inside, hauled more ice from Solano's, all the while casting a wary eye for The Three. They were nearby, I just knew it. No doubt. I hadn't told Da about the money from Tate. Would I ever? Or should I simply buy a gun, target practice with Jimmy and feel better about myself? Walk around, not afraid of those men. Or any man, for that matter. Or should I talk to him today? If he was willing, we could both go over at noon, and pick one out. On second thought, I'd go alone. This was my problem and probation wasn't ending for three more weeks.

I held the broom while Da talked to a customer. What kind of son would I be if I didn't confide in him first? Not a good son. But part of me didn't want to be *good*. I wanted to be my own man. Molly wanted a man who took chances, maybe even bullied people. That wasn't me, but I wanted her and I could change. Couldn't I?

And even if I didn't become a curly wolf, I could be a deputy sheriff. They needed to be brave and bold and rough and tough. I could do all those things. But damn, I needed a gun first. My entire life pivoted on that gun. I'd stop by the gunsmith's during my quarter-hour lunch. Enough time to see what he had. I wouldn't buy one today, but simply look.

Fortunately, we were busy and time raced by. First thing I knew, Da waved me out back to eat my sandwich and drink the milk Ma had insisted I bring, this morning. Milk was for children and I sure as hell wasn't a child, anymore. No siree. I was a man. I'd had a woman and everything. Someday, soon I hoped, we'd even get naked together. Did *children* do that? I thought not.

I left Da alone as I headed out the back door and made my way toward the gun dealer. With a fortune in my vest pocket, I could afford a really special weapon. Price would be no

object. The folded fortune burned against my ribs, as I walked through the alley. I'd have to be quick and probably have to come back tomorrow, maybe even the next day, to make sure I got the right one.

Two blocks up from our meat shop, I stepped onto the boardwalk, nodded to a man I recognized as a customer, and continued up the street, until I spotted the gun shop. A fluttering, empty feeling in my stomach and sweaty palms reminded me this was an occasion to be remembered. I sucked in air. This was it.

I stepped inside and stopped dead. There stood Purdy at the counter, talking to Mr. Krause. Both turned at the door opening. First thought was to back out and run. Instead, I closed the door behind me and nodded to the gunsmith.

"Be with you in a minute, Eagan." Krause nodded to a back room. He spoke to Purdy. "I'll get that firing pin. Be right back." He slid off the stool. "Eagan, take a look around."

Purdy leaned on the counter and looked at me. His homely face, the nose like a wedge of cheddar, rearranged itself into a sneer. "Well, well. Eagan Nolan. Out of jail, I see." He pulled in a drag on his cigarette and flicked the ashes toward me. "You come to buy your daddy a new gun? I mean since you threw his in the mud."

"Mind your own business, Purdy." Surprised I said that, I realized it felt good. Really good. Was I becoming unafraid? A second thought. I needed to be afraid of him and his friends. Together, they were stronger than me. "Thought the judge ordered you out of town."

"Nah. He said we're welcome any time."

I wanted to holler, "Liar, liar," but didn't.

Purdy took another suck on his cigarette, flicked it to the floor and squashed the butt like a bug. He pointed a finger at me. "We started a conversation. Needs finishin'. How 'bout now?"

Without thinking, I licked my lips. "That conversation's over. Best you leave town before the judge or Sheriff Wagner finds you."

Purdy chuckled, that low-throat rattle. "You owe me a new pair of boots. I'm thinkin' sixty dollars ought to buy me right fine ones."

"You boys doin' all right?" Krause called from the curtained room.

"Fine, just fine, sir," Purdy replied.

I lowered my voice. "You shot your own foot, Purdy. You pulled the trigger." Fury filled my lungs and my hands balled. I'd like to beat him senseless, right here. I wouldn't, though. Not in Mr. Krause's shop.

"On second thought," I said. "Any time you wanna finish the conversation, I'm ready." I wasn't sure who this new man was, but I liked standing up for myself. It was scary and exciting at the same time.

"We'll finish up, soon. Maybe not today, but soon."

Mr. Krause returned, a firing pin in hand. Purdy turned back from me and picked up the pin. He examined it. "Should do nicely."

"I see you're busy, Mr. Krause." I thumbed over my shoulder. "I gotta be gettin' back. Another day, sir."

He nodded. "Another day, Eagan."

What I wanted was to yank open the door, bolt into the safety of the street, rush back to Da where I knew I'd be safe. But I didn't do any of that. I inched open the door, stepped through, closed it firmly, and sauntered, looking over my shoulder the entire way.

* * *

DA PUT down his sandwich and frowned at me. "Ye feeling all right, boyo? Look at the state o' ye."

I knew I looked bad, like I'd spent days hoisting several in Sam's. Felt like it, too. I

closed the front door, glad to be inside. I'd prepared myself for a bullet or two in my back on the way over. I took my apron off the hook behind the door and tied it around my middle. Da stayed silent the entire time I was deciding whether to tell him or not. "I was right, Da. Ran into Purdy down the street—"

"Ye were on the street?"

I nodded. "Decided to take a short walk, after the sandwich. Saw him go into a shop."

"Did he see ye?"

Obviously, Da was concerned for me. I needed to be honest. "He did. Even spoke. Said the judge told him and the Clydes they could stay in town."

"*Ara!*" Shaking his head, Da greeted a woman stepping into the shop, the bell announcing her entrance.

Now that I'd relaxed a bit, my stomach reminded me I'd neglected it. I sneaked a few bites of my sandwich in the storeroom, chugged half the milk, then came out to help Da.

Exactly like this morning, the afternoon flew by. Customers came in thick and plenty. By closing time, I was tired. The calves of my legs complained. Da looked exhausted. He probably ached all over.

Da flipped the sign over with *Closed* facing out. I pulled down the shades over the front two windows. My favorite part of the day. He opened the cash register and counted while I swept, cleaned up melted ice spills, and placed the meat into the storage cases in back. With so many customers, I was surprised we had any meat left.

Da held up a stack of bills. "We did well today. I'm takin' this to the bank first thing in the morning." He folded the money and stuck it deep down an inside vest pocket that Ma had sewn specifically for that purpose. The coins he counted, replaced a few in the till drawer, and handed me the rest to put in my own pocket. I barely had room for all that silver jammed in with Tate's sixty dollars.

We stretched as we sauntered down Main. We'd be home in fifteen minutes or so and eating supper in another fifteen. My stomach gurgled at the thought of Ma's cooking.

Da stopped. "Did we lock the front door?" He halfway turned back.

"Don't we always?" I was sure he'd locked it, but then again...

He dug in a pocket and handed me the keys. "Would ye be a good lad and go check? I don't think anybody would come steal from us, but ye can never be too careful."

I agreed but also wanted to argue. Surely, he'd locked up like every night. Tonight, I wanted to go home and eat. Put up my feet. Go to bed early. Tiredness radiating from his eyes, Da had asked nicely. I was sure his feet hurt as much as mine, if not more. I tossed the keys in my hand. "Be right back, Da. Go on without me if you want. I'll catch up."

What I wanted to say was, *walk back with me. I'm afraid.* Instead, I threw my shoulders back and headed to the shop. It wasn't but five minutes to check, and even though the sun was setting, it was light enough to see. Da and me would be home a couple minutes late, but Ma would understand.

I twisted the doorknob. Locked tight. Should I check the back door, just in case? Why not, it'd only be an extra minute or so. It was locked as well. Tingles raced up and down my back. Was Purdy or the Clydes waiting? Probably. Maybe not. I surveyed the alley, right to left. No one but me back here.

I rushed as fast as I could out to Main and spotted Da waiting. Feeling the fool, I limped faster. We met, both relaxed. Two steps later and a gun barrel was shoved into my back, another into Da's.

"Stop. Hands up."

Purdy's voice. I'd know that gravely, smoke-infected voice anywhere. A quick glance at Da and it was Clyde Two who covered him. Clyde One had to be nearby.

Purdy reached around me, my back to him, and patted my vest. The coins jingled, muffled a bit by Tate's dollars. Moving around in front of me, Purdy kept his gun, fully cocked, against my belly. "Empty them pockets, boy. Hand it all to Clyde."

Clyde One stepped up, growling at me. "Want it all, Crip. Don't go holdin' out on me. He'll kill you dead." He cocked his head toward Purdy, then turned to Da. "Don't go playin' hero, old man. We'll kill you next."

This was one time I wished Sheriff Wagner would appear. Surely, he couldn't blame me for this. I didn't dare take my eyes off Purdy, but I hoped a deputy was close by. I hesitated. I carried Da's money and Tate's. I had no right to let it go.

"Get movin'!" Purdy backhanded me across the face with his gun hand. The extra weight hit my jaw and I spun, plowing into the dirt. I tasted blood from yet another split lip, while stars took up most of my view. I rolled over and sat, then was yanked up by one arm. "All your money, now!"

Clyde's hands dove into my vest pockets, the ones on the front first. He brought out nothing, as I knew he would. Jerking my hands up made searching the inside of my vest easier. Coins clattered as he pulled them out and shoved them into his own vest pockets. He handed some to Purdy, who jammed them in his pocket and then a fistful to Clyde Two.

"Ain't your money. We worked hard for it." Would my logic make him give it back and apologize? No, but I needed to say it.

Another backhanded wallop sent me reeling five feet. While I managed to stay upright, my face burned like Lucifer's fires.

"Leave him alone." Da moved in close to me and held up his clenched fists. "I'll take ye on."

Purdy snorted. "Old man like you?"

"Try me."

"Move again, we'll shoot 'im."

More stars danced in front of my eyes, and I must've

blinked a million times. Was that my da being brave? Tears pushed my eyes, but I squinted, hoping to keep them at bay.

"We said *all* your money." Clyde waved his gun at me. Now I had two guns trained at my chest. If I hadn't been so terrified, I would have kicked out or something. More importantly, why didn't I have a gun?

"That's all I got." I wanted to hold my hands out at my sides. I shook too hard. But apparently, Clyde had missed Tate's folded bills. There were only three and they folded down thin.

Purdy grabbed my hair and yanked me closer to Da. I couldn't breathe, think, react. I simply stood there, my hair in Purdy's fist, and gun jammed into my right temple. "Your turn, old man. Let's have your money."

"Don't have any. Put all I had in the bank this afternoon."

"Wanna keep your son alive?" Clyde One pointed his gun at me, too. He pulled the hammer back. The metallic click resonated up and down the street. "Empty them pockets."

Da's eyes pleaded with me to keep still. There was fear in them, but defiance, too. I'd heard he'd been a scrapper as a youngster in Ireland. Maybe that had never gone away.

He brought his hands down slowly. "Got nothin' worth anything." He pulled his vest open. "Told ye, *ye sleeven cur*...it's in the bank."

Clyde Two holstered his gun and patted Da's vest. His eyes widened when he felt the hidden folded bills. He plunged his hand into the pocket and Da brought up his clenched fist, hard and fast, clobbering Clyde's jaw with an uppercut. Clyde Two's head snapped back and he sank to his knees, then onto his face. Out.

I grabbed Purdy's gun and jerked it up. *Bang!*

Clyde One kicked the back of my knees, and as I went down, he used his gun to wallop my face. Again. I couldn't let him hurt Da, though. I rolled, grabbed Clyde's legs, and pulled him down. He thudded into the dirt.

Da and Purdy fought back and forth, Purdy's gun now lost to the street somewhere near Clyde's. Somehow, I managed to straddle Clyde One and pound his face. Undeterred, he pushed me off, sat on me, punching and pounding my face, until I knew I was unrecognizable. My lips had split in a couple of places, and my eyes had swollen almost shut. Blood ran down my face and into my mouth. I coughed.

Bang! I flinched but didn't understand that the shot was close by. Pounding in my head, throbbing headache walled out any other sound.

Bang! "Stop! Hold it, all of you!"

Clyde One released his grip on my shirt, but otherwise didn't move. I located Da standing down near my legs, Purdy in his grasp. Where was Clyde Two? And who had hollered "Stop"?

Boots and legs I didn't recognize stopped by my side, and suddenly, the weight lifted off my chest. A hand reached down, grasped my arm and I was yanked to my feet. All I could see was a badge on a shirt.

"Don't anybody move."

I turned my head as far left as possible and made out Sheriff Wagner's shape. Next to him stood Deputy O'Sullivan. Both with guns drawn.

"You…" Wagner pointed at Da. "Move back."

Open hands out at his sides, Da stepped away from a nose-bleeding Purdy, who glared back at him. Wagner pointed at Clyde Two, just coming awake. "You. Over here." He wagged his gun to his right, then wagged left. "Deputy, keep your gun trained on those two."

I moved two steps away from Clyde One, when the deputy grabbed my arm. "You're swayin' there, Eagan. Don't faint on me."

"I'm all right." I wasn't, but I didn't want to sound like I was hurt. My face and entire head throbbed, while blood now ran down my chin and onto my shirt. I shook all over, and despite being upright, still couldn't see much. My lunch sandwich threatened to come up. I was a mess, but how was Da? His cheek sported a glowing red mark, but otherwise, looked to be in good shape. Apparently, I'd taken the brunt of this fight.

Once the five of us were separated, Sheriff Wagner started with Da, asking questions about who did what. We took turns answering until the lawman needed clarification.

"So, let me get this straight." Wagner cocked his head. "Mr. Nolan, you and your son were walkin' home after a long day at work."

Da and I nodded in unison.

"And the three of you"—he waved his gun at Purdy and the Clydes—"were accosted by the Nolans. You said Mr. Nolan here blamed you three for assaulting his boy and making him spend time in jail."

They nodded, working to perfect a woe-begone look.

"That's not the truth, Sheriff." Da inched closer, his anger uncontained. "Did you listen to what I said? They took my money. Tate's coins from his vest. Have them show you. They got lots of coins that are ours."

Ignoring Da, Wagner stepped nose to nose with me. "Ain't you the one shot off Mr. Purdy's foot? Tried to drown this other fella in the stream?" He breathed out in anger. "Ain't you the one hauled into court? Ain't you on probation?"

I stared at Da, his fists balling. How did all this become my fault? Taking a chance, I pointed to Purdy. "He's got some of our coins like the other two do. We want 'em back. That's our money." Up until a few weeks ago, I'd have never been that bold. But these thugs had changed me. Them and Molly.

Purdy reached into a vest pocket and pulled out my coins. "These, Sheriff?" He hauled out the remainder, maybe ten. "These, I won at a poker game last night. Why, you can ask anybody at Sam's I was playin' with. These coins ain't the Nolans' here, they're from a couple saddle tramps what didn't take kindly to losin'."

"Fact is, Sheriff," Clyde Two spoke for the first time, "Purdy won so well, we helped him carry some of those coins." He pulled out a handful from his vest. "Those fellas sure as hell were mad."

"Sure were." Clyde One nodded. "I watched 'em ride out this mornin', still grumblin' about losin' all that money. Over in the hotel is where I saw 'em."

Da's face turned red. He shook a pointed finger first at Wagner, then Purdy. "He's got a mouth would make an arse jealous. You gonna believe them, Wagner? Coupla no-good *shite hawks,* who can't do anything but cause trouble? What kinda lawman are ye?" He looked at Deputy O'Sullivan. "Both of ye."

Following on Da's rant, I hollered at Wagner and then O'Sullivan. "That's *our* money. We work hard for that. They're lyin', Sheriff. They're lyin'."

Wagner stuck a finger on my swollen nose. "Mind your manners, boy." He turned to Deputy O'Sullivan, who'd been quiet this entire time. "Lock 'em up or let 'em go? It's gettin' to where there's no place in my jail for anybody else."

"Let 'em go? Let 'em *go*? Are ye thick?" Da lowered his voice to iron. "They attacked me boy and me. Stole our money. And you wanna *let 'em go*?"

O'Sullivan looked at me, my da, then the three men. "Don't see a need to lock up anybody, Sheriff. These three"—he pointed at them—"should be out of town by now. Judge ordered them out, remember? If we arrest them, they'll just be out, come sunrise."

Resetting his hat, Sheriff Wagner nodded. "Suppose you're right." He holstered his gun. "You three. If I see you around here tomorrow, I'll toss you back in jail. Understand?"

They nodded and grumbled.

Wagner turned to Da and me. "I don't believe any of you, but I'll let you go. Mr. Nolan, only thing saving you is you bein' a law-abiding businessman of Blanco Hill."

"What about me money?" Da held up his hands. "What they took? 'Tis mine, I'm tellin' ye. 'Tis *mine*."

"Have your name on them coins?" Wagner didn't wait for an answer. "Then how do I know for a fact it's yours?" A snicker jiggled his chest. "Just be glad I'm not tossin' you in jail."

Da growled, but otherwise stayed silent, his gaze burning holes through Wagner.

Wagner pointed a finger at me, again. "You. You're a rabble rouser, just like your horse-thieving brother. One more fight, I'll lock you up for good. You and Tate can share prison stories."

Well, hell. Fire and ice flushed over my body.

"You get me, Nolan?"

I nodded. Got it loud and clear.

CHAPTER SEVENTEEN

MA FUSSED OVER DA AND ME UNTIL I DIDN'T think there were any words left in the world. Both of us brushed off her fussing, in both English and Irish, but she was relentless. She daubed at the blood, swollen eyes, and bruised cheeks. Did I have any skin left? Whatever concoction she used brought tears to my eyes, its stringent smell making my nose run. Snot and blood cascaded down my chin and onto my shirt. Tears moistened my sore cheeks.

Da, first to be doctored by Ma, came into my room buttoning a clean shirt. "How ye feelin' there, boyo?" He peered at my right eye. "Gonna have quite the shiner, again, ye are. Ye shoulda seen him, Mairelle. Duking it out. Wild as a tiger. Our son's got *mór spine*." And he grinned.

Ma glared at both of us. "Only spine he's gonna need is to stay outta trouble." She daubed extra hard on my cheek. "Ye figure out how to be peaceful. Sure, look it, fightin' never solved any problems."

"But—" Da and I spoke together.

"There'll be no more fightin'. Either of ye." Ma slammed the cloth onto the table by my bed, fisted her hands onto her hips, and stink-eyed us. "*Ní arís!* Not again." She marched out of my room, mutterings following behind.

Da raised one shoulder at me. "Best get a clean shirt on, son. Even a tiger can't sit for supper like that."

* * *

To SAY I hurt all over was not an adequate statement. Ma had made her usual Monday ham and potatoes fare, which I could barely eat. My jaw wouldn't open wide enough for a fork, and I thought a tooth or two was loose. I ate small bits of potato, but the meat would have to wait. After supper, Da and I stood on the front porch, holding onto the railing. Ma had insisted she needed no help tonight, so she was busy clattering dishes in the kitchen. Normally, she hummed or sang sweet Irish ballads when cleaning. But not tonight. Pots and pans banged on the counter and into each other, and instead of lilts, mutterings took their place.

I stared into the warm night air, the frogs down by the creek harrumphing to each other. So many things I wanted to say. Needed to say. But nothing came out. Partly, my lips hurt, which had made eating a problem, and my jaw seemed to be out of whack, but mostly, I wasn't sure what to say. So there I stood, thinking, planning, wondering, but not relaxing.

Da glanced over his shoulder toward the kitchen. "I've been ponderin' on it." He lowered his voice to a conspiratorial whisper. "Maybe ye're right. May be time for ye to have a gun."

Had I heard correctly? I faced him, and he looked serious. "But you said—"

"I know what I said. And I was wrong." He pointed toward town. "Those fellas weren't foolin' around. I think if they hadn't taken our coins, they might've taken our lives. And we were lucky the sheriff came when he did."

I nodded.

"What say we take Wednesday afternoon off, close the shop, and go target practicing? I'll teach ye what I know. And we'll carry my gun 'til ye get one of yer own."

"But what about my being on probation? The judge?"

"Thought about that. Sure, look it. This is what they call extenuating circumstances. I won't have ye walk about town like a sittin' duck."

Smiling was out of the question, and my hands were bruised and swollen. I settled for a pat on Da's shoulder. "Thank you." Maybe now was the time to come clean about Tate's gift of sixty dollars. Maybe not.

"Ye're welcome." Da slid an arm around my shoulder and pulled me in. "Yer my son and I don't want nothin' happenin' to ye that, well, hasn't already."

I wanted to melt into his strong arms but gripped the rail instead. "Da, need to tell you something important. You always say, 'tell the truth, shame the devil.'" I waited for him to stiffen a bit and slide his arm off. I started softly, slowly. "Yesterday, Tate loaned me money. Enough to buy a hat and a gun. Today, when I was supposed to be having my lunch, instead I went over to the gunsmith. That's where I saw Purdy."

A long stretch of silence wormed its way along the porch and out into the darkness. Had I made a mistake? Should I have kept my secret? Should I have said he *gave* me money instead of *loaned*?

Da pushed off from the porch rail. "Figured as much." He patted my shoulder again, and I flinched. Even that hurt. "Yer brother's becoming a fine man."

He strode to the door and turned back. "Tomorrow, we'll go see Mr. Krause. Good night, son."

What had gotten into Da? Finally, he understood what I'd been saying all along. Maybe it took a couple of whacks for him to get it. I hated like the blazes for him to get hurt, but if that's what it took...well, so be it. But I was the one truly hurt. With all the aches and pains, could I even sleep tonight? I yawned. Probably.

* * *

VILLAINOUS RAYS of sun struck my face. Grunting, I turned onto my side and let the sun warm my back. My eyes flew open. Sun? On my face? I'd slept way too long. Why hadn't Da waked me? Pushing up, groaning, sitting in bed, every ounce of my body screamed and declared its pain. But I had to go to work and then buy my gun. What a glorious day! Now, if I could manage to get out of bed and stand, I'd be in fine feather.

It took a bit, but I succeeded to stay upright, wash my face, comb my hair, and dress myself. Sliding my feet into boots aggravated every sore muscle, every bump and lump, but finally, I had them on. No way could I bend over and pull the covers up to make my bed. For once, Ma would either do it for me, or leave it alone. I didn't care which.

I hobbled downstairs and followed my nose into the kitchen. Ma had made flapjacks and eggs for Da, according to remnants on the table. Standing in the front room and putting on his vest, he patted the money-filled pocket. "Going to the bank, soon's they open. Take what's left, anyway."

"Good idea." I followed him to the front door. "I'll be in right after breakfast, if that's all right."

"Take your time." Da opened the door. "Bet ye're a bit *banjaxed* from yesterday."

I nodded and wished he wasn't so right.

Ma made me fresh flapjacks and scrambled eggs. The tea was extra special this morning, sweetened with locally grown honey. That was a treat. She sat with me at the table.

"Son. I know ye've had a tough go the last few weeks. We didn't know what ye'd put up with. Wish you would've told us. But ye didn't." She placed a soft hand on my arm. "But fightin' isn't the answer. Look at ye. All banged up, bruised, and bloodied."

I put down my fork and looked into her concerned blue eyes. "What was I supposed to do, Ma? Let them take my money? Tate's money? Da's money? They got enough as it is."

"Let the law take care of it. The sheriff..."

I choked and shot a frown at her.

"I know how ye feel about him...he should do his duty. And there's always the deputy. He's said to be a good man."

I let "good man" settle around the room as I tried to eat. My jaw still didn't open wide like it usually did, but my teeth weren't as loose as last night. Maybe with just Ma and me talkin' open like we were, this was the time to discuss being a lawman. My future plans.

I played with my fork, part of a flapjack on the end. "Ma. I've been thinking. I wanna be a good man, but I'm not exactly sure what that is."

"That's easy, Eagan. 'Tis doin' the right thing, it 'tis. Takin' care of other people. Not fightin'."

"But Molly likes men who are curly wolves. Outlaws. Men who fight. Who are brave. I don't think I'm any of that."

"You're brave." Ma leaned away from me. "That Molly is a *caílin álainn*, she is. Quite pretty, sure, but she's trouble, that one. Ye stay with her an' she'll land ye in prison. Mark me words," and crossed herself.

I wasn't about to tell Ma what Molly and I had done. That's what a good man did. Kept the reputation of women to themselves. Tingles spread from my stomach downward. Suddenly, I wanted her bad. And naked.

"I'll think on it, Ma. But I've also been thinking about asking Deputy O'Sullivan if I could be his helper. Like a deputy to the deputy or something. Learn how to be a lawman. Think I'd like that."

Frowning, Ma's eyebrows knitted, her mouth turned down. "'Tis more dangerous than ye think. Fightin', shootin'. Is that what ye really want?"

One shoulder shrugged. The other hurt too much to move. "Not sure what I want, but I'm fairly sure I don't want to work in Da's meat shop the rest of my life." I added in a rush, "It's fine for now, but at some point, I want to be on my own."

"As well ye should." Ma stood, kissed the top of my head, the only part right now that didn't hurt. She picked up my empty plate and headed for the wash tub, tossing over her shoulder, "Ye're a good man, Eagan Carbry Nolan. A *fear maith*."

* * *

SHORTLY AFTER NOON, Da and I turned the *Open* sign around to *Closed* and headed for Mr. Krause

and his selection of guns. Something about the smell of the gun shop—the odor of black powder, oil on and in the weapons, the aroma of guns—brought a partial smile to my face. Smiling with a puffy, split lip was gammy, but here I was, ready to buy a gun. My very own gun. Despite my pain, I was in heaven. And Da was right beside me, asking questions, making suggestions.

Within an hour, I held my weapon of choice. A Colt 1861 Navy Revolver. Seven and a half-inch barrel. Thirty-six caliber. Used, but not abused. And it took paper cartridges which Krause sold here in this store. For the gun, he had asked fifteen dollars. Da said that price was a bit high, but Mr. Krause had simply shrugged, with a take-it or leave-it attitude.

I wanted to clutch my new baby to my chest. Stroke it. Caress it. Kiss it. But I'd wait until we were alone.

"Need a holster for that, Eagan?" Mr. Krause pointed to leather rigs hanging against another wall.

One caught my eye. Darker leather, a snake tooled end to end, and a holster that looked used but service-able. Hopefully, it would fit around my hips like I'd seen other men wear theirs. "How much for that one?" I pointed.

Krause took down the rig and handed it to me. "Sharp eye there, Eagan. It's a fine one. Leather, hand stitched. Try it on."

It fit perfectly. Enough room around my hips with a few inches left on the belt tail. I loved the way it creaked as I tightened the buckle. I slipped my Colt into the holster. Butter. It slid in and out like butter. Immediately, I was in love. "I'll take it, Mr. Krause." I hoped I had enough money, but surely it couldn't be more than the Colt.

Mr. Krause leaned back and examined my image. Did he see the gunfighter that I saw in my head? I certainly felt like one. Any moment now, I'd jump on my faithful steed and go racing off after bank-robbing outlaws. Far away from town, we'd meet in a canyon. I'd draw and fire, wounding but not killing the curly wolves. I'd drag them back into town, depositing them with the sheriff. Their pictures had been posted all around the territory and *I* was the one to bring them in. I'd receive a sizable reward for their capture. I raised my hand, waving to the grateful townspeople.

Da nudged my shoulder.

"Eagan? You heard me?" Mr. Krause snapped his fingers. "Said it'll be ten dollars. That's first-rate tooling there. That snake looks like it'll reach out and strike any second. Fact is, wouldn't mind having it for myself."

Joyous day! Could it get any better? Not only did I have enough to buy both the gun and the rig, but now I could also buy a hat! If I could jump for joy, or do an Irish jig like Ma did, I would. Instead, I simply beamed.

CHAPTER EIGHTEEN

THAT NIGHT, FOR SOME REASON, MA WASN'T AS happy with my purchase as I was. She sighed, patted my shoulder and mumbled something in Irish I didn't understand. Da chuckled at the mutterings but wouldn't tell. I spent the better part of two hours outside on the porch, getting to know my prized possession. I swear it spoke back to me.

Da and I took the next afternoon off, closing the store at lunchtime. We'd be gone the rest of the day, something we'd never done before, and I was giddy with excitement. Something new, different, and it involved my precious gun.

We stopped in at the house to saddle Horse, Kilkenny Canterer, Da had corrected me, and then headed over to the stable to rent another one. I'd ridden since before I could walk, and my confidence was palpable. Sure enough, the sorrel was easy to ride, responding to my light touch on the reins and gentle nudge in the flanks. I wasn't wearing spurs and certainly didn't need them with this horse. She was a fine one, indeed.

We trotted up a well-used road that, if memory served, led to the berg of Dripping Springs, known for a wide variety of successful ranches as well as loads of pretty girls. I'd heard there wasn't an ugly one in town. Jimmy, Zeke, and I had vowed to go there someday. But that was before Zeke got himself officially hitched to Matilda. Far as I knew, no date had been set, but he sure talked about her. A lot.

I chuckled. Probably like I did with Molly.

Up ahead, far away east of Blanco Hill, a stand of cottonwoods that must've been eighty feet tall lined one of the many streams in the hill country. Due to their compact and extensive leaf canopy, they shaded a good quarter mile of stream, in both directions. Beyond that lay a flat

meadow. Da surveyed the area, turning side to side, then completely around. "Good. No houses. Don't want people thinkin' we're shootin' at 'em."

I agreed. No need for angry ranchers or a sheriff investigating our practicing.

Da swung out of the saddle, tied the horse to a sturdy Texas bush and lifted his rig from around the saddle horn. I did like Da, tying my horse, to the same bush. Lightning, I think she was called. Both horses picked at the furry leaves.

Most importantly, I also lifted my new rig I'd carefully wrapped around the saddle horn and took my time buckling the leather belt around my waist. Like yesterday in the store, it fit so well I was sure it had been made only for me. It couldn't have fit any better. I slid the Colt into and out of the holster, until Da shot me a sideways scowl. The weight on my right hip was comfortable, so much so the gun felt like it was part of my body.

I untied the burlap bag filled with cans I'd gathered at

home and the shop. Must have twenty or so. Remembering from when Jimmy and I went shooting, I lined up five of them on a fat log that seemed made for target practicing.

Da and I went over the finer points of shooting, something Jimmy hadn't done with me. A couple instructions of Da's were word for word like Jimmy's. But still, I soaked it all in. If I was going to be a curly wolf—or a lawman—or maybe both, I'd need to know all this.

We plinked and plunked all afternoon, moving when the sun made us squint. I hit twice as many cans as before, and my confidence soared.

"Where'd you learn to shoot like that, Da?" We squatted on our haunches under the tree canopy and watched the stream water crash into boulders, then slide around on either side.

He gave me a half-grin while his eyes narrowed. For the first time, I noticed little lines dart from the edges of his eyes. Was that age?

"Remember I told ye I'd had a life before ye? Well, my da ran a butter-making business. I remember our mule goin' round and round, churning that golden cream. I helped as much as I could as a wee lad and then took over later when he died."

I leaned back. "You made butter? For a livin'?"

"*Rine mé*. That I did. Made a good livin', too." Da grew quiet, his breathing shallow.

I waited for him to continue, but when he didn't, I pressed further. "What happened? Why'd you come to America?" I held up a hand. "Don't get me wrong. Glad you did, but why?"

He half turned to me. "First off, the British government decided us small butter producers didn't have any quality control. Second, the Sassenach landowners wanted the quid for themselves. They'd formed their own company, and when I didn't sell to them and at a loss, they confiscated me operation and run me off." He shook his head. "Then the potato crop failed and your ma and me didn't eat regular. I couldn't let my wife and new wee one starve. So off we went to Amerikay." He patted my knee. "Haven't looked back since."

Surprised, I had more questions. "So, is that where you learned to shoot?"

"Not there. Not in Ireland. We weren't allowed guns. Nobody but English constables had them."

"But—"

"When we stepped off the boat in New Orleans," Da's eyes hardened. "I wasn't havin' English boots to my neck. I'd be a free man...one with a gun." He patted my still-sore knee. "First thing I did was buy one. Traded my hat and a bit of coin."

I had nothing to say. I'd never heard any of that before and it would take a while to settle in. Did Tate and Joe know?

Birds cawed as they settled into the branches overhead. Water gurgled around large rocks, its tune whispering to the world. I listened for fish to jump but realized they do that only in lakes or much larger streams. This was more of a creek than stream, and more than likely lacking anything larger than minnows. But the trees certainly appreciated the water. They were huge.

Da and I eased to our feet quietly, each lost in our own thoughts. I had no more bullets, Da had two left but wanted to save them. Each of the cans sported at least one hole, which made my chest bump out a bit. Many of those were my holes. The cans had danced and flown backward several times after I pulled the trigger. With more practice, I could get good.

In so many ways, I hated for this day to end, but I couldn't wait to tell Jimmy and Zeke. Could life get better?

We replaced the cans into the sack, took a long drink of creek water, swung up into our

creaky saddles and headed for home as the sun perched on the western horizon. We'd been out here much longer than I thought we would. More than likely, it would be dark by the time we got to town. I still had to return Lightning.

Yesterday, Da and I had agreed that I wouldn't show off my Colt. Wouldn't wear the rig around town. I still had a couple more weeks of probation, and we saw no need to openly defy the judge's order even though I thought he wasn't in town. So, I promised to keep it under wraps until I met the lawyer and judge in a couple of weeks to be officially freed. I could hardly wait.

Enough yellow kerosene light flooding from windows and the two saloons allowed us to easily navigate down Main. Three townsmen on the street waved to Da, who waved back. He was a popular fellow and I hoped someday to be like him.

While handing over the reins to the stable worker, I thought again about being like Da. He was well-liked, fair, honest and a good man. But Molly wanted something else. And I still wanted her. Part of me was well satisfied. Happy out, as Da would say. I had a gun, a rig, and a girl. Did that make me a man? The other part was still trying to navigate between man and

youth.

I'd need another meeting with Tate. He seemed to

have figured things out and it hadn't been easy. I'm sure he had advice to help me.

From the stable, Da and I walked our horse home, ready for a hot meal and then put our feet up on the front porch railing. Da would more than likely go to sleep out there and Ma would come out and rouse him. Tonight, I wouldn't be far behind.

Spotting our house, all the windows ablaze with welcoming light, I took Horse's reins. "Go on in and wash up, Da. I'll take care in the barn and be right in."

I walked into the stable and stopped short. Another horse took up half the space. Whose horse was that? I checked the brand, one I didn't recognize. A long lost relative? A county marshal coming to check up on me? I had no answers, only questions.

I did everything I needed to do for the horse—unsaddled her, brushed her quickly, filled the oat bucket, patted her rump, and said good night. I said it to the other horse, too. Why? Kindness, I guessed.

Curiosity coursing through my body, I limped as fast as I could to the back door, which was closer than the front, and slipped into the kitchen. Spotting no one, just a pot of bubbling stew on the stove, I peeked around the corner into the dining room. Empty. But voices sailed from the front room. One voice I recognized. Not Da's. Definitely not Ma's.

I stepped into the room to find brother Joe sitting on the couch, coffee cup in hand. He looked up at me, jabbed me with a brotherly stare, plopped his cup on the small table, then jumped to his feet and gave me a bear hug. I looked over his shoulder at Da, his eyes wide with an even wider grin, then Ma's smile as well, her eyes dancing with love and excitement.

Wriggling out of his embrace, I stood back, each of us

the same height. "Holy jumpin' frog legs, Joe! Good to see ya."

"Been here 'bout an hour he has." Ma stood. "Surprised all of us, he did." She ruffled his hair, although she had to reach up to do so. "Though the rover's not told us why. Supper's 'bout ready."

Da was still standing near the front door. "Surprised is a word, son. *Iontas.* Why didn't ye write? Tell us ye were comin'?" He sat in a chair across from the couch. "Your brother and I went target shootin' today. Ye coulda come along."

"If I'd been here, I would have." Joe retook his seat on the couch. "I was busy ridin' in from Fredericksburg."

Dying, simply dying of curiosity, I blurted out, "So why're you here? Are you staying?"

Joe's gaze swept the floor, the inside of his coffee cup, Da's face and then mine. "It's an after-supper discussion, I'm afraid. Not pleasant and I don't want to destroy all of Ma's hard efforts."

That certainly put a damper on all the good feelings. Something about his shoulders slumping, his sad words, his downcast mouth told me the news wasn't good. But all agreed we'd have to wait. Every day Ma worked hard, slaving away at providing us good suppers, and nothing should take away from the effort, unless it was more good news. And that didn't seem to be the case this time.

I did notice his fiancee, Frieda Aertker, was missing. For all I knew, they could've been married by now. A few months ago, he rode off to Denver with her family and I think he sent one letter saying he'd found a job up there as a telegrapher, like his old job here, and things were

swell. Short. To the point. *So* very Joe. That's all we'd heard until now.

Realizing Joe wouldn't say more, Da told him all about today's practice shooting,

mentioning how many holes I'd put in cans, the perfect weather, and even the gurgling water in the stream. I couldn't tell if he was nervous or simply wanting to share an amazing day. I filled in what he left out, and at times, Joe asked questions. It turned into a lively discussion even when Ma called us to the table.

Her chicken stew held carrots, potatoes, lots of chunky chicken, and she'd made bread rolls with honey butter to go with it. Once in a while, she made tortillas, which was a Texas staple in some households, but she preferred bread—rolls and such. Either was fine with me. There truly wasn't anything she made I didn't like.

We dug in like we hadn't eaten in weeks. Ma's cheeks reddened with all the compliments.

True to our word, we didn't ask Joe personal questions. But still, I could hardly wait. And I was hoping he'd say he was moving back. Having all three of us brothers close by, again, would be fun.

Supper over, we all pitched in helping with dishes. That chore was done and over in record time. Ma folded the dish towel and Da pointed toward the front door. "What say we take the night air?"

We traipsed out, each taking our usual places. Mine was perched on the porch railing. Although it was dark toward the trees and stream, our porch was golden yellow with two lanterns sharing light through the windows. Definitely enough to see each other with, but not too much.

Joe cleared his throat, and tingles raced through my stomach.

Leaning back against the rail, looking at Ma and Da,

Joe put his head down, mumbled something, then raised it. "I didn't write because I couldn't put it into words."

"Son, ye—" Da started but Joe raised a hand.

"Frieda and I got married."

An *ooh* and *aah* raced around the porch.

"Her parents insisted when they found out...well... well...she was in the family way. We hadn't been in Denver very long, but we found a justice of the peace and got married."

My folks nodded but kept quiet. A myriad of questions crowded their way to my mouth, but I held them back. Joe would explain. In time.

He ran a hand across his mustache, looked down again, cleared his throat again, and his eyes looked like they were holding back tears. His words were thick. "The baby came early. Way too early. It was a girl." Joe swiped at his eyes. "They died. Both of 'em. In my arms."

Ma's hands flew to her mouth. *"Ó Mo Dhia!"* She jumped out of her seat and threw her arms around Joe. "I'm so sorry, son. So very sorry."

I had no idea what to say or do. I'd never known anybody in his situation and barely knew anybody who'd lost a spouse. And a baby? At the same time? That had to have been hard. No wonder he wanted to save this news for after supper.

Da squeezed Joe's shoulder. The three hugged each other until Joe pulled away. "A few days later, her parents told me to leave. Said I was Irish and Catholic and wasn't welcome in their German family, especially after what I'd done to Frieda." He raised his swollen eyes to Ma. "I didn't kill her. I didn't. I would never—"

"Of course ye didn't, son. They were grievin', too. What they said was just their sadness speakin." Ma hugged him again.

"That's right." Da moved back. "It wasn't yer fault."

Joe nodded. "I know, but it feels like I did. Shoulda done something. Anything."

Ma took both of his upper arms in her tight grasp. "Look at me, Seamus Joseph Nolan. Look at me." She waited. "'Tis a sad thing it is, but women die in childbirth. All the time. Many women. 'Tis not fair, nor right, but that's the world. God's will. Not for us to understand. Grieve for a while, and then ye've got to get on."

Finally, I jumped in. "Stay here as long as you like. Your bed's still where you left it. I'll even take some of my stuff off." With that, I received half a smile.

* * *

JOE SHOWED up at the shop an hour after Da and I had turned the sign around. I handed him the broom and he took up the chore like he was born to do it. Before customers came in, we shared bits and pieces of the past few months. I told him about the three bullies who'd made my life miserable, about Molly, who'd made my life fantastic, yet confusing, and more about my gun, making him promise not to tell anybody.

"I'd like to meet this Molly girl." Joe leaned the broom against the back wall. "If she's got you flustered like you are, she must be something."

I continued to talk about her until customers came in, and I had to get busy. Joe hung around a bit longer, greeted some of the people he knew, then by lunch time, decided to leave. "I'm going over to the telegraph office, see if I can get my old job back." He opened the door. "See you at home."

Da and I wished him well. While I waited on customers, I thought about him working here at the store. There were days we could use an extra pair of hands. But not every day. When I got a chance, I'd talk to Da about him working part-time. Another thought hit me. Maybe I could have a full day off, maybe a Tuesday, which would give me a chance to properly court Molly.

The afternoon was busy, especially since we'd been closed yesterday. We sold more roasts and chicken than usual, it seemed. As much as I enjoyed talking to our customers, my mind was busy thinking about Joe and my gun. Images of Molly, naked Molly, crowded in and I found myself shaking my head a time or two. So much going on!

Da closed the door after Mrs. Winters left, wrapped roast in hand. He turned the sign around and sighed. "What a day!" He leaned back against the door. "Coulda used Joe today. Think he could work here part-time?"

"At least a day or two a week." I lugged the last roast out of the glass counter to put in the icebox in back. "Maybe I could give him one of my days. I wouldn't mind."

Pulling down the shade of the front window, Da turned. "Ye'd be giving up a dollar, ye know. But maybe he'd agree."

Banging on the door startled us both. Before either could reach it, the door opened and in stepped a fella I recognized but didn't know his name. His round face was flushed, brown hair sticking out all around from under his bowler hat, his eyes wide. He pointed up the street. "Mr. Nolan. Better come quick."

"What's wrong?" Da rushed to him.

"Your son, Joe." The man panted like he'd run across country. "Down at Sam's. Tearin' up the place. Somebody's gonna get hurt."

"Joe? At Sam's?"

The man stepped outside. "Deputy's there now, trying to calm Joe. Ain't workin'. Said to come get you. Quick."

Da and I slammed the door as we rushed outside. I'd never seen Da run as fast as he did then. I was left behind since I didn't run well, but I'd get there soon enough.

At Sam's, I froze just inside the saloon's batwing doors. I expected chaos with men shootin' off their guns, women screaming, people running around, beer mugs being tossed against walls. But, when my eyes fully adjusted to the dim light, there was Deputy O'Sullivan, hand outstretched near the bar. Saloon patrons stood across the room.

Standing on top of the bar, was my brother, broken whiskey bottle in his hand. He was glaring at the deputy and then anybody else who moved. "Back off!" he hollered to the entire room. "I'll slice you seven ways to Sunday."

Da moved in next to O'Sullivan and I stood slightly behind both of them. "What happened?" Da spoke out of the side of his mouth, keeping his gaze on Joe.

"Seems he'd had only a couple of beers, maybe whiskey, when an upstairs woman tried to sit on his lap. He pushed her off, rather roughly. When someone objected to him doing that, he did this." O'Sullivan turned to Da and then looked behind at me. "Know what caused him to act like this?"

Da nodded but didn't explain. "I'll get him down. Just keep everyone away."

O'Sullivan lowered his voice. "Better hurry. Wagner might show up any minute and then Joe's goin' to jail. Or worse."

Threading his way through the crowd, Da stopped

near the bar and looked up at Joe, still clutching the whiskey bottle, its jagged edges glinting in the lantern's light. Da put out a hand. "Son? How 'bout ye put down that bottle and climb down from there? Nobody meant to hurt ye."

"Da?" Joe narrowed his eyes and ran the back of his hand which held the bottle, across his forehead. "She's gone, Da. Ain't nobody like her. Never will be." He glared toward the stairs leading to the women's rooms. "Especially them."

"I know, son. I know. But come on down and we'll figure this out."

He swiped at his forehead again. "Ain't nothin' to figure. She's gone." Like lightning, Joe swung the broken bottle to his neck, pressed against his skin. "Maybe I should be gone too."

"Son, don't do it. Son, please. Put that down." Da moved closer. He stood a foot in front of the wooden bar. "That's not the answer."

"What *is* the answer, Da? I don't wanna live anymore." His hands shook which made the glass edges scratch his neck. "Least this way, I'll see her again."

I didn't think this was going anywhere. "Can I try, Da?"

Da nodded, as did O'Sullivan.

I edged closer to Joe, bumping into a man who moved back. "Joe?" I waited for him to look down at me. "You haven't truly lost her. She'll always be in your heart." I patted my chest. "Your memories. She'll always be with you."

"What d'you know?" Joe closed his eyes.

"I know she loved you. And she'll wait for you. Years from now when it's truly your time. Which isn't now.

She'd want you to be happy." I took a breath. "You know deep in your heart that's what she'd want."

Joe cocked his head at me, lowered the bottle. I reached up, and he allowed me to grip it. Without getting cut, I managed to take the shard and hand it to a man nearby. "Come down and we'll go outside and talk to Frieda. All right?"

He crumbled onto the top of the bar. Tears streamed down his face. Shaking, sobbing, he let me help him to the floor. Da took one arm, me the other and we led him through the still-hushed crowd. O'Sullivan followed behind.

The four of us stopped on the boardwalk. Joe bent over, his tears splatting on the wooden planks. He vomited again and again.

Deputy O'Sullivan looked away and then asked, "So, what's the story? This isn't like him. I've known Joe for a few years and—"

"His wife and baby died couple weeks back." Da patted Joe's back. "Got home last night."

"Frieda?" The deputy wagged his head and ran a hand across his mouth. "The Aertker girl? Frieda? Sorry to hear that. Well, hell." He gazed down Main. "Best you take him home right now. Don't need the sheriff stickin' his nose in this."

"Thanks, Tommy." Da nudged Joe, who stood upright. "Tell Sam I'll pay for any damages." He shoulderbumped Joe. "Let's go home, son."

* * *

WITH THE SUN barely peeking over the horizon, I dressed as quietly as I could, sometimes forgetting Joe was back now. When I dropped my razor against the ceramic dish, I was sure he'd startle, sit up, and scowl. But, no, he slept right on through.

Da and I sat at the breakfast table, not saying much. Dark circles under his eyes told me he had been up most of the night. He sipped at his coffee, which he usually slurped with gusto. Based on remnants on his plate, he'd picked at the eggs and bacon Ma had set in front of him. I cleaned my plate and felt a bit embarrassed that I was hungry and Da wasn't. Ma was quieter than usual, too. Instead of flitting around the kitchen humming, she solemnly arranged dishes and pans in the kitchen, then brought out a cup of coffee and joined us at the table.

We spent a good five minutes in silence, until Ma broke it. "I'll ask him to chop kindling today and a few other chores around here. He needs to take care of the horses."

Da nodded. "Tomorrow being Saturday, I could sure use him at the shop." He pointed a fork at me. "Eagan and I will have our hands full then and we could use the help."

"I'll tell him when he comes down." Ma sipped her coffee. "I won't let him sleep much longer. He needs to get on with life."

That was my mother. Practical. Hard at times, but then again, she had to be. Through her, Joe would be fine—eventually.

Da and I waved goodbye, like we did every day, and walked up the five blocks to the store. Something about this routine made me feel safe. Comfortable. I tightly gripped the bag of sandwiches Ma had made. Probably ham sandwiches today.

To our surprise, the store's front door was unlocked. Da and I looked at each other, he probably thinking we'd been robbed. I figured the Clydes and Purdy were in there waiting for me. We did a quick survey and nothing was stolen, nothing upturned, nothing missing. No one was hiding in the storeroom.

Da chuckled at the cash register, still sporting bills and coins. "Guess we forgot to lock up last night. In a bit of a hurry, we were. Played the *eejit*," he said and grimaced.

Relief unclenched my stomach. I remembered slamming the door last night, but not taking the time to lock up. Still, I wondered if anybody had come in, looked around and then left empty-handed. That thought gave me chills, like maybe they were still here. Just in case, I moved boxes and peered behind an ice chest in the back room. Nothing out of order.

The day was busy, like most Fridays, and in some way, I was glad to be busy. Took my mind off Joe and his problems but left me time to think about my own. I hadn't seen Molly in a while, but Sunday was coming in two days, and I could hardly wait. Would I get invited to dinner again? And would we be able to *inspect* her cattle like last time? Would this Sunday be Naked Molly Day? Parts of me tingled thinking about it, envisioning her without clothes, me without clothes, but mainly her. The feel of her skin all over mine made me lick my lips. I could kiss her anywhere. I—

"Need some help out here, son." Da's voice popped my daydream. Dropping back into the storeroom, I blinked into reality and rushed to join him in the crowded shop.

It was near time to turn that *Open* sign around, when Joe stepped in. He tipped his hat to the Widow Jenkins, choosing two pork chops for tonight's dinner. He waited for her to leave and I turned the sign. Both Da and I sighed as he pulled down the shade.

"What a day!" Da swiped a hand across his forehead, leaving a light trail of grease. "Glad we're busy, but I'm *knackered* with all the customers."

"Ma says you need me to come help out. Looks like she's right." Joe put his hands on his hips. "Needs sweeping. I'll do that now."

Should I ask him about last night? He looked a bit tired, but not overly so. A lot better than Da. Scrapes and cuts on his neck were the only evidence of Joe's antics at Sam's. And the marks weren't too bad. I'd save questions for later tonight, either on the porch or in the quiet of our bedroom. I remembered Tate and Joe sharing so many secrets that I was sure most of them were made up. As the youngest of three, I didn't have much to contribute. Nothing in my life, until recently, was interesting, much less worth being a secret to share.

Joe swept, I carted meat to the storeroom to the icebox and Da counted money. He stuffed the bills into the secret pocket in his vest, and within fifteen minutes, the three of us locked the door and walked home to a welcomed supper.

* * *

SATURDAY WAS THE USUAL, extra busy day of the week. Joe being there took the burden off Da so that he had a bit more time to spend chatting with his friends. Mid-afternoon, I was standing behind the roast counter, when in waltzed Molly, a younger brother in tow. My heart skipped a beat until I could barely breathe.

I came around the counter, and it took everything I had not to grab her and hug her with all my might. I smiled at her and nodded to the youngster, his name forgotten or unknown. I didn't really care.

"A pleasant surprise, Molly." My smile stretched my cheeks and warmth radiated through them. I leaned in and lowered my voice. "Missed you."

She nodded, looked around, then mouthed, "Me, too." Her smile was infectious.

Da spotted us, and from across the room, said, "'Allo, Miss Molly. Good to see ye. How're yer folks?"

"Fine, Mr. Nolan. Just fine. Ma sent me and Abe here to buy pork chops for tonight." She glanced at me. "And maybe a roast, if Eagan can join us for dinner after church tomorrow."

Certainly, my heart stopped. Another invitation to dinner? Could this be heaven?

"It's fine with me." Da smiled. "I'm sure it's fine with him too."

"Who's this, little brother?" Joe stood next to me, stuck out a hand. "Joe Nolan, Eagan's older and *wiser* brother. Born in New Orleans but lucky enough to live in Texas. I'm—"

"This is Molly O'Malley. And she's taken." I swatted at Joe's hand, but Molly took it anyway, both chuckling.

"Eagan's mentioned you." Molly glanced at me and then back at my brother. "You're taller than I pictured."

Joe stood straighter and threw his shoulders back, chest out. "Tallest of us three." He leaned in closer. "And the best looking."

That Joe was friendly to Molly, who was a girl, surprised me after last night's shenanigans. I wondered if the beer and whiskey had made him react like he did. Or had he simply been exhausted from the long ride? Whatever the cause, I sure as hell didn't want to see it again. We hadn't talked about this, but I was sure Da and I would keep a sharp eye on Joe for the next couple of months. Until…I wasn't sure when, but two things I did know: I didn't want him in jail, and I didn't want him killing himself.

I stood back a bit while Joe and Molly chatted, their back-and-forth banter light and comical. They seemed at ease with each other, which made me smile. Plus, simply being near Molly brought warmth to my entire body, along with tingles. I couldn't wait until tomorrow and naked—er, dinner.

"Can we go now?" Molly's brother, forgotten until now, tugged on her skirt. "I wanna go play."

Molly, desperate to ignore the pulling and whining, finally gave in. "In a minute. I need to buy some things."

"Here," Joe and I said in unison and pointed to the chops counter.

If Molly was going to stay longer, I'd have to find something to placate the whining child. What did I have? A meat cleaver? I chuckled. No problem there. The store didn't carry anything for kids. String?

Molly and Joe's laughter angered me. I'd have to make it clear that Molly was *my* gal and to keep his paws off.

Again, as I watched her leave the shop, wrapped roast and chops in hand, I wondered about my brother. For a man who'd just lost a wife and baby, so broken up and desperate the night before, how could he flirt with Molly? I had to admit they made a good-looking couple, but Molly and I were handsome together, too. More so than Joe.

As the three of us walked home that evening, I turned over in my head who I could talk to about Joe and his encounter with Molly. Da didn't see most of their conversation, as he was busy with other customers. How about Ma? She was a girl, after all. Maybe she'd have an idea what happened. Settled. I'd talk to Ma.

After supper, I volunteered to help Ma clean up. I'd clear the table and dry dishes while Da and Joe took their accustomed places on the front porch. While we worked, I confided in Ma about Joe and Molly. She nodded, smiled, frowned, and asked questions. I answered as best I could, but for the most part, was clueless.

"Joe's tryin' to put away the faeries, son." Ma handed me a soapy plate. "Your brother's got too many emotions, all scrambled together, right now. Don't read anything into his playin' with Molly."

"Sure looked real to me."

She patted my arm with a wet hand. "He's sort of practicin' with women again. Talking to girls. Just like ye did. Remember?"

I did remember. And it wasn't that long ago. Awkward, shy, nothing of substance to say. Heart-pounding fear, nervousness. Oh yeah, I remembered. And cringed.

CHAPTER NINETEEN

I SHAVED EXTRA CLOSE, MADE SURE MY CLOTHES were clean and pressed, even polished my boots. This morning, with the sun pouring through the bedroom window, I looked in my shaving mirror and could see every bump, bruise, and blemish on my face. Would Molly mind? Would she get naked despite the light green fading bruise under my left eye? Or my split lip with a hint of a remnant scab? Would she kiss me?

Joe stuck his head in the door and sniffed. "You're kinda overdoin' the smell-good stuff little brother. Don't want to drown yourself in it."

What did he know? Molly liked it strong. Or so I assumed. I stood back, re-tucked my shirt, and presented myself to Joe. "What d'ya think?"

Head cocked to one side, he gave a cursory hair-to-boots survey. "A bit overdressed for church. Priest might throw you out." He ducked as I tossed the hairbrush. "Breakfast's ready."

I rushed through breakfast, helped Ma with dishes again, ran a wet towel over my teeth, and stood on the porch, waiting. And waiting. Would it ever be time to walk up to church? About the time I was ready to leave without them, the rest of the family finally met me on the porch. They kidded me the entire trek about my eagerness. No one had the slightest hint that within a few hours, Molly and I would be naked. Somewhere. I hadn't worked out that part yet, hoping Molly knew a secluded area of the ranch. But I was sure fate would intervene, and we could get naked, unobserved. Just us two.

The priest took his sweet time going through the homily, singing, lecturing, and having us kneel, stand, kneel, stand, and sing some more. The hour was pure torture. Several times, I looked at Joe, then Ma and Da and they seemed contented to listen to what the priest said. Da even nodded a time or two. If the service wasn't over soon, I'd have to get up and leave. Or feign passing out. Something to get out of here and go to Molly's. Anything.

To save my sanity and pass the time, I concentrated on what Molly would look like naked. I hadn't truly seen much of her body, touched it more than seen. Familiar tingles worked their way around my body.

My carnal thoughts were interrupted when the congregation stood, everyone speaking in soft tones, but I caught, "see you next Sunday" and "wasn't that a grand sermon" and other familiar phrases. Must be over.

Joe nudged my shoulder. "Let's go."

But I couldn't stand up, just yet, without it being quite obvious exactly what I'd been thinking about. I was aware of holding up traffic but I didn't care. I kneeled for a good two, three minutes, as if in solemn prayer, mumbling and muttering, as if piety had suddenly hit me hard.

Finally! Time to get on with my life. I stood, shook a pant leg, worked my way through the parishioners still milling inside the church and excused myself while I flew down the steps and waited outside. I nodded to people coming out and exchanged a basic, "Howdy."

And then red-haired Molly, followed by at least twenty shorter redheads, with her folks behind, traipsed down the steps. We moved back so other people could get by. Molly stood next to me. I could hardly breathe.

Her ma gave me a quick smile. "Glad you can come to dinner again, Eagan. I know Molly's been looking forward to it."

"Thank you for inviting me, ma'am." Thankful my manners had kicked in, I added, "I had such a pleasant time before, I'm looking forward to being with your family again." I almost said, *being with Molly again*, but that would bring the wrath of her da down on my head. I was glad my mouth hadn't betrayed me.

My folks, Joe too, stood with Molly's family and chatted. Could we just go? Why did everyone have to stand around talking? I had courting to do. Serious, naked courting.

Molly's da caught my eye. "You ready? I'll bring you home this evening."

No way could I sit next to Da O'Malley having Molly's scent all over me. I hadn't truly thought about getting there and back until now. My brain kicked in. "I'll ride my horse over. That way, I won't bother you with the return trip." I nodded at Joe. "He's got a horse, so if Da needs one, he can use his."

And then Joe, not being helpful at all, piped in. "Good idea, brother. Let me ride with you. My horse needs a good stretch." He turned his back on everyone and spoke softly to me. "Don't worry. I won't stay. Just need to get out for a bit."

I nodded, raising my hand to shield my eyes. Should've bought a hat along with a gun. "Mr. O'Malley, I'll be out there soon as I saddle my horse." I turned to Molly. "See you in a flash."

She gave me a sensual wink. My toes curled.

* * *

JOE and I rode at a gallop, canter, trot until entering the ranch gate, then we walked. I was glad I'd remembered the route because, truthfully, I hadn't paid much attention last time. Three of Molly's siblings stood on the porch waving.

"Hi, Uncle Eagan."

"*Uncle* Eagan?" Joe chuckled as he swung out of the saddle. I was already tying my reins to the hitch rail.

"Howdy!" No way could I name any of them.

Joe stepped next to me and ruffled a redhead. "I'm Joe. What's your name?"

The little bugger rattled off something that I tuned out. Molly had stepped onto the porch, and I focused on her. Out of the corner of my ear, I heard one of the children say, "Joe, you wanna see our chickens?"

I started to wave them off but decided to let Joe handle the poultry. I stepped onto the porch, and glanced behind me at poor Joe, engulfed by red-haired chickens, more coming by the second, all clucking, pecking, and trying to lay eggs.

I stepped inside the house with Molly in the lead, where I was met with roast aromas. Not only roast but carrots and potatoes. Bread! Someone had recently baked bread. The O'Malleys sure knew how to eat.

Molly pointed to the kitchen where I followed her, helping this time to set the heavy roast on the table. The carrots and potatoes followed. Molly hollered for everyone to wash up and come eat.

Her ma turned to me, wiping her hands on her apron. "Would Joe like to stay for dinner, too? We have plenty."

Well, hell, not Joe. He said he wouldn't stay. "I'm not sure, ma'am. He probably has something to do this afternoon."

"I'll ask him." Molly disappeared into the front room.

Within moments, a rush of chickens, along with Joe, carried in on the tide, were all seated at the table. I glared at him, but he simply shrugged. Besides the food, the best part was sitting next to Molly. Joe sat across the table, two of the younger children on either side. I briefly wondered what he thought about that since his own child had died. Maybe, at some point, he'd tell me. But right now, I was angry at him for staying. I'd be a caring brother later.

Molly's da asked a couple of general questions of Joe, to which he responded carefully.

He talked about living in Denver, working as a telegrapher, and that was all he mentioned. No one asked more specific questions.

Dinner at last was over and I couldn't truly recall the taste. Molly and I offered to help with clean up, but her ma, instead, enlisted the help of the next two oldest children. Joe thanked the O'Malleys for a fine meal and made his way out the door, followed by a half dozen clucking chickens.

I waved halfheartedly at him and enjoyed seeing his horse's rump trot out the gate. Turning to Molly, I smiled, my cheeks stretching. "Wanna go inspect your cattle again? Got any new ones?" That was for anyone possibly overhearing the question. Meaning, her da.

"Let me tell them we're going down to the herd, and I'll be right back." She raised up on tiptoes, her lips grazing my cheek.

She returned to the porch and slid her hand into mine. "I need to help Ma mend Abe's pants, but not for an hour." Molly whispered, "Plenty of time."

Whoo hoo. Not that I knew how long it would take to get Molly out of her dark-green skirt and matching blouse, but I had faith. We sauntered over two rounded hills and stopped halfway between the herd I spotted in the distance and where I knew the ranch house stood. She squeezed my hand.

"Did you get a gun?"

I nodded.

"Did you shoot it? How was it?"

"Yes, and it was grand. Da and I went out and shot all afternoon." I wrapped her in a bear hug. A gentle one. "Got into another scrape with those men and Da decided I needed to defend myself."

Her eyes lit up like Chinese fireworks. "A scrape? Did you throw punches and such? What did you do? That's where Joe's scratches came from?"

Two entirely different events. I'd have to sort them out for her and then get naked. "They attacked Da and me. And yes, I threw punches and ran them off."

"Joe?"

I looked down. No escaping her questions. "Joe's had a rough time in Denver. First night back, he went to Sam's and got into a scuffle. Broken whiskey bottle cut him." That's all I would say on the subject. It was not where I wanted to go with this conversation and the precious hour we had.

She tightened both hands. "Scuffle? Broken whiskey bottle?" Her words rushed out. "Did the law come? Did he get arrested?"

I sighed. Last time. "Yes, the deputy was there. And no, Joe didn't get arrested." I held both of her arms. "Look. We don't have much time. I can't show you my gun just yet, since I'm on probation for another week. But I will soon's I can." I nudged her toward a stand of trees in the distance. "How about those steers?"

She stepped a few feet and stopped. "This might not be the best time to get naked, Eagan. I know I promised, but not today."

All the light and air in the entire world fizzled out. I could hardly breathe. She was welching on our deal. "Why not?"

Hesitating, she started and stopped. "There are some things women do, once a month. This week happens to be my turn."

I had no earthly idea what she was talking about. Sewing? Cooking? No, they did that every day. "*What* is your turn?"

Her cheeks reddened. "Ask your ma." She continued walking. "But we can still kiss. And you can touch me in places." She squeezed my hand. "I'd like that."

My entire world turned black. While I liked kissing and touching, I wanted *naked*. I'd planned on naked. Could I rip her clothes from her and see her flesh? Was I that kind of man? Part of me was.

We made it to the trees, and I leaned back against one, disappointment dripping from every pore in my body.

She leaned against me. "Tell you what. Next Sunday, you come back, bring your gun, and we'll get naked. I promise."

So, what was so different between this Sunday and next? I hated her for the game she was playing. Maybe it had something to do with Joe. Maybe I should have been arrested again. Maybe I should have let The Three beat me again.

I held her and kissed her a time or two, but the spark wasn't there. My hand strayed down her chest, worked its way under her shirt, and felt the firm roundedness of her womanhood. But it wasn't the same as being naked. Still, I enjoyed it and she said she did too.

And then, we were done. If I couldn't go any farther, I lost interest. She buttoned her blouse and smoothed her skirt, which didn't need smoothing. Kissed me again, took my hand and we walked away.

CHAPTER TWENTY

Was that her way of saying I wasn't curly wolf enough for her? I gripped the broom, swept at the boards in front of the store, and considered. Although seeing her naked had been my top priority, maybe her welching on the deal was a good thing. Gave me time to step back and truly think. If I was being honest with myself, I wasn't curly wolf material. I didn't like not obeying the law. I didn't steal or lie—very often—and wanted a career as an honest man. Which left out being an outlaw. Robbing banks and stagecoaches was not my idea of a good time or the best way to make money. Despite what Tate wanted, for the three of us brothers to be a stagecoach-robbing gang, I liked working hard, like Da and now Tate, and Joe for that matter. Hard work was the only way.

Leaning on the broom, an idea struck me. Today, I'd go see Deputy O'Sullivan and ask him how to be a deputy to the deputy. Hell, I'd be eighteen in a couple of months and what better way to learn a trade, besides meat cutting? I'd have to work part-time, since I worked full-time at the store. I couldn't tell him I had a gun yet. My probation hearing wasn't until Wednesday, and I wasn't about to do anything to jeopardize my freedom.

It was Monday, a busy day, but not like Friday's. Everyone stopped by on Friday. Shoulders pulled back, I'd tell Da what I planned and maybe he'd let me have more than fifteen minutes for lunch.

To my surprise, Da gave me half an hour, more if I needed it. He didn't give me much hope of becoming a deputy to the deputy, but he didn't discourage me, either. Da cautioned me about my gun, and I assured him I'd stay quiet.

At noon, I found Deputy O'Sullivan off to one side, sitting at a small desk in the sheriff's office, pencil in hand, papers spread out across the top. He glanced up and smiled when I stepped inside. A long look around revealed no Sheriff Wagner. I let out an audible sigh.

"Eagan! Good to see you." O'Sullivan put down the pencil, rose and stuck out a hand. "What brings you this way? You all right?"

I took his outstretched hand. Strong, and were those calluses? So, he did more than push papers. Good to know. "Fine, Deputy. I'm fine."

He pointed to a chair in the corner. "Pull up. Have a seat."

Sitting across from him was awkward and I wondered why he was being so nice and glad to see me. His wide face and bright light-green eyes emitted an inner joy. I'd have to ask. But I only had a few minutes and I'd waited long enough to make this decision. First, I decided to talk business.

Seems he had other ideas. He leaned forward, then

back. "How's Joe doing? I was worried about him. Glad you talked him down from the bar."

This wasn't where I wanted the conversation to go but was sure I could circle back. "I think deep down he's in agony." Surprised those words surfaced, I continued. "He rode out to Molly's place and seemed to enjoy talking to her and her little brothers and sisters. Even played with them."

"Molly? Who?"

"O'Malley. Molly O'Malley. I've been seeing her, and—"

"O'Malleys. They bought that old Douglas ranch couple months back. Run a nice herd of yearlings?" He snapped his fingers and pointed north. "Met Mr. O'Malley time or two. Red hair?"

"That's them. All of the kids. And there's a passel. Molly's the oldest." Simply saying her

name and thinking about her made my chest ache. Maybe next Sunday...

O'Sullivan nodded.

Something compelled me to continue. "You'd think that someone who'd just lost his wife and unborn baby wouldn't want to be around a family like that. But he even stayed for dinner."

The deputy nodded again. "Probably his way of coping. Putting things in perspective."

Exactly what Ma had said. All right. Ma and the deputy were smarter than me. I needed to change the subject, something I was never good at. "Listen, Deputy."

"Why don't you call me Tommy when there aren't others around?" One eyebrow rose. "Gotta sound official out in public."

My turn to nod. "Listen, Tommy." I started again.

"Now that I'm almost eighteen, I've been thinking about becoming a lawman. Like you." I rushed my words, like they were about to escape unleashed from my mouth. "Don't want to be a meat cutter the rest of my life. I wanna do something with my time on earth. Something meaningful. Like you."

He held up a hand. "Whoa, there, Eagan. Too many compliments."

"Seems to be more to my liking than being a curly wolf."

"A curly wolf?" Tommy leaned back. "What gave you that idea?"

I studied the top of his desk, the rest of the room, my hands. "Molly."

"And she wants you to be a curly wolf? An outlaw? She wants you in jail or dead?" Tommy frowned, a strand of dark hair hanging over one eye. He pushed it back. "Doesn't think much of you, does she?"

"Guess she wants an action man. Doesn't care which side of the law he's on." I took a breath. "But...is there a way I can be a deputy to the deputy? Here? Maybe help out at night or weekends? I'm still working full-time at Da's shop."

It was Tommy's turn to scan his desk, papers covering most of the top. I could tell by the dipped eyebrows and the pursed lips that he was considering my proposal. He picked up a pencil, put the eraser end to his lips, put it down, then played with it between two fingers.

"Interesting idea, Eagan. You know, when Sheriff Becker hired me couple years back, there were two of us deputies. Now, there's just me. Could use another hand sometimes."

"I'm the man for the job, Tommy." My shoulders

pushed back. "I don't mind fighting, getting bruised up. I mean, you've seen my face a time or two. And I won't back down. I can be a good deputy, Deputy."

"You got a gun?"

Icy cold shivers ran through me. What to say and could I do it without letting on? "You know I'm on probation until Wednesday. Why would I have a gun?" Did my voice waver like I thought it did? Most importantly, I didn't lie.

"Right. Sorry. Of course." Tommy pushed back his chair and stood. "Tell you what. When Wagner gets back to the office, which oughta be in the next couple of hours, I'll mention it." A wide smile took up part of his face. "He's gone out to see his sweetheart, Miss Van Zant. Gertrude, I think he said. And when he comes back, he's always relaxed and happy. I'm sure you know why."

I didn't, but pretended like I did. Relaxed? The courtings I'd had with Molly did not relax me. Confuse, yes. Cause anxiety, yes. But relaxed? Never. Maybe when I got older.

Tommy extended his hand again, and I gripped it. I'd like working with him.

"By the way," Tommy released me. "Your probation meeting's gonna be here in this office. Judge didn't see it necessary to shut down Preston's saloon again. It'll be Sheriff Wagner, your attorney, and of course, you. Your folks if they want to come. And me."

"Thanks for letting me know." Most of me was relieved I didn't have to stand in a courtroom again, although most times it was the Frontier Tavern. The judge liked that saloon because it was smaller, he'd said. More intimate. I didn't like it either way, small or intimate.

I opened the door, and Tommy pointed his pencil at me. "See you Wednesday at ten. Meantime, I'll talk to Wagner."

My boots barely touched ground as I limped back to the shop. I mulled over what Tommy had said and came up with a shred of hope I could become a lawman. Wouldn't that be grand? Ma would be so proud.

In between customers, I told Da what the deputy had relayed. All good news was my take on it. As I cut up roasts into smaller pieces, I thought about Molly. She wasn't good for me, like Tommy had said. But I couldn't keep my thoughts or hands away. Something about her drew me in, and I was helpless. I'd thought yesterday we were over, but her hand in mine as we walked back to the house and her aggressive kiss before I rode away, told me different. I'd been too disappointed at the time to see it. But I understood now.

* * *

TEN O'CLOCK WEDNESDAY MORNING, I stood in front of Sheriff Wagner's desk, staring at Judge Rickets sitting there instead, whose long arms took up about half the desktop. In his right hand he gripped a sheet of paper, another in his left. Wire rim spectacles perched on the end of his long nose.

To my right stood my attorney, Mr. Tubman and on my left was Sheriff Wagner. Behind and to my left was Deputy O'Sullivan, and directly behind me were Ma and Da and Joe. We filled the office, leaving scant room for the door to open and close. Despite the open window, I tugged at my collar. My face pulsated warmth, and unless I breathed deeply, thought maybe I'd pass out. Not only would that be awkward, but it would also be embarrassing. If that happened, no doubt the judge would extend my probation. I sucked in warm air.

Rickets read and harrumphed over the paper in his right hand. Finishing, he did the same with the paper in his left. All of us standing, we fidgeted, shifting our weight ever so slightly. Waiting was impossible. My future hung on his words, and they wouldn't come.

After what seemed like days, weeks, months, Rickets put down the papers and looked up at me. "Well, Mr. Nolan." He tapped the top paper. "Seems you've kept your nose clean this past month. No fighting. No shooting a gun within city limits. No shooting at all. Says here, in this statement from your attorney, you're a model citizen."

I nodded to the man next to me, offering a silent thanks. How he knew I hadn't caused much trouble was surprising. I hadn't seen him since the trial a month ago.

"Sheriff Wagner"—Rickets pointed to the other paper—"says the same thing." His gaze roved up and down my body, head to boots and back up. "Hard to believe a rabble-rouser like you and your brother, Tate, could stay on the straight and narrow for four weeks. But I guess you did."

"Yes, sir." Maybe I shouldn't have spoken, but the words popped out. "I have." All right, that was a lie, but I hadn't started any of it.

Judge Rickets located a third piece of paper. From my point of view, upside down, it had names and lines on it. Rickets picked up a stylus, opened an inkwell, and signed one of the lines. He turned the paper around to me. He pointed. "Sign here and you're off probation."

I signed in my best penmanship. Thanks to Ma's insistence, I made my E's and G's

perfect. I handed the pen and paper back to the judge,

who blew on the wet ink. He extended a hand. "Glad to see you become a worthwhile citizen, Mr. Nolan." We shook. "Stay out of trouble." Then he waved me off. "You're free to go."

The best day of my life! I turned to Ma and Da who gave me a two-person hug. I shook hands with Joe, the deputy, and a short one with a reluctant sheriff. My attorney also gave me a quick handshake and then stepped outside, quickly disappearing down the street. Hopefully, I'd never seen him again, or need his services.

I needed to ask Da about paying for the attorney since he got the bail money back. Did he charge for showing up today, even though he didn't do anything but stand next to me? I'm sure there were a ton of behind-the-scenes meetings and things like that he'd done, but that discussion with Da was an issue for another day. Today, I was a new man.

I stood on the boardwalk with my family. It was too early for lunch, too late for breakfast, which I had barely touched this morning, and too early for a drink, which sometimes I'd get served at Sam's, depending on the bartender. I thought back to the last time Joe had been drinking and the result wasn't good. I could skip a beer celebration. Looked like it was back to work.

As if knowing my thoughts, Da patted my back. "How 'bout you take the morning off? Come back this afternoon?" He turned to Joe. "Wanna fill in?"

Shrugging, Joe gazed toward town. "No. But haven't heard back from the telegraph office if they'll hire me. Guess I got nothing better to do."

While that wasn't too gracious of Joe, it was about what I expected. His emotions ran from surly, to mean to cheerful in two seconds. I never knew which Joe would show up. Ma had said to give him time. I'd like to give him a punch in the puss, but since I was now a "model citizen," I'd have to be understanding, too.

"Thanks, Joe. Appreciate you stepping in." I decided to take the high road and be syrupy nice. "I'll come in, right after lunch."

My family waved as they walked away. Now that we'd gone our separate ways, I had a little over two hours that were all mine. What to do? I could go see Molly. No. I nixed that idea immediately. I wasn't sure where I stood with her or she with me. I needed space.

Jimmy! My best lad. He'd want to know what the judge said. I waved a second time to the family's backs and started the other way to the stable where Jimmy shoed horses. He was more blacksmith than stable worker with arms to prove it. I admired him for his muscles.

About halfway down the street, I turned at my name being called. Deputy O'Sullivan was running to catch up. I waited, half expecting bad news.

"Eagan!" He stood in front of me, trying to catch his breath. His face blushed a deeper red. "Need to talk."

"Sure, Tommy. I'm free, 'til after lunch."

He took in a long breath and blew it out. "Guess I don't do much running. Sorry." Tommy cleared his throat. "Talked to Wagner, the other day, about you working with us. After a lot of discussion, he agreed he'd try you out. On probation."

I chuckled. "Seems like I'm doing a lot of that lately." Something didn't sound logical, though. "He said it was a good idea? Why? Thought he hated me."

Tommy glanced down the street toward his office. "Doesn't like your brother, that's for sure. But he doesn't know you. We talked about you and your family and finally Wagner saw why you might be good to have on our side. I mean, you're young. Real young."

"So are you."

He raised one shoulder. "Twenty-four. Not young. Not old."

That made him two years older than Tate. I didn't think of Tate as young or old. He simply was Tate.

Tommy shifted his weight. "You can go into the saloons and men won't think of you as a threat. You can see what's going on easy. What's that big word?" He studied the sky. "Infiltrate. Yep. That's it. You can infiltrate. Wagner agreed."

I knew what that word meant. And he was right. Looking this young, nobody would take a notion that I was a card sharp or gunner ready to make a name for myself. No, I'd be a "kid" who got away with being in a saloon. Put one over on the bartender. This was indeed a glorious day. Ma and Da would be so proud. "What about my limp? The way I walk? I can't run as fast as you did just now."

"Considered that. Don't think it'll be an issue." Tommy looked down at my leg. "You can ride, can't you?"

"Like I was born on a horse." I wasn't lying. That was the one thing I truly was good at.

Thumping my chest with the back of his hand, Tommy grinned. "Usually, when we go chasing after bandits, we don't run. We ride. You'll be fine."

And just like that, I was a lawman. Hallelujah!

"Plan on starting Friday evening. Just a couple hours should do it. Saturday, too." Tommy pulled out a shiny badge that read *Deputy Sheriff. Gillespie County. Blanco Hill.* How that six-pointed bronze pin managed to squeeze all that information on there was remarkable, but nevertheless, it was plain to read.

I grinned, smiled, beamed, and shook his hand. I wanted to give him a hardy bearhug but decided against doing something so rash. I mean, here I was, a brand-new deputy sheriff who was ready to give hugs to men. Instead, I stepped back and willed my eyes not to tear up.

"Thank you, Tommy. Thank you. I'll make you proud."

"I know you will. Just remember, Wagner's watching you. And now the town will be too." Tommy smacked my upper right arm. "See you Friday. I'll stop by the store around six."

My boots didn't touch the boardwalk as I sailed toward the stable.

CHAPTER TWENTY-ONE

TRUE TO HIS WORD, FRIDAY, TOMMY STOPPED BY the store right when Da was turning the sign around. I'm not sure who was more excited about my first day being a deputy-to-the-deputy, Da or me. Ma was nervous. She'd told me to be careful and to watch out and so many other words of caution. But she'd packed me an extra sandwich for supper, which I couldn't eat. Nerves had tightened my stomach, and for the life of me, nothing would go down. I said goodbye to Da as he locked the front door. He walked one way, Tommy and me the other.

Our first stop was down at the end of Main, Sam's Emporium, the largest saloon in town. Largest of eight. If there was going to be a fight, it would be at Sam's. For some reason, all the rowdies gathered there. The rowdies and the upstairs ladies. The other saloons didn't seem to provide that sort of service for their clients. They did have barmaids, who wore shorter skirts and served drinks, but that was all they served. Most men seemed to know that, and while they might say something off-color, generally, they kept their hands to themselves. And the barkeep's shillelagh ensured it.

Which left all the problems down at Sam's. I hadn't brought my gun, which Da said I should leave at home. No sense inviting shootings, he'd said. And Ma wholeheartedly agreed. Now, I almost felt naked without it, although most men in Sam's weren't heeled, either. Of course, Tommy was, but he was an honest-to-goodness lawman and was expected to have a gun.

In the next week or so, I'd tell Tommy about my gun and see if I should wear it. But for now, it was safe at home in the top drawer of my dresser.

For the next two hours, we circulated among the men and barmaids at Sam's. Nobody looked too drunk or violent. Card games revealed no cheaters. No big winners, either. Even the faro table was relatively serene, surprising for such a usually noisy game. Spanish Monte, which I knew little about, didn't have a huge draw either. We made the rounds of the other saloons and found them nearly empty. Nothing much going on. We also walked Main checking business doors to be sure they were locked. Part of me was disappointed. I'd expected much more.

"It always this quiet, Tommy?" We'd stopped a block down the street from Sam's,

where I dropped onto a bench. My feet and legs screamed at me, like a small petulant child wanting attention. I wanted to wrench off my boots and rub my feet, but that would never do. Not by a deputy sheriff. I'd do that when I got home.

He nodded. "Most times, it's relatively calm. But be prepared. When the ranches finish roundup, it gets damn interesting around here. Jail fills up fast."

Feeling like I should know this, I had to ask. "When's

round-up?" Would Tate come into town, blowing off steam, getting arrested? By me?

"Couple more weeks from now and then again in the spring." He chuckled. "Don't worry. You'll earn your pay, then."

I got paid? That hadn't been a big consideration, figuring this trial period would be for free, but now it was more like an added bonus. This just kept getting better and better. I didn't have the courage to ask how much. I'd simply be surprised when the coin arrived.

We spent the next hour hiking up and down Main until Tommy pointed toward my house a few blocks away. "Nothing else to do here. See you tomorrow."

Going home, I limped extra hard, exhausted, but the happiest I think I'd ever been.

* * *

SATURDAY WAS SIMILAR TO FRIDAY. I worked all day at the meat shop then, right before dusk, Tommy and me made our rounds. Weekends, especially Saturdays, were supposed to be rowdy, full of miscreants and men letting off steam, but not this evening. If anything, it was quieter than the day before. I was partly disappointed and partly relieved. I needed to ease into this lawman business without having to fight a man bigger than me. And most of them looked bigger than me. Probably stronger, too. And they'd been drinking.

I thought back to Joe and his drinking. That had caused, or nearly caused, all sorts of problems.

I leaned against the end of the bar and surveyed the clientele. Basic, ordinary, run-of-the-mill men in for cards, a drink, and maybe some female companionship. Nothing untoward. Which led me to think again about my brother. This past week Joe had been more polite and rational than before. Was he starting to "come around," as Ma had predicted? I hoped so. He still didn't have a regular job, but he'd come into the shop often to help. We needed his extra hands and if things worked right, maybe he'd come work most of the time and I could be a lawman more than two nights a week. I'd keep fingers crossed.

I had no idea walking up and down Main would be so hard on my body. Especially my feet. My legs complained when I got home, and Ma would have a large pan of hot water ready for me to stick my feet in. Then she'd go to bed. Still energized, I'd sit up until well past one soaking my feet and thinking about what I'd seen, done, and of course, Molly.

Molly. I'd see her tomorrow morning at church. And then what? Would I go to her house for dinner? Would I be invited? Would Joe go? Would this be naked Sunday? I tried to get excited about the prospect of seeing her undressed and lying there under a canopy of leaves, but my eyes kept closing and my head bobbing.

* * *

SOMEONE SHOOK MY SHOULDER. "Rise and shine, little deputy. Time for church."

I grunted, growled, and rolled over, taking the sheet with me. I opened one eye and caught a disgustingly happy ray of sunshine right in my face. I growled again. My brother's back was the target of my glare.

"Not going." Had I actually mumbled that out loud? And why would I go? Molly. If it wasn't for her, I'd go back to sleep. But with the off chance we could get naked today, they couldn't keep me at home.

"Ma," Joe yelled out the door. "Eagan says he's not going."

I threw the sheet back and jumped to my feet. "Am, too. Changed my mind." I pushed him out the door and hollered. "Be ready in five, Ma."

My legs barked while my feet complained. Sliding my feet into boots was torture. I hobbled downstairs knowing I couldn't survive the day in such agony. Unless Molly...

By the time we'd made it to church, my leg muscles had relaxed some, and I had gained a bit of spring to my step. It wasn't much of a spring as I was wanting to be asleep right now. But knowing my woman was close by, I pushed down fatigue. Would I get used to being a lawman? My chest puffed a bit thinking about it. In a hurry, I'd left my badge at home, but I'd remember to wear it next week.

I endured hours and hours of sermons, singing, kneeling, praying, more sermons, and forcing my eyes to remain open. I tried concentrating on what the priest said, quietly counting the pages in the hymnal, envisioning rearranging the shop's storeroom. How much more ice should I buy tomorrow?

A sharp nudge on my shoulder and a whisper in my ear. "Whist! You're snoring." That would be Da on my right.

With a congregational "amen," I groaned to my feet, then perked up. Molly time!

Winding my way down the aisle, nodding to neighbors and people I'd seen in the store, I made it past the back row where the O'Malleys sat. Empty. Figuring they were already outside, I inched out and down the steps. No slew of red-haired chickens or Molly. Her ma and da were absent, too.

More than disappointed, I asked one or two women if they knew about the O'Malleys. Most shrugged until one said she'd heard two or three of the children were sick. Common summer colds, but too sick for church. So, that meant Molly was either sick, too, or home taking care of the flock. Did I want to visit? See how she was doing or stay away?

Ma stopped next to me. "I see Molly isn't here today."

"Her family's sick."

She patted my arm. "Best stay away. You don't want to come down with what they've got. Especially now that you're a *leas-sirriam,* an employed man o' the law." Her eyes gleamed.

I hadn't considered that. Not only did I have a responsibility to Da, but now to the entire town. All right, for their sakes, I'd go home and take a nap.

* * *

THE NEXT TWO weeks flew by. Working at the shop, then walking the streets and saloons took a toll on my body. Tired. I was tired. And a bit grouchy, I'd been told. More than once. I hadn't seen Molly and it seemed like every customer who came in couldn't make up their mind. I pulled out roasts, chops, bacon, Hamburg steak, chicken. Everything we had in the store. And then they'd buy one pork chop. One. What was wrong with these people?

At church, no Molly or any of the O'Malleys. Were they that sick? I stood on the sidewalk in front of the church, staring toward their ranch. Should I take a chance and go see? Joe stopped at my shoulder.

"You know. I could go out to their ranch and check on them." He glanced at me. "Isn't that what good neighbors do?" Joe reset his hat, reminding me I needed to get one. "I can ride out now and be back by dinner."

"Aren't you afraid of getting sick? I mean—"

"Nah. I'll stay on the horse and holler. Should be fine."

Joe had that look on his face that said no matter my feelings, or the facts of the matter, he was going. I gave in. "I'll tell Ma and Da where you went. Don't take too long, they'll worry."

He waved over his shoulder as he jogged toward home and his horse.

* * *

JOE SLAMMED the front screen door, just as we took our places at the dining table. Aromas of oven-baked pork chops and green beans swirled around my head. If Joe's sappy look was any indication, he smelled them, too.

He quickly washed his hands and face, then sat with us. We said grace and got down to serious gobbling. The way Ma baked those chops was exactly the way Heaven made them, I was sure.

Joe spoke over a forkful of cubed potatoes. "The O'Malleys all have colds or some such. Not sick enough to call on the doc, but none of them feel well enough to go to town. Told 'em I'd bring by groceries tomorrow."

"That's gran' of ye, son." Ma nodded and smiled at Joe. "Thoughtful, ye are."

"You see Molly?" I couldn't stand not knowing.

"I did. She came to the porch. We hollered at each other." Joe's smile lit the room. "She's feeling fine, but she stayed away from me. Said to tell you howdy and she's sorry."

Wasn't her fault her family was sick. Why else was she sorry? I stewed on that through dinner and while helping Ma clean up. Joe and Da sat on the porch, despite dark clouds and the threat of rain. I dried dishes thinking about Molly and a nap. A nap *with* Molly. Now, that held possibilities.

Kitchen cleaned, my duties over, I headed upstairs for a nap without Molly. Hopefully, I'd dream about her where she would be there in spirit.

By the time I stirred, the sky had turned a light purple, sunlight fading fast. Downstairs, Da sat in his chair reading a Beadle and Adams adventure novel, Ma in her chair mending a shirt.

I cast around for Joe and assumed he was in the barn. No, his horse simply stared back at me as if saying she was bored. Our horse munched on straw.

Back in the house, I had to ask, "Where's Joe?"

Ma looked up over her needle. "Walked into town. Said he'd be back in an hour or so."

Wondering why he didn't wake me so we could go together, I poured myself a glass of buttermilk and sat in the front room thinking. Over the past couple of weeks, since he'd been back, he'd become more of his old self. Not as much arguing, bad language—even around Ma— and sarcastic outbursts. He mentioned his wife only once or twice, which I took for a good sign.

Way after dark, Ma warmed up leftover chicken stew for the three of us. Stomach full, I stretched out on my bed, knowing I'd have to be up in a matter of hours. Sunrise came early. Despite wanting to stay awake until Joe returned, my eyes slammed shut.

Rustling and something clunking on the dresser opened my eyes. Pitch dark but a form moved in the room. "Joe?"

"Shhh."

All right. He was home, and I was going back to sleep.

What felt like only minutes passed, until sun smacked me in the face. Joe was passed out on the other bed, and I wasn't about to wake him. No doubt he'd be crabby, and I didn't want to start a Monday like that. I dressed as quietly as possible, and he didn't stir.

* * *

MONDAY at the shop was like every other Monday. Busy, but not too busy. Constant customers kept me on my toes, but I managed time to straighten and clean.

The remainder of the week was uneventful. I'd almost forgotten to keep an eye out for Purdy and the two Clydes. I hadn't seen them around and figured they'd moved on like the judge had demanded. I had enough to worry about—Molly, the store, deputy duties—without worrying about The Three. Hopefully, by now they were harassing people in jail, where they should be.

Friday finally arrived, as did Tommy, just as Da turned the shop sign around. I pinned on my badge, mentally shined it, and stepped into the street. Da waved as he headed in the opposite direction.

We stopped at Sam's first, where we were met with nothing but calm. Three different card games were in play, a woman hung on a man's arm, two men leaned against the bar. Pretty humdrum. We headed down to the Frontier Tavern at the other end of town.

"Been meaning to ask you, Eagan." Tommy walked next to me. "Didn't know Joe was seeing Molly."

I slid to a stop. "Joe?"

"Your brother."

"What?"

"Uh oh."

My head shook. "What?"

Tommy thumbed toward the Frontier. "Saw 'em in here, last Sunday, and then again Wednesday, I think. Looked cozy."

My hands automatically fisted. "You sure?"

His voice turned soft and low. Apologetic. "She was on his lap."

"And you didn't think to tell me before now?" Why did I turn on Tommy? Wasn't his fault.

He held up a hand. "Thought you knew."

"Well, I didn't." I studied the sign over the tavern's door. "Suppose they're in there now?"

Tommy shrugged and pushed open the batwing doors. No Joe. No Molly. We proceeded to check each saloon but found no brother of mine courting my woman. When I got home, I'd have a talk with ol' Joe. He'd have a black eye by morning.

CHAPTER TWENTY-TWO

NEXT MORNING, WE BOTH HAD BLACK EYES, although mine was a bit darker than his. He sure threw a hard punch, one right into my jaw and another against my temple. My split lip, the third I'd had in the past couple of months, throbbed. However, I'd held my own and clobbered him a time or two.

We sat silently at the breakfast table, glaring at each other. Fork in hand, I envisioned stabbing him, but that would never do at Ma's table. I thought back to last night, when I'd returned home, fuming, footsore, mad at myself, Molly, and especially Joe. I'd pulled him out of bed and hauled him downstairs, through the front door, down to the stream. Barefoot, he'd pranced around, trying not to step on too many sharp rocks.

He explained it was Molly's idea. She liked the rough and rowdy sort of men and he fit the bill. She'd been all over him. He missed his wife terribly and had given in. He knew it was wrong, he apologized, but couldn't help himself. She was so very persuasive.

I called him a back-stabbing sumbitch and meant

every word. In return he'd called me *le chat*, whatever that was. It sounded French and I was sure it wasn't nice. We punched twice more, then I accepted his third apology. That last one sounded pretty sincere, if a bit muffled, due to his swollen lips. At least they weren't split with blood running down his chin like mine was.

Sipping tea, thinking coffee would have been better, I realized neither Ma nor Da had

asked why we were battered and bruised. Good on them, because I was still ready to tear off Joe's arm and beat him with the remaining bloody stump.

Breakfast was quietly tense, with Ma and Da making small talk. I tried forking scrambled eggs past my lips, but I couldn't open my jaw wide enough. Inside, I chuckled at Joe trying to do the same. We made quite the pair. In that instant, I almost felt sorry for him. Almost.

And then it hit me. Molly. All this was her fault. Joe had simply become a stooge for her getting what she wanted. As he'd said, it wasn't all his fault. I'd nearly fallen into that trap as well. Thinking about her skirt up around her waist, her bare skin, that feeling of—

"'Bout time to head for work, boys." Da stood, finished his tea and smiled at Ma. "Thankee for breakfast, *acushla*. 'Tis always a blessin' to have ye with me. I was a lucky man when I met ye."

"Yeah, ye were." Cheeks turning red, Ma flapped a hand at Da and rose to gather dirty dishes. She spoke over her shoulder. "Actually, *I* was the *knacky fancier*."

Would I have a relationship like that? Ever? Certainly not with Molly. However, she was so...so soft and a good kisser and willing to lift a skirt and even promised to get naked, although she reneged on that deal. But still, all in all, she was exciting. Sensual. Tempting.

I thought about her all the way to the shop, Joe and

Da walking slightly ahead of me. Last night, walking up and down the boardwalk with Tommy, had about worn out my boots. My feet hurt like the devil had set them on fire, which made my limp worse. Soon, I'd have to buy new boots and a hat. Maybe Monday I'd have time.

We opened the shop on time with two customers already lined up outside. I wheelbarrowed my way down to Solano's, bought twenty pounds of ice, and managed to wheel it back, without tipping over in the ruts. Fortunately, the rain we'd had a couple nights ago hadn't amounted to much. Wagons hadn't furrowed the road and I managed to dodge the road apples no

one had yet swept to one side. I wasn't sure who, exactly, was selected for that task, but it was an important one. Without a street cleanup, I could only imagine what Main would look like in a week. I pictured foot-deep manure, packed hard all up and downtown. Probably harder than the concrete path I'd seen in San Antonio the one time I visited there.

Joe and I kept our distance during the day, which wasn't hard as there was a steady flow of customers until closing time. After a long day on our feet, Joe turned the sign around, locked the door and leaned against it. "What a day. Looking forward to supper and bed."

Da riffled through the cash register, extracting a wad of bills. "Me too. Wonder what your ma's made."

"Don't matter." Joe untied his apron, hanging it on the peg behind the door. "Long as there's plenty to go 'round."

Da mentioned to Joe how much he appreciated the help and since it was Saturday, paid him. He whipped out five one-dollar bills and two silver one-dollar coins. Half expecting to get paid, I stayed close by, waiting for Da to give me the same or more.

Instead, he shook my hand. "Couple more weeks, boyo. Your debt will be paid."

Well, hell. He hadn't forgotten about the "bail" money like I had. I'd moved past that and now I was off probation.

"You mean money for the attorney, Da? Was he more expensive than bail? And why didn't you tell me you got the bail money back?"

Da leaned on the register and eyed me. "Looks like I underestimated ye, boyo. For that, I'm sorry. I am. In fact, I'd been meaning to tell ye Mr. Tubman did come at a pretty penny, but worth it as he got ye off. In confidence, he thought ye'd be going to prison for six months but promised to do his best. And he did."

Joe nodded. "Money well spent."

Dumbfounded, I couldn't figure out what to say. Do I thank Da? Or stay mad at him for not being truthful from the beginning?

As if reading my mind, Joe shoulder-bumped me. "I'd say thanks to both Da and that lawyer. I know he asked me some questions about you."

"He did?" So, Tubman had been asking around. I reconsidered Da. Just because he forgot to tell me, didn't mean I was ungrateful. I'd have to find a way to tell him. But not now.

Da closed the register. "Couple more weeks, Eagan. Couple more."

At least I still had the rest of Tate's money. I hadn't counted it recently, but if memory served, I had about twenty-five dollars left. Definitely enough for a hat and boots. I know I smiled because my lip bled, and my cheeks hurt.

At least none of the customers asked about my bruises. They were probably used to them by now.

Seemed like something on me was always purple, green, black, or swollen. I was constantly a mess.

I was certainly ready to go home, eat, put up my sore feet, put a cold compress on my face, chat a bit more with Da, and go to bed.

But I couldn't, now that I was a deputy. Tommy would be stopping by any minute, and I had to be ready. I untied my apron, hung it up, and pinned on my badge. That was the best part of the day—putting on the star. Plus, today I'd brought my new gun and the rig, like he'd suggested I do. I felt like a real man.

There was no telling what would happen tonight. Tommy kept regaling me with stories of wild men, shooting, causing havoc, but all I'd seen, so far, were men playing cards and drinking beer. I was ready for excitement. Not a lot, but some.

Tommy arrived on time, so I waved goodbye to Da and Joe as I marched away next to the deputy. In the past couple of weeks, we'd become friends. I guess you had to if you counted on your partner to save your life if ever the need arose. I hoped it didn't, but I was ready for adventure.

First stop was Sam's, at the west end of Main. A bit more lively than yesterday, I counted four card tables in play, two women hanging on arms, and maybe ten men lined up at the bar, each with a beer mug or whiskey glass in front. Judging by the loud voices, they were busy telling stories to the bartender and swapping tales with each other. Laughter sailed up and down the wooden deck. Tommy smiled and patted my shoulder. Maybe next week would be the end of roundup.

Sun setting and spreading its last rose-gold hues on the town, we stuck our heads into the other saloons. Nothing going on. Final saloon before we headed back was the Frontier Tavern, which doubled for a courtroom. Tommy and I pushed open the batwing doors, stepped in, and I froze.

On the far side, against the wall, sat Purdy, beer glass in hand. On his lap, perched Molly. I couldn't move, couldn't breathe. Tommy pointed. "Isn't that—"

"Molly!" Was that me shouting? Had to be, because I'd run to the table, grabbed her arm, and yanked her off his lap.

"Hey! Watch it, Eagan!" Molly ripped her arm out of my grip. "Get your hands off me."

"What are you doing with this sumbitch outlaw?"

Against my left shoulder, I felt Tommy standing there, ready to back my play. Directly in front was red-faced Purdy, snarling, fists clenched.

He leaned in within inches of my face. "What the hell you think you're doing, Nolan?" He chinned at my badge. "Just 'cause you're a pretend lawdog, wearin' that shiny new badge of yours, that fancy-dancy gun belt, you figure you can come bustin' in here, harassing me and my girl?"

"*Your* girl? Like hell! Molly's *my* girl."

Purdy plowed a fist into my lower left jaw. I spun, crashed against a table, but somehow kept my feet.

Tommy's grip on my arm kept me from swinging. "Hold on, fellas," he said. "This won't solve anything."

Maybe not, but it'd feel damn good planting my fists into his face and watching blood gush down his nose. My gun warmed against my hip. Should I pull it out and use it? Better sense kept it holstered.

Tommy stood between us, arms held out. "Molly, you sit right here." He chinned toward a nearby chair and waited while she indignantly plopped down. "Eagan, move back."

He was right. Shouldn't be fighting. I pulled in air, took the deepest breath I'd ever had, lowered my fisted hands, and took exactly two steps back. Still close enough to launch at Purdy, but far enough away to be respectful.

Spinning his pointed finger, Tommy spoke to Purdy. "Hands behind your back. I'm arresting you for assaulting a peace officer."

"Assaulting? Peace officer?" Purdy laughed loud. "Who? This two-bit meat chopper? He's no peace officer. Hell, not even a glorified—"

"Enough." Tommy pulled out handcuffs from his belt. "A day in jail'll help you see clearly."

"Jail?" Purdy glared first at Tommy and then me. "I'm sittin' here havin' a drink and this yellow-bellied *tomball* comes up and harasses me. And it's *my* fault?"

Tommy locked the iron around Purdy's wrists and pushed him toward the door. He spoke quietly to me. "Eagan, I can handle Purdy. Looks like you and Molly need to talk." He pushed Purdy through the doors as I followed. "Check Sam's on your way home. Thanks for your help tonight."

Tommy growled at Purdy, who begrudgingly walked toward the sheriff's office. Molly joined me outside on the boardwalk, and I turned to her. "What makes you think—"

"What gives you the right to bust in on me like that?" Molly's freckles stood out even in the dim kerosene lights. "I'm not your property. Yeah, we had a good time. You and me. But you..." She eyed me up and down and sneered, like I was a rotten piece of meat. "You—"

"I thought you liked me." I was grasping at straws, trying desperately to understand.

"Sure. I liked you enough to let you touch me. All over. Even the special parts. You liked that, didn't you?"

Of course, I did. But I wanted to see her naked, even more. I nodded, my mouth refusing to make words.

"That's all you did. Touch me. I want somebody rowdy. Somebody who takes what he wants. A real man. Not *un chat* like you." Molly's lips curled up and I thought she was going to spit on me.

There was that word again. I'd have to find out what it meant. Her harsh words sat on my chest, crushing not just my breath, but my entire life out of me. What could I say in response? In defense? In retaliation? Nothing. I was a big *gobshite* standing there, mouth open, being emasculated by a tiny, yet busty, feisty red-haired woman.

"We're not a couple. You and me." Molly jabbed a pointed finger down the street, more toward where Purdy had been led. "I've moved on."

That much was obvious. First Joe and now Purdy. I pointed to the backs of Tommy and Purdy. "He's an outlaw. An evil man. Your folks don't want you—"

"What my folks don't know is fine with me. They don't really care what I do. Got lots of other kids to worry about."

No doubt that much was true. "I thought we—"

"You were a passing tumble. Good for a couple of laughs. You were good at fondling me, really got my kicks from that, but—"

"I loved you." Where the hell did that come from? "Thought I did. But why didn't you tell me we were done? Why'd I have to find out you'd thrown me over for my brother and now Purdy?"

She shrugged. "That's just the way I am. I like men touching me, caressing me, and I like them being rowdy.

That's just who I am." She double shrugged, turned, and started up the boardwalk. She stopped, turned to face me, and hollered, a shrill, gut-wrenching decree for the entire world to hear. "And you're *never* gonna see me naked!"

That was embarrassment beyond endurance. How could she announce it to the world? Chuckling roiled out of the Frontier Tavern. If I could have been swallowed up by the street, I would have welcomed the chasm. She spun back around and marched away.

My heart puppy-dogged with her. The bottom fell out of my world. Painful. It was painful to hear those words. The tirade. The belittling. How could she?

I stood on the wooden walk, in front of the tavern watching my lady love stride away. She'd made it crystal clear I'd never get to see her naked. Most probably never talk to her again. I might see her in church, which thinking on it, made me smile. Irreverent Saturday nights, pious Sunday mornings.

What would I say to her folks, tomorrow morning, assuming they showed up to mass. Hopefully, by now everyone was well enough to attend mass. Would I tell them I'd found her sitting on bully-boy's lap, beer mug in hand? Maybe. Possibly. Probably. A slice of my hurt feelings to get back at her for being so cold-hearted.

My legs were more numb than the rest of me. I stood there, like I'd been hit with a deaf and dumb stick, and waited a good five, ten minutes before slowly heading down toward Sam's. It was still a bit early, but a beer sounded good right now, to help drown my broken heart. But I was on duty. And deputies shouldn't be drinking while on duty, even those who'd been humiliated in front of the entire town. Maybe tomorrow after church I'd stop by. Yeah, that was the answer. I'd get good and sloshed tomorrow afternoon. Joe could help get me home. I perked up a bit at that plan.

Nothing new was going on at Sam's. I chatted with the bartender about how dead it was, and he mentioned probably next weekend being end of roundup. And I should be braced for the onslaught of hellbent-for-trouble cowboys blowing off steam.

I thanked him for the warning, took a last look around, nodded to two men at a nearby table, and stepped into the night. The moon hadn't risen yet, which made the world dark. I could barely see my hand. Only two street lanterns had been lit and they were at the other end of Main. Fortunately, I'd walked this route at least a million times, so I knew every inch of this hard-packed road.

Within three blocks of my house, I was busy deciding whether to get a glass of milk and a sandwich before going to bed or simply milk. Maybe I'd forgo milk and head for bed. I was exhausted and this Molly encounter had drained me.

On my right, a stream gurgled a nighttime lullaby. A stand of trees, Texas oak, stood nearby like army sentinels guarding the town. Since it wasn't far from home, my brothers and me had spent many happy hours here playing pirates and army men. I'd always liked it this slice of Heaven.

"There he is. Right on time."

Clyde Two. I'd know that croaking crow voice anywhere. I walked faster. Maybe they'd follow me home, and Da and Joe could help take care of them. I considered running, but that would make me seem like a coward. I wasn't a coward, but I was tired of getting hit. I limped as fast as I could.

Purdy and Clyde One stepped directly in front of me.

Purdy? Wasn't he supposed to be in jail? Did somebody bail him out already?

I slid to a halt, choosing not to try to sidestep them. It would simply become an awkward dance and I wasn't ready for those games. "Why aren't you locked up?" I gave Purdy my best glare.

He cackled, rubbed a dirty hand across his mouth. "That lawdog changed his mind. Said I didn't do nothing he wouldn't do." Purdy shrugged at Clyde One. "Let me go."

He was lying, that much was obvious. So why did Tommy release him? I'd find out tomorrow, but now I needed not to be at the end of more fists. "Let me pass. I have no truck with you right now."

Purdy snorted. Clyde Two stood next to his brother. From out of the dark, a woman softly said, "What are you waiting for?"

A woman? Sounded like Molly. A quick glance revealed nobody. The world was too dark and not even the stars helped put light where I needed it.

"Finish him off, so we can go play." Had to be Molly.

Finish? That sounded ominous. I heard, more than saw, three men make an arc in front of me. Thank God I'd brought my Colt tonight. I yanked it out of the holster, aimed at a darker blob to my right.

"No need for gunplay, men." Did I sound strong? I hoped so, because inside I was trembling. "Let's go our separate ways. Live another day."

"You ain't gonna live any longer, Deputy Nolan. Not one more breath."

Bang! A flash of golden light arched across the dirt. The bullet zinged past my ear and I ducked.

Changing directions, slightly, I aimed for the man.

Bang! Oranges and reds shot from my gun. I dove for cover behind a tree. Kneeling, I peeked around the trunk.

"Oww!" A voice, could be Clyde One's, pierced the dark. "I've been hit!"

"Sumbitch, law dog!"

The two men opened fire, the night lighting up like Chinese fireworks gone berserk. I returned the favor until running out of bullets. Had I brought more? I fumbled with my gun belt and found two.

If I hadn't been shaking so hard, I could've reloaded. As it was, one bullet fell to the ground, the other still in my hand.

Bang! Icy fire raged across my head, across the left temple. Blood ran into my eye, blinding me. I felt my other bullet slide into the chamber. Lifting the gun, I fired. My head crashed into the tree trunk.

Everything went dark.

CHAPTER TWENTY-THREE

BY THE TIME I OPENED MY EYES, A FAINT GLOW
had appeared on the eastern horizon. Scraping dried
blood out of my eyes, I could just make out my hand in
front of my face. Moving, every part of my body hurt,
screaming.

Pushing up to my feet, I stood leaning against a tree. I
patted my head, picked out pieces of dried blood from
my hair, and tried to make sense of my world. Sore. I was
damn sore. I pushed away last night's attack and focused
on Tommy. Where was he and why was Purdy out of jail?
And then like a bucket of cold water, it hit me. I shivered.
Was he dead?

As fast as I could hobble, head on fire, I stumbled my
way back up Main to the sheriff's office. Unfortunately,
at this hour, no one was on the street. No one who could
help. As usual, the door was unlocked. "Tommy?" I
stepped inside. No one at either desk. "Tommy?"

"Here." The voice was soft, pain filled.

I followed the sound to the farthest cell. Tommy lay
on the floor, both wrists handcuffed to an iron bar. Dried

blood covered most of the right side of his face. I squatted on the other side of the bars. "Thank God you're alive." He probably felt the same.

"Key's in the top right drawer."

I wasn't sure which key, but we needed two since the cell was also stoutly secured. I looked way in the back of the drawer and found three keys on a ring. Sure enough, one opened the cell door, the other the manacles.

I helped him up to the cot, where he groaned and patted the lump on the back of his head. I looked closer. "Purdy do this?"

Tommy moaned. "The Clydes came in behind him. One of 'em sure packs a wallop."

I nodded. "Shot one of 'em last night. Don't think I killed him, though." I gripped his left arm and lifted. "Can you get to your desk?"

We wobbled to the outer office where he sank into the chair. I stood leaning against the wall, afraid if I sat, I'd pass out. As it was, the office spun.

"You shot him?" Tommy frowned at me and picked at dried blood on his face. "What happened?"

I relayed the ambush, leaving nothing out.

"Damn," Tommy held his head. "I picked a bad time to be napping. What time is it?"

"Near morning."

He frowned at me. "Why're you here? Shouldn't you be—"

"Guess they thought they'd killed me. Thank goodness for a hard head. Came to my senses a few minutes ago. I was worried about you. So, I came here."

"Well, hell." Tommy studied me out of one unswollen eye. "You see the doc yet?"

I fingered my head, recoiling at the touch. "Guess it's

not all that bad. I'm sure Ma'll fix me up. But you look worse off than me. Maybe you should go."

He held his head and wagged it slowly. "I'll be right as rain soon. But those weasels. Have any idea where they set off to?"

I shrugged. "Probably in some cat house sleeping it off. Right now, I don't care. I'll find 'em later."

"Hope they don't find you first."

Every muscle in my body shook. Tired. I was tired. Exhausted. My head thundered. The severity of nearly dying swallowed me. I pointed toward home. "I'll go get some sleep. See you this afternoon?" Obviously, Tommy and I were the only ones in the office. "Where's Wagner?"

Tommy shrugged. "Not here, so my guess is with the girlfriend. He's not around too much lately these days."

Good news, since revenge was rampaging in my chest. I turned to the door.

"Eagan." Tommy pointed at me. "Thanks for worrying about me. You're a good pard to ride with."

Quite the compliment, but all I could do was hold my head and groan. I stepped into a red and gold sunrise. Hobbling home, I considered what I should tell my family. I would give details, later.

But most of the way I thought of revenge. Sweet revenge. What would I do? Killing may be the answer. But that was too quick. This revenge, whatever it was, needed to take a while.

Maybe I'd shoot Purdy in the foot again. Both feet now. But the other two? Clyde One? A bullet in the arm? Was he the one I'd shot? If I shot him again, he wouldn't die, probably, but he'd be out of action for months. Clyde Two? Maybe push his face in deep mud and run over him with my wheelbarrow couple times. Yeah, those had possibilities.

By the time I opened the front door, I was lathered in revenge. And plans. Lots of plans. My family was at the breakfast table if dishes clanking and chit chat was any indication. The door closed harder than I'd intended.

"Eagan? That ye?"

Ma. Before I could answer, she rushed to me and gave me a tight hug, then stood me back at arm's length. "Gracious Good Mother." She reached up to touch my head. I'm sure the dried blood on my cheek looked worse than it was. "*Cad é a Tharla?* Are ye all right? Here, come sit."

Da and Joe stepped in behind Ma, everyone eyeing me up and down like a steer that had

survived the slaughter pen. I kind of felt like one, too.

On the way over, I had decided to tell the truth instead of hiding it. I was still sore Da hadn't told me earlier about the bail money. It wasn't fair to keep me in the dark like that so, not wanting to be like them, I figured my folks deserved honesty—to know what really happened last night. And that Ma should be glad I had a gun.

I gave them a shortened version, but didn't leave anything out, except that Molly was there. I'd deal with her on my own terms.

Ma fussed over me like I hoped she would. "Get out of those dirty clothes, while I find the liniment and bandages." She spoke over her shoulder. "Joe, go heat some water." Back to me. "Then I'll fix you a nice breakfast." Her eyes smiled at me. "You'll sleep while we're gone to services this morning. Place'll be nice and quiet. You'll feel better."

Perfect. Exactly what I'd hoped for.

* * *

BUT SLEEP WAS ELUSIVE. I tossed and turned, recounting the ambush. What could I have done differently? Was it my fault? I should've been more alert. But my excuse was I was tired and shook up by the Molly tornado. Not one of my better days.

A gentle hand rocked my shoulder. "Supper time, boyo. Time to get up." Apparently, I had slept.

Supper time? Had I heard Da right? I'd slept all day? I'd missed after-church dinner? I washed my face, unwound the bandage from around my head, inspected the painful crease in my scalp, smoothed my clothes, all while the heavenly aroma of baked chicken seduced me down the stairs.

I loved Ma's Sunday chicken. She put some sort of spice on top, baked it whole for I didn't know how long. This evening, we had green beans and stewed apples with it. I eased down to my chair, head beginning to pound in earnest.

Joe shoved a forkful of beans into his mouth and spoke over it. "By the way, Molly says to tell you howdy. Wondered where you were today."

"Molly? She was at church?"

Ma put down her fork. "Why wouldn't she be? Her family's all healthy now."

I cleared my throat. "Sorry I missed her." Like hell, I was. She was indeed a piece of work, as they say. I thought back to "irreverent Saturday, pious Sunday." Yep, that was Molly."How'd she look?"

Joe eyed me over his milk glass. "Fine. Real fine." There was a question at the end of his statement I chose to ignore. He sipped. I'd tell him later.

"I miss anything else?"

The three of them looked around at each other and shrugged. Joe forked a piece of chicken. "Nothing special. Same things."

I nodded. "You see Tommy? Or Sheriff Wagner?"

Da's eyebrows dipped. "No. Why?"

"It's just that Wagner has a girl outside of town and he's there more than here. Tommy was up late. Since he was on duty, figured he wouldn't get much sleep, 'til Wagner came back." I saw no need to tell them about Tommy getting whacked, too. I picked up a fork. "Just wondering how Tommy was doing."

The meal resumed. Joe sipped his milk, slurping, more to irritate Ma than bad manners. Joe put down his glass. "Didn't see either one. But there was no need. Pretty quiet Sunday."

Chicken melted in my mouth along with the stewed apples. If this was Heaven, I was in it. "Next Sunday'll probably be different. Tommy and a couple barkeeps are thinking it'll be the end of fall roundup. Lots of cowhands, drovers, and such will come in to blow off steam. I'm wondering if Tate will come."

"T'would be lovely to see him again." Ma smiled. "Hope he stops by before enjoyin' the...the evening."

I chuckled at Ma. What she wanted was for him to be happy, but to be happy, here. Not in the saloons or bawdy houses that were sure to spring up overnight. Would he go to one of those? A saloon, absolutely. But the other? I liked to think of Tate as sensible.

Da nodded and finished his chicken. "If that's true, then Friday and Saturday at the store will be quiet. Nobody ventures out when the rowdies are in town." He pointed a fork at me. "You remember last spring? Ranch hands, cowboys all up and down Main. Shootin' their guns. *Goin' on the gargle*. Drunken brawls. All of 'em, *fluthered* and *banjaxed* and *arseways*."

I nodded. Vaguely aware of the revelry, wasn't sure where I had been. Probably Da had kept me at home, away from the trouble. Wild bullets were known to hit windows and people and horses, at random. Safest place would be away from town.

Revenge ideas exploded. Stray bullets. Drinking. Drunken brawls. And I'd be right in the middle of it. A smile stretched my cheeks.

* * *

THAT NIGHT, Joe and I went to the stream to toss rocks into the water. Our usual place of plotting. I kneeled at the bank and told Joe in detail about the ambush. Inch by inch I was becoming madder and madder. Somehow, I'd get revenge, and by damn, Joe could help.

We talked over plans, and he had some good ideas. Some were too drastic. I wanted the men embarrassed and humiliated. And if they died...well, that's what they'd intended to do to me. They were bullies and needed to know what the receiving end felt like. After a lot of scheming, we came up with an idea that we expected to work.

Monday, we decided, we'd go target shooting again. Tuesday, I'd have Da teach me the finer art of bare-knuckle fighting. Wednesday, sparring with Joe. Thursday, more target practicing.

Friday would be a busy day getting ready.

Saturday would be glorious.

But first, I'd have to be near death to do it.

CHAPTER TWENTY-FOUR

Figuring Da and Ma were fed up with The Three's shenanigans, and the fact they beat on Da a couple weeks back, and tried to kill me Saturday night, Joe and I sat down with our folks and shared our plans.

"If I'm thinkin' right," I started off as the four of us sat in the front room, each balancing a cup of tea. "Those outlaws think I'm either dead or about dead. That's what they wanted. It was plain to see. And I'm worried they'll come after Da and maybe even Joe, next."

"And they don't seem all that worried about the law." Joe smoothed his mustache.

Ma crossed herself and looked at all three of us. "Mary and Joseph, let it not come to that."

"Right." Joe eyed me. "Eagan being almost dead keeps him out of the picture until Friday or Saturday. Here's what we're thinking."

Between us, Joe and I described how I'd stay home the next few days and customers who'd come into the store would ask about me. Da would tell them I'd been shot, ambushed, and didn't look like I'd make it. I was afraid if I'd "died," the shop would need to be closed and a funeral planned. This way, simply being shot up "real bad," no need to do any of that.

"I know that's going to leave you short-handed, Da, but Joe'll fill in and I think this plan'll work. Take care of these *gobshites* once and for all." Oops. I said a bad word. In front of Ma. Surely, I'd go to Hell for that. At least to my room. I looked over at her. A tinge of a smile slid up the right side of her face. I relaxed.

Da nodded. "And since it's round-up time, customers will stay away Saturday. I'll tell everyone we're closed that day, anyway. Will that help?" He crossed one leg over the other. "Did that with the spring round-up."

Joe pointed his cup at Da. "As Eagan said, I'll help out since I'm not working. Do what I can." He turned to me. "I'll also have Tommy stop by here, so you two can plan more."

"If Tate comes into town, he can help with his cowboyin' skills." I twirled an imaginary rope over my head and launched the lasso at Joe. I missed and he grinned.

"What about Tommy? And Sheriff Wagner?" Da uncrossed his legs and leaned forward. "Surely, they can't endorse shooting, killing, and general mischief."

That was the only piece of the plan I worried about. Tommy would be easy to convince, Wagner, not so much.

My gaze swept the rug. "I'll have to think on that more, Da." I looked at my family. "But what I need now, is to be almost dead."

* * *

MONDAY DAWNED OVERCAST AND GRAY, almost like a storm was on the horizon. Almost, but no purple clouds or smell of rain dotted the area. It was simply gloomy. Perfect. No need to have a happy day, when Ma, Da and Joe were so sad, so worried about me.

Although my head still throbbed and at times things blurred, I enjoyed breakfast with them and waved goodbye from inside the house. Ma and I cleaned the kitchen before she headed out to her usual Monday sewing circle. Of course, to the women, she'd be mighty worried about me and trying to be brave in front of them. I figured by noon, the entire town would be full of Eagan close-call gossip. Maybe, I'd even die, depending on who told who. In a morbid, perverted way, this was fun.

But more than fun, I hoped with all my being I'd get revenge and those men would consider new, better ways to live out their lives. I still didn't want to kill anybody, but I'd shoot one to death if need be. Revenge was going to be sweet.

Tommy knocked softly mid-afternoon. I let him in, and Ma greeted him with a cup of hot tea. I wasn't sure he liked tea but he accepted it politely and sipped at the steaming liquid, while he and I plotted and planned.

We sat in the front room, Tommy and I, talking. I wanted to make those men pay for humiliating, harassing, stealing from me—almost killing me for real. Shooting Purdy in the foot wasn't nearly enough payback.

As we chatted, both Tommy and I held our throbbing heads. He'd said he was fine, but dark circles under his eyes and one hand constantly rubbing his head revealed him as a liar. More than likely, he felt as bad as me.

This morning, with full sun on my shaving mirror, I'd examined the bullet's path along my head. I'd lost hair in a line and a soft scab was forming on my scalp. The trench along the right side was deep enough to make me shiver. I'd been lucky. Damn lucky. Another half inch and I'd really, truly be dead.

"If we—you, Joe, Tate—can get Purdy or the Clydes out of Sam's, since you're the wronged one, you can call them out to a duel. With guns. I think the judge might be agreeable to that. Especially if you didn't kill 'em."

So, there was hope I could get revenge, after all. "How soon 'til the circuit judge comes back?"

Tommy studied the ceiling. "Probably two, three weeks." He looked at me. "And if they survive Saturday night, they'll spend the rest of that time behind bars. They'd hate that."

I chuckled. "They would." I remembered the night I spent locked up next to them and all the curse words I'd learned. I wasn't sure some of them were even real.

Putting down the almost-empty cup, Tommy stood. "I gotta be gettin' back."

I stood, too. "Thanks for your support."

He smacked me on the shoulder. "That's what pards're for." He stepped toward the door. "I'll let you know if anything changes. By the way, I've already heard you might not make it."

"That's sad. And I was so young." I hung my head and chortled.

"Can't wait to see you come back from the dead." Tommy opened the screen door. "It'll be glorious."

* * *

THE FOUR OF US sat at the dining table after supper, chatting. Da had reported that throughout the last two days, he'd mentioned to customers that we'd be closed Saturday, due to fall roundup. Without exception, each person nodded and agreed closing was a good idea. They vowed to stay home, windows shut, doors locked for a couple of days. If town got as rowdy as I'd heard, then my plans were more than perfect. Maybe a few drunken cowboys would even help. Saturday was turning out to be perfect. If things went as intended.

Joe's grin stretched his cheeks. "Eagan, Ma, guess what." He thumbed over his shoulder. "Guess."

I couldn't help myself. "You got better looking, while getting ice at Solano's?"

"Uh uh. Looks like I got my old job back." He smiled wider. "Mr. Whalen over at the telegraph office said the fella he hired in my place when I went to Denver? Well, he's quitting tomorrow. Wants me to start Wednesday. Even got a bit of a pay raise."

Ma raised her fork. "*Iontach!* 'Tis gran', son. 'Tis gran. Good on ye!"

We tinked cups and congratulated him, until the excitement fell out. That meant, for three days, Da would be by himself. Maybe Ma could go help.

Keeping my plans in mind, Da and I spent at least an hour that evening with him showing me how to bare-knuckle fight. If I couldn't use my gun, for whatever reason, I needed to know how to use my fists and wits. He explained the differences between ring boxing and barroom fighting. And since I didn't have a lot of muscles, he emphasized speed over brute strength. Joe sat in, too, and the three of us pranced around the front room, jabbing and bouncing. Ma *tsked* in Irish and English and excused herself to bed earlier than usual.

* * *

TARGET PRACTICING WOULD BE HARDER to pull off because it was outside. I couldn't chance being spotted, so I *shot* everything inside the house. Especially flies, that dared to intrude. I also got a curly bug and three moths.

Both Joe and Da reported the town was upset about my near death and a few men had vowed revenge on The Three. I hadn't considered someone besides my family and Tommy would be outraged, but it looked like being a *good boy* with a popular da was working out. Maybe the townspeople would help me string them up on Saturday.

* * *

WEDNESDAY DAWNED MUCH brighter than the past two days and I was feeling tons better.

My vision had cleared, and the head hurt only when I thought about it or touched it. I was definitely on the mend. That night, us three men duked it out in the living room, while Ma fussed in the kitchen muttered Irish epithets, then went to bed early, again.

* * *

THURSDAY, Tommy stopped by to tell me Sheriff Wagner planned to stay in town through the rowdy weekend. Already, two ranch outfits had come whoopin' and hollerin' into town. One outrageously drunken drover was busy sleepin' it off in the jail. Tommy said he was surprised the man was still alive, considering all the cowboy had consumed. He'd visited all eight saloons before trying to make love to a chair on the boardwalk, then throwing up and passing out.

No incidents of shooting or anything like that—yet. But more was sure to come.

* * *

FRIDAY. As usual, I helped Ma clean the kitchen after breakfast. Turning my attention to the barn, darting about and staying out of sight of passersby, I mucked out the stalls, replenished the oats, and curried both horses. I didn't plan on needing them, but things didn't always go according to plan.

After the noon meal, shouts of ecstatic cowhands, along with whooping and gunshots, pierced the quiet. Even from five blocks away, I could hear their joyousness. Tonight was going to be raucous. What would tomorrow be like?

I sat on the couch, felt the scab, glad it didn't hurt like the last few days. Just as I stood to get a glass of water from the kitchen, the screen door squeaked open. My hands immediately fisted. Purdy? The two Clydes?

No. There stood older brother Tate, wide grin on his tanned face.

"Howdy there!" Tate lightly punched my shoulder. "Heard you're dead. Or almost." He dropped his saddlebag and stuck out a hand. "Glad to see you're not."

"You and me both."

Tate batted away an extended hand and pulled me into a tight bear-hug.

After Ma gave him a once-over and asked a million questions, Tate and I sat in the living room. I shared my plans and how he fit in.

"So, let me get this straight." He sipped hot tea, then set down the cup. "You want me to lasso each of those fellas, one at a time, haul 'em outside, one at a time, and string 'em up? Like in to a noose?"

I nodded. He got the picture.

"And they're gonna let me do that?"

"Probably not. But Joe'll be there to help."

Tate frowned and thought. "I think you're crazy. But then what?"

"Joe ties their hands, I put the rope around their necks, and we leave them for Wagner. And if one tries to shoot me, I shoot back. Probably wing 'em." I shrugged. "Or not."

"And the sheriff and deputy are all right with this?"

"Tommy is. Says it's self-defense. Wagner...hard to tell. I haven't talked to him, yet."

Tate glanced out the window. "I'd like to string up Wagner myself. Maybe my rope'll accidentally go around his neck, too. Tighten, 'til he can't breathe too good."

I shot him a look, knowing he was all talk. Couldn't blame him for hating Wagner, though, he'd been nothing but cruel to Tate, but still...

CHAPTER TWENTY-FIVE

TOMMY AND I WALKED UP AND DOWN MAIN AT dusk, ducking into Sam's at least six times and the Frontier Tavern three. Only one man from town recognized me and said he was glad I hadn't died. Everyone else we ran into was from out of town.

Those outhouse rats, the three bullies, had made themselves scarce. I hadn't seen even Molly, who I figured would be hanging on Purdy's arm, laughing at his stupid jokes, batting her baby blues at him, lifting her hem. On our seventh visit to Sam's, we elbowed our way up to the bar, men crowding the wooden structure, one frilly-clad woman trying to climb on it. Before either of us could help her back down, a stocky ranch hand swooped her up and carried her back to his table. The two hollered and laughed the whole way.

Tate came over with a half-full beer mug. Knowing he had no idea what the bullies looked like, at home, I had told him in detail and then drawn a rough sketch of each. We laughed at my artwork, but admitted he might be able to identify them, if and when they came in.

"Thought I'd stick around here," Tate shouted over the noise and used his mug to point around the room. "Some of these boys I work with are from Carmichael's ranch. But I'll watch for your old fellas, come find you when they get here." He sipped. "Might take a few more of these, though."

I glanced toward the batwing doors. "Joe's supposed to be by soon." I leaned closer to Tate. "Da's hanging out by the shop. Doesn't want anything happening to it."

"Like one of these cowboys'll bust in and steal pork chops?" He laughed long and loud. Tommy and I chuckled. Tate patted my shoulder. "I think not, little brother. The shop's most likely not in any danger."

Actually, I had to agree, but Da had every right to be concerned. He'd even brought his gun, including a gun belt I didn't know he had, complete with holster and bullets.

Bang! Bang! Gunfire from up the street only served to make Sam's patrons louder. Tommy charged outside, and I followed. Men and women roiled out of the various saloons, and one cowboy on horseback shot his revolver toward the sky.

Tommy pointed. Those bullets had to come down somewhere, and often, it was on an innocent victim's head. Together, we corralled the cowboy, yanking him off his horse.

"You're under arrest." Tommy slapped handcuffs on the man. "Sleep it off in jail."

The man bowed to Tommy, gathered and handed him the reins, then lay in the street, curled into a fetal position. He was snoring before I could get him to his feet. I dragged more than walked him to jail.

Still hadn't heard from Joe, or Tate for that matter, but the street was filling up fast. Horses raced up and down Main, men waving their pistols, hollering, fancy women laughing and screeching. Robust, off-tune, tinny piano music spilled out from all eight saloons. The entire town, it seemed, was ablaze in golden kerosene light, illuminating scores of drunken cowboys.

They were all having the time of their lives. "Letting off steam" was an understatement. Now, I understood why Da was concerned about his shop.

With the drunk sleeping it off behind bars, nothing more for me to do. I pointed toward Sam's at the end of the street. "I'm goin' back. Maybe Tate just hasn't seen them yet."

Tommy nodded and turned. "Maybe you're not the portrait artist you think you are." His quick smile made fine lines around his eyes crinkle.

I smacked his chest with the back of my hand. "Let's go."

Dodging horses clomping on the boardwalk, men dancing in the street, and women egging them on, we threaded our way back to Sam's. I pushed in on the door just as Tate pushed out. He cocked his head toward the back of the barroom.

"Just came in. The three of 'em. And Molly, too. She's on a lap. They're over in that corner by the stairs."

I glanced behind me at Tommy. This was it. Now my plans would come together. They'd finally get what was coming to them. I lowered my voice to Tate but didn't need to since no one could really hear me. "You see Joe?"

Tate nodded. "He's down at the shop. Said to tell you the *neckties* are done, and he'll keep an eye out for when it's time. He'll come runnin'."

"Wish he'd stayed here." I thought he knew to stick around.

"He's worried about Da and the store. Even the telegraph office." Tate raised both eyebrows at me. "Don't worry. Things're fine. Got my lariat down behind the bar."

Edging in front of me, Tommy surveyed the crowd. "Got 'em. In the back." He took a breath. "Here we go. All right, Tate. Do your thing."

Tommy and I backed onto the boardwalk, bumping into a couple cowboys. I waited on the other side of the door, listening for Tate to start. Seemed like ten minutes passed.

"Ain't you the one they call Purdy?" Tate's voice flew across the room. I made it out loud and clear. Conversations quieted and chairs screeched across the floor.

"What's it to ya?" I'd recognize Purdy's voice anywhere.

"Understand you nearly killed my little brother the other day." More chairs scooting. "I'm here to see you pay."

"Nolan? He ain't dead?"

"You ain't the pistolero you think you are." A pause. "Step outside and take your beatin' like a man. Nobody, but nobody messes with my brother."

Two, maybe three men pushed their way outside, glancing over their shoulders. Inside, chortles, but also a few *go ons* flew to my ears. Tommy nodded at me like this was all right. Briefly, I wondered where Sheriff Wagner had hidden himself, but as long as he stayed out of this, I figured I wouldn't end up in jail, myself.

A *whoosh* and some *olés* filled the night.

"Get that rope off me!"

I peeked over the top of the batwings in time to see Tate tighten up the lasso around Purdy's chest and arms, pull him off his feet, and drag him toward the door. I laughed, recalling cowboys doing that same thing to reluctant steers during branding time.

"Shoot 'im, Clyde! What the hell you waitin' for?"

I hadn't thought a lot about that and should have. Of course, the Clydes would be heeled. From my viewpoint, neither of the men could get a clear shot at Tate. A drunk fell into Clyde Two and both went to the floor. Clyde One twisted back and forth as if choosing who to help.

Tate dragged Purdy out through the doors, across the boardwalk, down the steps and into the street. Most of Sam's emptied out following Purdy, who'd somehow managed to draw his gun.

I kicked up, and the weapon flew out of his hand and into darkness.

Like the lasso expert I expected him to be, Tate smartly wound the rope around Purdy until he couldn't move. I stepped in close, surrounded by at least a million men and women all encouraging me.

Purdy sneered. "So, still breathin', I see."

"Save it, Purdy." I couldn't see the Clydes among the crowd. Surely, they'd be close by. Tommy was at my left shoulder.

Purdy tried to wriggle out of Tate's rope. "Snivelin' coward, Nolan. You're nothin' but a crippled, snivelin' coward. Oughta be six feet under by now."

Hoping Tate had him secured, I leaned down, nose to nose with Purdy and his foul breath. "You've bullied me, beat me and my da, and now tried to kill me." I holstered my gun, still warm in my hand, and patted my treasured badge. "I'm a lawman, and you're gonna pay. You're gonna hang or go to jail. Which'll it be?" Where was Joe with the noose?

"Let me loose and I'll fight ya."

Tommy whispered in my ear. "Might be better'n trying to hang him. Here comes Wagner."

Well, hell. This was not going the way I wanted. But all right. I nodded to Tommy, then Tate. "Let him go."

Tate took his time unwinding the rope. To Purdy, I lowered my voice to steel. "Just you and me. No guns. Just these." I held up my fists, the knuckles already sore from sparring. "If your friends, there, try anything, the deputy'll shoot 'em. Dead."

Purdy glared at me and breathed out. "All right. Bare-knuckle. To the death." He scrambled to his feet. We handed our gun belts to Tommy.

"No!" I frowned. "Toe the line in a ten count or out."

Purdy's face relaxed. His shoulders slumped. "Fine. Be over soon enough, scarecrow."

Purdy nodded to the Clydes, who'd managed to push through the throng and stand close. He spun back to me and clobbered my chin with an uppercut. My head snapped back, and I blinked at stars. I returned with an uppercut of my own, my fist meeting his jaw. He staggered back, I staggered forward. I punched his paunchy belly and he *oofed* over, but straightened up with a headbutt to my nose. Blood gushed into my mouth and down my chin.

A stronger blow took me to my knees. I hit the ground and tried to breathe. Rage smothered me. Images of me in the street, my britches yanked down, my money in their hands, the bullet tearing across my head. I became an animal.

I launched myself on top of him, taking him to the ground. I punched and pounded until I couldn't lift my arms. Couldn't roll over. Couldn't think. I laid across Purdy, now quite still, and sucked in what little air I found.

Many hands pulled me off. They set me on my feet, some still clutching my arms like I would fall without their support. Through red goo, I spotted Da and Joe in the crowd, Da with barbed meat hooks in hand. Joe clutched a burly noose.

I blinked down at Purdy lying in the street, his face a mishmash of blood and dirt.

I frowned at the image on my right. A blurry Tommy nodded at me. Wagner, a scowl claiming his face, stood on the other side. He leaned over and spoke to him, who nodded, then the sheriff shoved his way out of the crowd and disappeared.

On my left, stood Joe. Tate, on Joe's left, shook his head. "Might be dead, Eagan. You got him good."

I shuddered. I didn't want him dead. Just gone.

Tommy kneeled by Purdy. "He's breathing, Eagan. Just barely." He hollered to no one in particular. "Help me get him over to the jail."

Clyde Two sucker-punched my kidneys. I spun to my right, directly into Clyde One's fist. I reeled back. Before my vision cleared, both Clydes were running down Main, like the true

cowards they were.

I struggled to get my gun from Tommy. "Stop! You two!" They were about ten yards from me, heading for darkness.

I yelled again. Clyde Two pulled up, turned, and fired his gun. Yellow and orange spires arched through the air, a buzz near my ear, the bullet dinging into the wall of Sam's Emporium. I brought my gun up to eye level, aimed, and pulled the trigger.

Bang! So satisfying and yet, so terrifying.

Clyde Two grabbed his side and kneeled. The other

Clyde continued running into darkness, abandoning his brother to his fate.

I stood stock still. Was I breathing? Sounds around me blended into nothing but noise. Whooshing in my ears. Shouts. Still, I stood, frozen. I'd shot a man.

Tate gripped my upper arm. "Eagan? Eagan? You all right?" I looked at him but didn't see him.

A soft hand ran down my chest. "Knew you were a fighter, Eagan. So brave, too." Molly's words in my ear made no sense.

I shrugged out of Tate's grip and turned to the woman I thought I had loved. With a pleasant smile, I put my hand over her face and pushed, hard. She landed in the dirt, a fresh pile of road apples under head, and her blue skirt up around her waist. Laughter, shouts of "Olé!" and other jeers danced around my head.

One long, last look at her, I wagged my head.

Now, if I had the energy, I'd go home.

But I wasn't going home. Tommy smacked my shoulder. "Let's get Clyde." He pushed his way through spectators, me wobbling right behind. Clyde Two still knelt, a couple of men standing nearby offering him a drink to "ease the pain."

I grabbed Clyde's arm, and not very gently, yanked him to his feet. "How's it feel, now? You're goin' to prison for a long, long time." Tommy handed me his handcuffs, and I slid them on Clyde's wrists. The *click* of the lock almost made me cry. It was that satisfying.

Tommy handed me my leather gun belt. I buckled it around my waist and slid my gun into the holster. With Purdy unconscious in the street and a mangled Clyde in my clutches, all I needed was the other Clyde in hand and my life could go be back to normal. Whatever normal was.

"Let's go, Clyde." I tugged him toward jail, Tommy on the other side when then came a shout from the dark, behind.

"Hey! Lookie what we found!"

Tommy and I turned to see the other Clyde being manhandled by a group of drunken men. Around Clyde's chest was a lasso. He wasn't going anywhere, now. A beaming cowboy stood next to him, the end of the lariat in hand. I chortled.

Tate appeared next to me with a trussed-up, groggy Purdy in tow and pointed at the cowboy. "You got 'im, Sam! You got 'im!"

Sam pulled Clyde One closer to me. "Thought you'd want this critter, Deputy. Found 'im out behind the jacks, over yonder." He pointed behind him into the darkness.

Of course, I wanted him. But more important, he'd called me *Deputy*. That acknowledgment felt almost as good as knowing those three desperados would spend most of their lives behind bars when the judge knew the whole story.

Joe stepped up, a satisfied grin on his face, and dropped the noose around Clyde's neck. He didn't tighten the rope, didn't need to. The message was clear.

The entourage of myself, Tommy, Da, Tate and Joe, along with about a hundred celebrating men and women, marched Purdy and the two Clydes up to the sheriff's office.

I opened the door and there stood Sheriff Wagner, jail keys in hand. He moved back, allowing us easy entry. Once the three were deposited and Doc allowed in to see them, my brothers, Da, Tommy, and I stood with Wagner in the office.

"I'm impressed, Eagan." Wagner stuck out a hand. "Didn't know you had it in you to fight like that."

I ducked my head, then brought my sore shoulders back and glanced at Da. "I had a good teacher."

I took Wagner's hand. We shook.

"Glad to have you on board, Eagan. Might have to make you a permanent deputy."

Despite a split lip, broken nose and swollen cheeks, my smile reached ear to ear.

Now, it was time to go home.

CHAPTER TWENTY-SIX

"Afternoon, brothers. Thought you'd sleep all day."

I opened my eyes, only to figure out, according to the sun, it was around noon. Joe lay in the other bed, snoring. Tate stood in the doorway, cup of tea in hand, fresh clothes on and smooth cheeks shining. But dark purple under his red eyes spoke volumes.

This morning, I ached everywhere. Top to bottom. Inside to out. My hair hurt. Even if I had wanted to, I couldn't have gone to church. No way. Working my jaw and finding it sore, I mumbled, "Sleep? Like to. But somebody came in and woke me up." I pushed to a sitting position using all the strength I could muster, complete with a couple of low oaths, quiet enough that Ma wouldn't hear.

Tate sat on the edge of my bed, making the frame creak and mattress dip, and pointed toward town. "Quite the event last night. At church, people were talking about nothing else. All three *hombres're* still locked up tighter'n a..." He shot me a glance and grinned. "Well, they won't be gettin' away anytime soon."

"Shhhh...would yer wheesht?" Joe rolled over.

Tate ignored him. "You're quite the hero, Eagan. Quite the braw lad. Everybody says so."

"Me?" I frowned. "Why?"

Tate leaned in close. "'Cause they say you're as good a fighter as Gypsy Jem Mace, and *almost* as good lookin' as your oldest brother." He shrugged. "At least, that's what the women are sayin'."

Right. I'd liked to have believed him but knew better. "Purdy?" My swollen lips made his name sound more like "pretty."

"Doc says you did a right savage number on him. He'll live, though."

"Clyde Two?"

"Doc says he'll live, also. Missed all the vitals."

Relief washed over me. Nodding, parts of last night's memories made me smile. "Think they got the message?" My busted chops couldn't form more words, even though I had lots of questions.

"I'm sure they did. According to Tommy, they're already tryin' to make deals on their attempted murder of a peace officer. And extra special since they violated the judge's exile order."

Tate patted my shoulder and then stood. "I gotta be headin' back to the ranch in a couple of hours. I was hoping the three of us could talk before I go. I think y'all be interested."

"Sounds like a proposition." Joe rolled onto his side. "I'll pry these eyes open, then come down."

I hated to see the three of us split up, again. At least Joe was still here. Maybe Tate had a plan, where I'd see him more often. Something exciting, where I could use my new gun skills. My knuckles hurt too much to consider any more pugilism, any time soon.

"I'd like to know what you're scheming now, big brother." In all the years I'd known Tate, which was my whole life, he was always planning for something bigger, better. This time, I was old enough and tall enough to be interested.

And...I was a deputy.

A LOOK AT BOOK THREE:
BATTLE AT THE PEDERNALES

Joe Nolan wants one thing—to catch the men responsible for wreaking havoc on his beloved town.

In the wake of his wife's passing, Joe Nolan's resolve is put to the test when he finds himself on the losing end of a bank robbery. Determined to preserve the community he holds dear, he teams up with his brothers and Deputy Sheriff Tommy O'Sullivan to hunt down the masked perpetrators.

But as the thieves continue to elude capture, Joe finds himself grappling not only with the relentless pursuit of justice but also with his own grief. With each heist, the robbers grow bolder, leaving Joe and his allies racing against the clock to uncover their identities and put an end to their reign of terror.

As tensions mount, Joe confronts his deepest fears and makes a daring stand to protect the town's future. And in a high-stakes showdown, he risks everything to reclaim what was taken…and ensure that justice is served.

AVAILABLE AUGUST 2024

ABOUT THE AUTHOR

Growing up in southern New Mexico, Melody Groves' mind raced with characters from the Old West–gunfighters were her favorite. Now, her novels reflect her fascination—and ties—from that era.

As a New Mexico Gunfighter re-enactor, Melody loves to entertain visitors at Albuquerque's Old Town, allowing them a glimpse into earlier times. Her books reflect her passion for rodeo and her appreciation of historic wooden bars. Yes, bars—the front and back wooden structures, which Melody feels are just as amazing as rodeo performers.